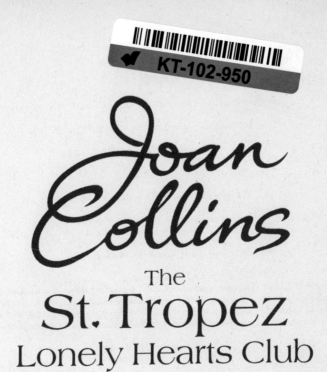

Joan Collins

The
St. Tropez
Lonely Hearts Club

Constable • London

CONSTABLE

First published in Great Britain in 2015 by Constable

This edition published in 2016 by Constable

Copyright © Joan Collins, 2015

3 5 7 9 10 8 6 4 2

The moral right of the author has been asserted.

A CIP catalogue record for this book
is available from the British Library.

ISBN: 978-1-47212-296-4 (paperback)

Typeset in Goudy Old Style by Hewer Text UK Ltd, Edinburgh
Printed and bound by Clays Ltd, St Ives plc

Papers used by Constable are from well-managed forests and other responsible sources.

MIX
Paper from
responsible sources
FSC® C104740

Constable
is an imprint of
Little, Brown Book Group
Carmelite House
50 Victoria Embankment
London EC4Y 0DZ

An Hachette UK Company
www.hachette.co.uk

www.littlebrown.co.uk

Witty, clever and beautiful, Dame Joan Collins possesses a singular star quality that has come to define what it means to be a living legend. As an actress, author and producer she has built a career that places her in the unrivalled ranks of an international icon.

Dame Joan has appeared in more than sixty feature films, dozens of plays, both in the West End and in the US, and many television series, including creating the role of Alexis Carrington on *Dynasty*, one of the most highly rated television dramas of all time. Her novels and memoirs have been bestsellers worldwide. She is a regular diarist for the *Spectator* and a contributor to the *Daily Mail*, *Sunday Telegraph*, *Sunday Times* and *Harper's Bazaar*.

Also by Joan Collins

Memoirs
Past Imperfect: An Autobiography (1978)
Katy: A Fight for Life (1982)
Second Act: An Autobiography (1996)
Passion for Life (2013)

Nonfiction
The Joan Collins Beauty Book (1980)
My Secrets (1994)
Health, Youth and Happiness (1995)
My Friends' Secrets (1999)
Joan's Way: Looking Good, Feeling Great (2002)
The Art of Living Well (2007)
The World According to Joan (2012)

Fiction
Prime Time (1988)
Love and Desire and Hate (1990)
Too Damn Famous (1995)
Star Quality (2002)
Misfortune's Daughters (2004)

For Jackie.

I will never forget you.

Introduction

The French Riviera is a place of sublime contrasts. Running from San Remo, just past the principality of Monaco, and almost to Marseille at the west end of the coast, each village, town and beach has its individual charm. Most villages have looked the same for hundreds of years, yet some of the larger towns – stately Monaco, and the grand old city of Nice with its stunning boardwalk, elegant Promenade des Anglais and its splendid hotels and superb shops and restaurants – have combined the best of modern architecture with nineteenth-century grandeur.

And then there is Saint-Tropez.

That humble and holy name conjures up an idyllic paradise where hedonism reigns and wealth and beauty conquer all, supposedly. Some have called it a cultural bone-yard, for the seven deadly sins abound in this happy hunting ground.

The myth of Saint-Tropez is known worldwide, but its reputation as the *de rigueur* party spot of the summer is comparatively recent. Although the sleepy little port village had existed for thousands of years, it wasn't until the 1950s that it started hitting the headlines, thanks to sex kitten Brigitte Bardot, the most nubile of post-war stars. Brigitte and her husband Roger Vadim discovered the delights of the nearby beaches of Pampelonne – then almost inaccessible thanks to the thick brush of parasol pines and tangled seaweed – while on location for Brigitte's first starring role, . . .*And God Created Woman* in 1955.

On what would end up as the most famous of all Pampelonne beaches, a tiny hut, owned by the de Colmont family, cooked lunch every day for Vadim's film unit. After the film crew left, the de Colmont family decided to keep cooking but to invite only those they knew and liked. Shortly thereafter, Bernard de Colmont created Le Club 55, named after the year of its birth, and it soon became the most sophisticated and exclusive beach club in the world. The elite of the world have done nothing to erase its unpretentious primitive charm, and it is a mecca for not only the denizens of Saint-Tropez, but for the summer season's visitors.

In the 1960s, the newly named 'jet set' finally discovered the delights of Saint-Tropez and its lush, gorgeous sandy beaches. Millionaires, playboys, film stars, heiresses, high-class hookers and low-rent boys descended on this elite paradise, and the party hasn't stopped yet. Some twenty years later, fat-bellied tourists in their buses and trailers, backpacks eternally glued to their spines like bizarre camel people, also descended in droves, marring the beauty and tranquillity of the village and its surroundings.

But Saint-Tropez has expanded significantly. In the past twenty years the environs of this charming village and the nearby villages of Ramatuelle, Gassin and La Croix-Valmer have spread like octopus tentacles via the new speedy roads and concrete apartment complexes, giant superstores and, saddest of all, McDonald's eating establishments.

Most people only think of Saint-Tropez beaches as filled with topless hookers, heavy hitters and illicit sex. That goes on in some of the more decadent beaches, such as the recently defunct Voile Rouge, where groups of rich playboys thought nothing of paying €10,000 for a jeroboam of champagne, which they liberally squirted over their squealing, scantily clad lady friends. Lunches at some of these beaches begin around three p.m. and rarely finish before eight or nine p.m., complete with floor shows and fashion parades of the flimsiest beachwear and wild, uninhibited dancing on the tables and bars to the heaviest of rap beats.

In the hills above Saint-Tropez lie some magnificent and expensive villas, many owned by billionaires who only spend as little as one or two weeks a year in their houses. Between November and February, the village is home to only five thousand souls. As the sun shines brighter, the Parisians and foreigners arrive to un-shutter their villas until, by June and July, more than 35,000 people are squeezed into Saint-Tropez. Add to that the daily influx of some 50,000 tourists and the pace becomes frenetic as the beat goes on.

This tale is about one sizzling summer season in this bacchanalian utopia, of sun, sin, sex and scandal, and the people who made it happen.

PROLOGUE

Lying face down in a pool, August 2015

How has it come to this? Me, the stud of Saint-Tropez. Twenty-nine years old. Handsome. Devilishly amusing. Big dick. Every woman in Saint-Tropez gladly accepting my advances. Well, not every woman, but I am seldom turned down. Think of an Italian Brad Pitt crossed with the brooding Latin sex appeal of a Benicio del Toro and that's me. The ultimate fuck machine, constantly horny, my body a factory of raging hormones. I don't like to boast . . . well, actually I do.

And my singing. Certainly I am no Julio Iglesias, but by the light of any silvery moon, my guitar playing and mellow, sensuous sounds have charmed many ladies (and the occasional man) into the sack. Sure, there are plenty of husbands and lovers who are insanely jealous of me, but I haven't lasted for nine years as a gigolo without knowing how to avoid them. After all, I am the stud of studs, the adored of the bored, the life and soul of every event, 'the second coming of Sinatra' . . . even I admit that was a bit over the top, but Maximus, my PR, my agent – well, my pimp – actually had a hangover that morning after the night I sang at Charlie Chalk's black and white ball and had no regard for originality when he thus described my performance to *Gala* magazine.

Joan Collins

That was one of the last nights I performed, while that ancient bitch Sophie Silvestri shot daggers at me.

I can hear people yelling and police sirens near me now, but I'm worried about the black silk Valentino shirt I'm wearing. My dear *fidanzata* bought me that as a making-up present last year for throwing my Etro bags off the back of her yacht. Now utterly ruined, soaking and blood spattered. I picture the wild-eyed Russian cow with her threats of 'I will kill you, you stupid wop-bastard', but she and I both know that her hands shake far too violently with the DTs caused by two bottles of Grey Goose a day to have done this.

My thoughts drift to the husbands. I'd cuckolded several by July, but none of them seemed to care as they traipsed off to the golf courses with their pot-bellied pals. Except the American mega-mogul, whose gorgeous trophy wife I slept with twice.

There have been hundreds, no thousands, of visitors in Saint-Tropez this hot summer, and I have rubbed shoulders with many of them. I have rubbed almost all other parts of my body with many of them too. We attend the same parties, lunches and dinners over and over again. Same people, same faces, same dialogue.

So how has it come to this? Is this the end?

Chapter One

Cannes Film Festival, May 2015

As I attempt to sweep up the red-carpeted steps to the Palais des Arts, the agonising pain in my hips makes me feel faint. I clench my teeth, as well as the hands of Frick and Adolpho, my two faithful style gurus who support me, one on each arm, whispering encouragement while I smile for the sea of lenses.

'Courage, Sophie. Be brave, cara – you are still the most beautiful; don't let them see your pain,' Frick encourages.

'And wipe the lipstick off your teeth,' hisses Adolpho.

And of course I won't, can't, let them see the effort it has taken me to strut up those velvet-sheathed stairs in six-inch Louboutins and a dress I haven't worn since *The Princess and the Playboy* in '68. Gina has let it out several inches in the waist and hips, but even with the steel corset it's torture. 'You must suffer to be beautiful.' The words of my mentor, the great director Charlot Benedicto, ring in my ears as I recall his insistence on having me strapped in corsets to play the young Marie Antoinette. 'She would have remained standing even after they chopped her head off,' I joked behind his back. Always behind his back. The corset had taken my then twenty-three-inch waist down to eighteen inches, and I had worn it the whole ten-hour shooting day, unable to eat or go to the bathroom. I also cracked a rib but never complained. Not to his face, at least.

I smile again at the cheering crowds of paparazzi, and fans pushing behind them, who line the staircase. How ugly most of them are. Where do they come from with their werewolf teeth, their hideous tattoos, their greasy hair and their pierced ears, noses, tongues, and nipples? And fat! So many are bursting out of their jeans, their white bellies exposed in all their cellulite ugliness, wearing nothing but T-shirts with stupid slogans that mean nothing. Not one elegant jacket, not one nice shirt – just shorts and jeans and crop tops and pale ugly skin spilling out of them, but with the occasional brilliantly dressed transgender fashionista, like a cherry on stale icing.

At the top of the steps a civilised crowd awaits. Amongst the coiffed, gowned and black-tied, I glimpse Deneuve and Depardieu, and make a gigantic effort with the last few stairs. Both my hips are now torturing me. Why hadn't I listened all those years ago when I was warned that the acrobatic exercise videos I was making, each one featuring my more and more excessive contortions, would eventually cripple me? 'Your bones are like Swiss cheese,' the blunt American doctor had pronounced. Did I detect a note of suppressed delight in his voice? Was I to be his retirement pension? 'If we don't give you two hip replacements within a year, you'll be in a wheelchair for the rest of your life.' He sounded slightly too pleased about that.

The rest of my life? How long will that be? I'm seventy-four now but I feel 104, and by the time I get to 104, I'll probably be long dead. But of course I don't look my age. No way. Frick and Adolpho see to that. Naturally, when I'm slopping around with the dogs and cats in overalls covered in dog hair, I look like an ancient Jane Fonda in Barbarella. Only my faithful menagerie and Frick and Adolpho help keep me sane and vaguely interested in what passes for a life. They don't care how I look and only insist I hide when the postman comes or the occasional fan or paparazzo manages to sneak into my remote property, concealing themselves behind the olive trees and trying to steal a snap.

What vile creatures they are, knowing that a photo of one of the most famous sex goddesses of the 1960s, now gone to seed, would fetch a fortune with the tabloids. 'Sophie Silvestri's so faded, she's almost invisible,' one cruel reporter had written. How nasty these people can be. One managed to ooze his way in through the oleander bushes last week while I was deadheading my hydrangeas. He'd begged for a photo, even offering to pay me, so I haughtily gave him my best Bette Davis line: 'I admit I've seen better days, but I'm still not to be had for the price of a cocktail or a salted peanut' before throwing him out.

That Davis woman, she sure had a way with words, and we'd had a few when I was playing the second lead in one of her movies. She accused me of stealing her boyfriend. Boyfriend! Fifty if he was a day, and I only flirted with him because he was the director of photography and giving me great lighting, so I occasionally gave him something else in my dressing room during lunch break, careful not to smudge my make-up.

I was so gorgeous then, I had to fight 'em off. Why are people so horrible to the elderly? Being beautiful and getting old is like being rich and becoming poor. One day they'll be old (if they're lucky) so why should they be so unkind? There should be a law against ageism. There are laws against racism, homophobia, sexism and the mocking of midgets – sorry, vertically challenged. So why can't we be polite to the over-sixties?

But the fans still try to break in. Usually Frick and Adolpho and my dear dogs manage to get rid of them. Of course, there was the unfortunate incident a couple of years ago when my favourite Doberman Pinscher took a little snack out of some fat fan's fanny. The idiot was bending over behind the bougainvillea bushes, camera posed, ass in the air – naturally dear Faustus couldn't resist the temptation of that gelatinous white builder's cleavage.

The Saint-Tropez gendarmerie hushed up the potential scandal, of course. The man looked like a pervert anyway, and Captain Poulpe and his daughter Gabrielle used the persuasiveness of truncheon and their posse of grim-faced goons to banish him from our lovely village for ever. Dear Captain Poulpe. He has always been one of my biggest fans. I think he has a tiny crush on me too. Sadly he's on the point of retirement, which is what I should probably have done years ago.

I wince as I make the top step and air-kiss Deneuve on both cheeks. The bitch looks far too good and, as I kiss, I try to check behind her ears, but all that real blonde hair (double bitch) gets in the way. After all, we are almost contemporaries. The crowd cheers, the cameras click, the flashes flash insanely, recording the moment when two queens of the French cinema reunite, and I feel the instant rush of adrenalin that these events still give me. After all, I am still a star.

CHAPTER TWO

La Recoleta Cemetery, Buenos Aires, February 2015

Nicanor Di Ponti was lowered to the ground as his entire family and his beautiful wife Carlotta wept, the tears running down her oval face. The drizzle of the Argentine summer rain was as steady and copious as the tears of the mourners, but the tears, like the rain, did not all come from the same cloud. In Carlotta's case, the tears were tears of freedom, tears of joy.

Carlotta had met Nicanor when she was a sixteen-year-old virgin from a poor family and he was a twenty-nine-year-old sex addict from a rich one. They had married and had a baby girl and their marriage seemed storybook, although sadly – and despite herculean efforts by Nicanor – Carlotta was unable to give him the male heir he longed for. They lived in mansions around the world, paid for by the vast sugar-cane fortune that the Di Ponti family had established, but which Nicanor's mother had made into a global brand. With its distinctive image of a gaucho riding free on the plains of the pampas, Di Ponti sugar was the staple in every supermarket, kitchen and restaurant in the world. How far from the truth that was, Carlotta often thought. What if they knew that the handsome man in the gaucho photograph, which Nicanor

had posed for when he was twenty-two, was into kinky bond-
age and hardcore sex?

∞

*I had never seen anything so beautiful as the villa that Nicanor took me
to on our first date. I had been sitting by the fountain in the middle of
our village square, thinking for a long time that my life had been 'one
step forward and two steps back'. Ever since I left school last year, I'd
been working in the chocolate factory owned by the powerful Di Ponti
family. They owned practically everything in the village and the
surrounding towns and villages too.*

*Nicanor was driving a very fancy car, red. The top was down and
the wind was blowing his thick black hair into a pompadour. I recognised him immediately. 'Gaucho' – his photograph – was on every bag
of sugar and on every wrapper of the delicious chocolate bars sold
everywhere. However, they were not so delicious when I worked ten
hours a day in the factory that made them.*

'Want a ride?' he asked, the sun glinting on his blue-mirrored glasses.

*I couldn't see his eyes but I knew they were black, black as the night
that comes so quickly in our village.*

*My mother had brought me up to never accept anything from strange
men, but this was no stranger. This was 'Gaucho' – a man admired
and worshipped by all young girls and women in Argentina, his face on
the front of every carton of sugar.*

'Where to?' I asked, wondering if I sounded too eager.

*'We'll go see the countryside,' he laughed, and I had never seen such
brilliant white teeth before. He was wearing a red polo shirt that
matched the colour of his car, which featured a black horse inside a
yellow shield on the bonnet.*

He asked me my name and what I did for a living, and I told him.

*'That's not good enough for a beautiful girl like you,' he laughed. I
blushed. 'Are you a virgin?' he asked.*

I blushed even more fiercely and hung my head. My mother would kill me if she knew I was talking so freely to a man. But he wasn't just a man – he was 'Gaucho' – he was almost a God!

'Of course,' I replied, 'I'm only sixteen.'

'Good, that's very good,' he said. He had a kind smile.

We drove around to his family's sugar-cane plantation and he spoke most amusingly of places I had only heard of – Paris, Vienna, Capri. He seemed to have travelled the globe many times; his stories were captivating but they also made me laugh a lot.

I became worried that it was getting late and I asked him to please take me back to the village.

'Only if you promise you will go out with me tomorrow,' he replied.

I was stunned. 'Gaucho' asking me, Carlotta Perez, a poor girl who worked in one of his factories, to go out with him? What else could I say but yes?

I told my mother I was going to go visit my cousins in the next village, and Nicanor arranged to pick me up in a quiet grove near the windmill.

He was in a different car this time. The windows were made of black smoked glass and it looked quite old.

'It's a classic Bentley. I collect vintage cars,' he informed me as I clambered in. He didn't offer to help me. My mother had told me to expect men to help me, but I was young and agile and, after all, he was 'Gaucho' and everyone did things for him.

We drove for miles until we came to an enormous pink villa perched on a hill with a beautiful view of the sea.

'Where is this?' I whispered. I tried not to be afraid even though it was getting dark, but it seemed he sensed my fear and put a hand on my knee.

'Don't be frightened, amor. This is our summer house – come.'

When I stepped inside the gorgeous villa I couldn't stop staring at the magnificence of it, at the many oil portraits of men in old-fashioned clothes who all looked very much like Nicanor and the dim lighting from golden sconces that illuminated them.

'Those are my ancestors,' he said, then ushered me into a room which had bookshelves covered in books. A deep, comfortable, dark-green velvet sofa stood in front of the grand fireplace.

'Sit,' he commanded, 'and I will get you a drink – prosecco and peach juice – okay? It's called a Bellini. It's a specialty from Harry's Bar in Venice.'

'I . . . I don't . . . I'm not allowed to drink,' I stumbled.

'Nonsense, you're sixteen. Of course you can drink – you must.'

He filled two crystal glasses at a dark wooden bar and brought them over.

I sat beside him and I gazed into his deep black eyes, and although I was apprehensive I felt a wonderful feeling of excitement.

'To us,' he declared, raising his glass.

I took a tentative sip from mine. It was delicious. The tart taste of the prosecco was offset by the sweetness of the peach juice.

'I just need to make a couple of long-distance phone calls,' he abruptly announced. 'Amuse yourself with this, mi amor – I'll be back shortly.'

He handed me an enormous illustrated book bound in deep burgundy leather. I opened it and almost choked.

It was full of the most explicit images of men torturing women – of a woman being ravaged by a massive dog and of men doing things to each other which I could not understand, much less imagine.

And that was the last thing I remembered.

I regained consciousness to the morning sounds of birds waking up. It was dawn. A TV flickered black and white shadows in a corner and an early newscaster was droning on.

I was sprawled on the sofa. There were bloodstains on the green velvet and a broken champagne glass on the floor. My stomach felt like lead and there was a throbbing ache between my legs. I picked up my *underwear, skirt and blouse and quickly pulled them on. I started hyperventilating. Where was Nicanor and why had he done this to me? Was he lurking somewhere upstairs in his darkened house, perhaps waiting to pounce on me again? I wasn't going to wait around to find out.*

My head throbbed, and when I touched it I could feel a bump the size of an egg. The painful memories suddenly rushed back. I had a flash of the images in the big burgundy book. Before I even finished it, I'd passed out. And then . . . and then? Had he done those things to me? I wasn't about to wait to find that out either. Oh God, he'd drugged me and . . . raped me? Why? Why would the great 'Gaucho' do this to me – an innocent sixteen-year-old? I never wanted to see him again.

∽

Carlotta had to get out. She dressed hastily and crept out of the library, but when she tried to open the enormous, copper-studded mahogany front door, she found it firmly locked. The villa was vast, with many windows that looked out at the verdant land-scaped gardens, but as she dashed through the empty rooms draped with tapestries and paintings of Nicanor's frowning ances-tors, she found these windowed sentinels firmly locked.

She found her way downstairs into the bowels of the house, hoping against hope that there would be an open door or window or perhaps a kind-hearted staff member who would let her escape. As she opened the basement door to a shining kitchen outfitted with the latest technology, Carlotta heard a low growl emanating from beside an incongruously old-fashioned Aga.

Suddenly two giant Dobermans jumped up from their cushions and raced towards her, barking furiously, teeth bared in a fero-cious snarl, saliva dripping from their dark jowls. Carlotta screamed and, slamming the door on the beasts' angry faces, slumped to the floor and started to weep uncontrollably.

∞

Suddenly I felt him beside me.

He was naked and he was – oh! I couldn't bear to think what he'd done with that thing. Even though he was wearing a dressing gown, that huge thing stuck out from between his legs. It had hurt me so much and I couldn't bear to be near to him.

'Where are you going, you pretty little girl?' he whispered, holding on to my shoulders tightly. 'Come back to bed, mi amor.'

I struggled to free myself, but he was so tall and so strong that I couldn't. I burst into tears of anger.

'How could you – how could you have done this to me? Why?' I wailed.

'I want you for my wife,' he said simply. 'I've been watching you for weeks. Come, my darling girl, let us talk.'

I couldn't believe what I was hearing. He made me sit down in the vast kitchen, shooing the now silent dogs into the corridor.

'Breakfast – you need food.'

Suddenly he had become so kind and caring – I didn't know what to think. I was terribly confused. My head was throbbing, as was the pain between my legs. I watched him fry eggs and chorizo. And then he explained.

'I need to take a wife, Carlotta, before I turn thirty, and I wanted my wife to be young and a virgin. I could not take your word for it, so I had to find out the only way I knew.'

I was stunned, 'So you raped me? This was how you wanted to find out if . . . if . . .?'

'No, no – it wasn't rape. It was . . . well, you didn't refuse me.'

In my muddled mind I thought maybe he was right, and he was being so sweet – so nice and so kind now.

12

'I couldn't wait for our wedding night to find out, Carlotta, do you understand? So now I can propose to you.'

I nodded, even though I found this all more than strange. Gaucho was proposing to me? Of all the women I had seen him with in the celebrity magazines – actresses, princesses, heiresses – he wanted me? It didn't make any sense.

Then he did the strangest thing of all – he got down on one knee and, taking my hand, he asked, 'Will you marry me, Carlotta? Will you become my loyal, my obedient wife?'

I was no longer a virgin. This man had raped me, but I was also a very poor girl who had little prospect of any good fortune in the future – I would be doomed to a life of poverty like my parents. He was 'Gaucho', the handsomest, richest man in San Miguel – maybe all of Argentina.

∞

Nicanor held her tight, murmuring into her ear, whispering how he loved her and wanted to make her happy. Carlotta closed her eyes. Then he gently picked her up and, mounting the marbled staircase, took her back to her bedroom.

'My darling, mi amor, don't cry, please,' she heard Nicanor's voice, considerate and charming, and looked up at his handsome figure in the paisley silk dressing gown. He cradled the sobbing girl in his muscular arms as she wept on his shoulder. 'There, there. Please don't cry, my little pet, my little darling butterfly.'

'Butterfly? Why do you call me that?' Carlotta said as she brushed the tears from her cheeks and attempted to struggle free from Nicanor's strong embrace, which tightened as he held on to her, rocking her lovingly, his warm breath on her neck.

'Because you are frail and delicate as a butterfly, and because you try to fly away from me,' he answered as he held her tighter. 'But butterflies can be caught with the right net, isn't that so, my darling?'

Carlotta nodded. Nicanor's voice was soothing and the scent of his skin calmed her in spite of her fear. As he continued talking to her in a soft, soothing voice, she felt herself melting and he, aware of her imminent surrender, bent his head to her parted lips. As he kissed her delicately but with passion, she felt herself succumbing.

'I want you,' he whispered into her hair. 'I am sorry about what happened before, my darling. I didn't mean to hurt you. I adore you. Something came over me. I desired you so much – too much, my love. And I want you to want me too. Please, my love, please give me another chance.'

Nicanor set her gently down on to the silken bed. His lips travelled to her breasts, which he freed from her simple blouse. Carlotta started to respond. His lips were so soft and warm as he licked and sucked her nipples. She had never felt anything like this before. Then his hand crept down between her legs. She couldn't believe she could feel this much pleasure.

Having caused her the most agonising pain just a few hours ago, he was now giving her the most exquisite sensual delight she had ever experienced. He didn't try to enter her, his fingers had found her pleasure point and within minutes Carlotta experienced her first orgasm. It was so intense that she screamed with the joy and the pain and her tears started to flow again.

After he had finished with her he had immediately fallen into another deep sleep punctuated by snuffling snores. Making sure he was fast asleep, Carlotta crept out of bed and felt her way to the bathroom. She closed the door softly, marvelling at the huge mirrored and pale marble bathroom en suite to Nicanor's bedroom, and drew a bath.

She luxuriated in the vast bathtub with the gold-plated taps and buttons and switches that turned on all manner of jet streams and showers; they would pamper every part, and help to heal her aching body. She sampled the delicately scented soaps, oils and lotions that surrounded the marble-topped bath. They were delicious, and as Carlotta lay back in the foamy warm water, the thought crossed her mind that maybe she could become accustomed to this sybaritic lifestyle.

Marry him? Of course she would.

∽

Carlotta didn't dare tell her mother what had happened with Nicanor. She went through the next few days in a daze, constantly reliving the night of pain and passion with Nicanor in an alternating haze of disgust and anticipation. But as the days passed, the anticipation turned into disappointment, as she heard no word from Nicanor.

After a week in which disappointment turned into doubt and then to despair, Carlotta took a ride on her bicycle to the outskirts of the village where the Di Ponti villa stood, in all its baroque majesty. Shielded from the road by the tall pine trees, thick foliage and luxurious flowering shrubs, all that was visible were the tall golden spires on the rooftop.

Carlotta sat beneath a gardenia bush and took a *queso fresco* and tomato sandwich wrapped in greaseproof paper from her rucksack. She was wearing faded red espadrilles and a second-hand pink and white striped halterneck sundress that she had bought for ten pesos at the local market.

The sun dappled her lightly tanned shoulders as she leaned against a pine tree, watching a yellow butterfly dart amongst the foliage, and considered her options. She wanted to see Nicanor again. She yearned for him. Against all her better judgement, she had wrestled with her conscience for hours each night as she lay in bed thinking about that extraordinary night.

Yes, Nicanor had taken her by force. Yes, he had hurt her, but after subtly questioning her best girlfriend Livia after school one day about sex, Livia had confided, 'Losing my virginity hurt like hell, Carlotta, but after that it was heavenly.'

Carlotta ruminated as she gazed up at the blue summer sky and the scudding clouds. The memory of the feelings she had finally experienced with Nicanor had become her most prevailing thought. She had known little real affection in her life. Her father had left her mother shortly after Carlotta was born and her mother blamed the new baby for his disappearance. Consequently she gave little heed to Carlotta when the baby cried or when, as a toddler, she hung on to her mother's skirts, hoping for a crumb of affection but receiving nothing. Her grandmother was more affectionate and loving, but the old lady suffered from painful arthritis and her withered old limbs didn't make cuddling Carlotta comfortable.

As she lay in bed at night, her hands strayed to that place whence Nicanor had extracted such deep pleasure, and she found herself climaxing gently to images of his mouth on her body and his lips on hers. She knew these were wicked thoughts and actions and she tried to banish them, but it was difficult when every magazine she scanned there he strutted, the 'Gaucho', with his handsome, insouciant gaze, his tight trousers outlining his manhood, one hand on his hip, the other holding the harness of a fierce black stallion.

On the outskirts of the village, Carlotta had passed another giant coloured poster of him proclaiming the values of Di Ponti sugar while astride a horse. He looked supremely confident, supremely male, and Carlotta realised she was supremely smitten.

Suddenly there was an excruciating roar and a posse of leather-clad young men on motorcycles zoomed past her, the noise of their exhausts so loud that she had to put her fingers in her ears. After they had ridden into the distance in a haze of fumes, one of the cycles stopped, turned, and came back to where Carlotta sat. As the rider stepped down and removed his helmet, Carlotta's heart leaped.

'My butterfly, I'm so happy to see you here!' Nicanor smiled broadly. Bending to hug her, he took a huge bite of her sandwich and sat down beside her.

'Oh, what are you doing here?' she stammered. 'I thought you'd forgotten about me.'

'Forget you? My gorgeous butterfly – never. You have been in my thoughts the whole time. I've been on a trip,' he laughed, then took another bite of her sandwich as Carlotta gazed at him open mouthed.

My God, but he was even more handsome than ever in his black leather jacket and trousers. His raven hair clung to his head in tight curls that accentuated the darkness of his eyes.

'Miss me?' he grinned, his mouth full of Carlotta's lunch.

'Ah, ye-es . . . yes, I did but, why . . . why didn't you call me or send a message . . .?'

'My darling – I thought of you when we were on the road with my gang and I couldn't . . . well, you know what it's like when you're in a group. We went all the way to Punta del Este,' he laughed. 'God, we had fun!'

Carlotta took a sip from her water bottle and kept silent. She didn't know what to say and remembered the advice of her ancient grandma: *If you don't know what to say – say nothing.*

Misinterpreting her silence for reproach, Nicanor looked repentant. 'I'm sorry, my love, truly sorry. I'm a rat, I know, but it hasn't been that long, has it?'

'Ten days,' said Carlotta weakly.

'Then let's start making up for them right now,' he declared and, taking her hand, led her deeper into the dense foliage until they came to a grassy clearing surrounded by flowering bushes and smelling of hibiscus. He laid her softly on the grassy mound and looked into her beautiful innocent brown eyes. 'How lovely you are,' he breathed as he brushed her parted lips with his.

Undoing the halterneck tie, his hands pushed the straps of her sundress to her waist and his lips eagerly found her soft mounds. It was useless to resist, and besides, Carlotta loved the feel of his mouth on her breasts, the touch of his hand on her loins, which felt heavy with desire. In seconds she came, her cries mixing with those of the Andean gulls that circled above them.

'Hush, hush,' he whispered, entering her while she still quivered with ecstasy. 'Hush, my little butterfly. We have our whole lives ahead of us to make love.'

∞

They married four months later, on Carlotta's seventeenth birthday, in a lavish ceremony in Buenos Aires at the Metropolitan Cathedral. Society, royalty and A-list celebrities ensured that the wedding received maximum coverage in *People*, *Vanity Fair* and *Hello!* magazine. Carlotta was a ravishing bride in a pure white Alençon lace wedding dress by Valentino.

Her jet-black hair, held on her forehead by a hundred-carat antique diamond necklace that had been in the Di Ponti family for nearly two hundred years, flowed down her back, covered in a downy soft veil embroidered with tiny butterflies.

The gown had a thirty-foot train and was carried by a dozen tiny tots, all distant relatives of Madame Elsa Di Ponti, the fearsome matriarch of the Di Ponti clan and mother of Nicanor.

'The most beautiful bride I've ever seen,' Adolpho breathed in admiration to his employer and mentor, the legendary screen star Sophie Silvestri, as they watched the couple walk up the aisle.

'She's short.' Sophie was hard-pressed ever to give a good review to a beautiful woman, particularly one of only seventeen summers.

'Petite,' answered Adolpho. 'A perfect little package, I would say.'

'Well, since you bat for the other team, I don't think you're much of a judge of female flesh,' said Sophie, checking her immaculate *maquillage* in a jewel-encrusted *minaudière*.

'*Shhh!*' hissed the famous record producer Khris Kane, who was sitting behind them.

'I think she's a little beauty.' Adolpho turned to look at the newly-weds as they passed the flower-covered aisle in a flurry of confetti and petals.

Sophie turned to him. Snapping her compact shut, she adjusted the blonde confection of her wig and the tiny hat tilted over her famous blue eyes and sneered. 'A little! A *very* little beauty she may be, but she's bitten off far more than she can chew with this marriage.'

'What do you mean?' asked Adolpho, nonplussed.

'Darling, *everyone* knows Nicanor Di Ponti is a complete bastard and an absolute degenerate.'

They stood up as the congregation began to shuffle out into the brilliant sunshine.

'Everyone *knows*,' whispered Sophie. 'The family have tried to hush it up for years. Apparently he almost killed a young girl a couple of years ago. The Di Ponti family had to pay the girl's parents a fortune to buy their silence.'

Adolpho stared at the receding figures of the laughing bride and groom as they exited the church to shouts and cheers from the excited crowd outside and the blinding flashes of the cameras.

'Then,' Sophie bent to whisper in Adolpho's ear, 'he was caught in a New York hotel last year with three girls all under the age of sixteen and with enough heroin to service a drug addict for a month.'

'How come he wasn't arrested?'

'Diplomatic immunity. The Di Ponti family have a lot of influence, darling. When it comes to the drug offences of the rich, it's easy to turn the other cheek if the rich grease palms with enough silver.'

'Well, he looks ecstatic with the new bride,' said Adolpho.

'Yes, the perfect picture of happy newly-weds,' answered Sophie, graciously acknowledging the cheers of the crowd as she came out of the cathedral. 'Just you wait and see,' she whispered.

∞

For Carlotta the honeymoon period did not last long.

They flew to Las Vegas – a strange choice, thought Carlotta. She had tried to influence her new husband to go somewhere more romantic, but what Nicanor wanted, Nicanor got. Their honeymoon suite was garish; as big as an arena, complete with four bedrooms, a fully stocked wet bar and a butler who discreetly slipped tightly wrapped packets of white powder into Nicanor's pockets whenever he was asked.

After a desultory bout of lovemaking on their wedding night, Nicanor had disappeared to the baccarat and blackjack tables. She had gone with him the second night, but the noise and clatter and flashing lights of the casino gave her a headache, and playing blackjack, which she did badly, or roulette, at which she consistently lost, frustrated her. She tried the slot machines but the intense monotony of pressing a button over and over again to get a line of matching fruits bored her to tears.

The front windows of the huge rooms overlooked the Vegas strip, where lonely Carlotta spent hours sitting with binoculars, helpfully provided by the hotel, to gaze at the passing throngs. In their Lycra shorts and flashy cheap T-shirts, most of them were so fat that Carlotta wondered how they could even walk.

She persuaded Nicanor to get tickets for Cher's show at Caesars Palace, but on the appointed night he simply disappeared, so she watched her favourite star, cavorting on stage in gorgeous Bob Mackie gowns, all by herself.

That night she couldn't sleep then Nicanor showed up stoned and stinking of vodka at four a.m.

'Where have you been?' she asked. 'I looked everywhere for you. I had to go and see Cher alone last night.'

'Oh, you poor baby,' Nicanor spat out sarcastically. Throwing off his sweat-stained silk shirt. 'Feel sorry for *me*, why don't you? I've just lost thirty thousand dollars on that crappy poker game – Texas hold'em.' He drawled out the word in a hideous impression of a mid-Western accent.

'Well, I think that serves you right.' Carlotta sat up in bed defiantly, emboldened to stand up for herself. 'We're married and we should do things together.'

'We should? We *should*? Ha!' Nicanor stalked towards the massive four-poster bed, which was festooned with hanging ropes and mirrors on the ceiling and on the walls at either side. 'Don't you dare tell me what I *should* and shouldn't do, woman!' He raised his hand and hit Carlotta so hard on the cheek that she yelped and fell back whimpering.

'Oh, yes, go on – cry, why don't you? D'you want to cry like the silly little idiot you are? Then I'll give you something to cry about, you stupid little bitch!'

Horrified, Carlotta saw her husband rip off his trousers. Without preamble he tore off her flimsy nightgown, then threw himself on top of her. Where once he tenderly licked and kissed, now he bit her breasts so savagely that they bled. He plunged into her with

21

the atavistic roar of a wild animal, and thrust so hard that she screamed with pain.

'Stop it, Nico – stop it, please!'

'Why should I?' he growled. 'You're mine, I can do what I want with you. You belong to me now.' He thrust harder and grabbed her breasts, squeezing them violently as she moaned in agony.

'Stop it, Nico, stop it! You're hurting our baby!'

'Our *what?*' Nicanor stopped abruptly and stared at her with bloodshot eyes.

'Our baby,' cried Carlotta. 'Nico, I'm pregnant.'

'Oh, my God! Oh, my God!' He rolled off her and sat on the edge of the bed, his head in his hands, his flaccid penis hanging forlornly on his thigh. 'When did you . . . are you sure?'

'Yes,' said Carlotta quietly. 'I went to see a nice American doctor today because I suspected and it's true – I am.' She smiled pleadingly, hoping that now perhaps Nicanor would become the tender lover that he had been before the marriage. 'I'm only seven weeks but it's definite.'

'Then you must rest,' he slurred, as he staggered up and walked shakily to the bathroom. 'I won't bother you again, my dear.'

∽

Throughout Carlotta's pregnancy, Nicanor had seldom come near her. They returned to San Miguel, where the family doctor told her that, given her young age, barely seventeen, and petite build she must spend the next six and a half months confined to her bed. Carlotta was lonely and horribly confused.

Her mother, despite being happy now that the Di Ponti family had bought her a cottage on the outskirts of the village, rarely came to visit. Madame Elsa was seldom at home, busy socialising in all the jet-set spots of the world, and Carlotta's grandmother, racked with arthritis, couldn't make the journey. Therefore

Carlotta's only visitor was her schoolfriend Livia. Livvy had married her boyfriend and was divinely happy. She visited often, regaling Carlotta with tales of family gatherings and outings to the beach, pizza restaurants and the movies – all things Carlotta could no longer do.

When Carlotta's daughter Flora was finally born, Nicanor couldn't hide his disappointment. 'Why couldn't it have been a boy?' he whined. He started blaming Carlotta for 'the mistake', as he referred to the child. When she asked him if he still loved her he replied bitterly, 'To quote Prince Charles, my dear, "Whatever love is" – quite apt for a Brit, I thought.'

Nicanor's desire for a son became more and more obsessive. His monthly lovemaking, if you could call it that, was timed to Carlotta's menstrual cycle. The doctor had told the couple which were the optimal times of the month to conceive, so for three days in the middle of her cycle, Nicanor pounded relentlessly into his young wife. These couplings were completely without affection or even a modicum of lovemaking. He seemed to think that the rougher and more brutal the sex, the stronger the chances were of producing a boy. She had endured his perversion as long as she could until, after a near-death episode involving a vodka bottle, she decided that a sexless marriage was preferable to what he demanded. This was reinforced by her doctor who informed her she was badly scarred by the incident. Carlotta became resigned to the fact that he found satisfaction elsewhere. 'Just not in our house,' she had requested.

Carlotta's life revolved around her gorgeous baby Flora, and eventually she gave in to the blandishments of the Buenos Aires socialites and started frequenting their gossipy lunches and get-togethers. She adored her daughter and spent her days involved in charities helping the poor and destitute of San Miguel. But she was not happy. It was an empty life, and when she brought up the subject of divorce, Nicanor refused to even consider it.

'You have your new life – I have mine, and if you divorce me I will see to it that you don't receive a penny from me or my family,' he threatened.

His jaunts with his motorcycle buddies became more frequent and, heedless of her request, he constantly brought under-age girls back to the villa, where he would abuse them, often so loudly that the sounds of the young girls' sobbing penetrated Carlotta's bedroom – despite being as far away from her husband's vile den as it could possibly be.

'One day – one day it will all end,' Livvy told her comfortingly.

'But how?' sighed Carlotta, watching the now six-year-old Flora play with her favourite parrot. 'How can it?'

∞

The official cause of Nicanor's death seven years later was a heart attack, but everyone wondered how someone so young, so vital, could have had a heart condition. Carlotta had found his body hanging by a black silk stocking from a rafter in his lair; a chair overturned and an orange stuck in his mouth, while a terrified teenaged whore in a Nazi cap wearing one black stocking and a garter belt screamed her head off. His family was shocked with the suddenness of his death, even though his debauchery was common knowledge among the elite of Buenos Aires.

With the help of the family lawyer, Carlotta had managed to brush the potential scandal of her husband's death efficiently under the Aubusson carpet, and salvage Nicanor's reputation, but not without first taking some graphic photos of the death scene. No longer the ignorant and naïve girl she had been before their marriage, she made sure to show his immediate family some of the photos, in the event there was any resistance to his will, which left her a very handsome woman in every aspect.

A month after Nicanor's funeral, and to escape the animosity of her in-laws, she thought about taking her daughter and her fortune away and start a new life abroad. Why had she never found the true love that her childhood dreams had foretold? A life in the dissolute world of the mega-rich of Buenos Aires had never dimmed her romantic hopes. She had stuck it out with Nicanor because she had no choice – and, truth be told, that life was infinitely preferable to the poverty she would have had to endure if she hadn't married him.

Last year, when she and Nicanor had attended the Grand Prix in Monaco, she had met a charming Italian, Maximus Gobbi, Jr. Gobbi had given her his card and said smoothly, 'If you ever need anything at all, my dear, I would be only too happy to assist you.'

CHAPTER THREE

Monte-Carlo, May 2014

Maximus Gobbi heaved his enormous bulk out of the rented vintage MG. This exercise consisted of several false starts, a copious amount of groaning, and left him with a ripped shirt and a face flushed from exertion. He adjusted his crumpled peach linen suit and lumbered up the white marble steps of the Hôtel de Paris.

The sun was shining, the birds were singing and Monte-Carlo was buzzing at this time of the year. The Cannes Film Festival was just finishing and this was the opening day of the Monaco Grand Prix.

Maximus had no intention of doing something as plebeian as sitting in the stands to watch the race. The noise alone would drive him up the wall. No, it was far more interesting to be a guest at the celebrity-studded luncheon thrown by the Russian oligarch Sergei Litvak, who collected stars as some people collect rare paintings.

Maximus strolled through the opulent foyer and turned into the large dining room where the hundred or so invitees, the *crème de la crème* of the jet set, gathered to gossip and sip their morning cocktails. He quickly scanned the room with the expert eye of a hunter, missing nothing and no one. He pretended not to notice the B-list reality-star couple, awkwardly huddled in a corner with their year-old child inappropriately frocked up in a black chiffon tutu and biker boots.

His glance settled for a second on Mina Corbain, the rock-star singer who was rising quickly to the top of the charts under the auspices of mega-manager and producer Khris Kane. Mina – a gorgeous young sprite of a girl in her late teens – was Khris's latest discovery. Though she had not yet reached the superstar status that would entice Maximus to say his first *buongiorno*.

Then he spotted the ageing diva Sophie Silvestri surrounded by several fawning acolytes – she was definitely worth a good morning peck on the cheek and a mini-grovel. Even though Max hated the bitch, she was a huge celebrity, screen icon and legendary beauty, who stood up to Father Time and, in spite of half a century in showbiz, was still at the top of her game.

'*Buongiorno, bellissima,*' Maximus beamed and kissed the goddess's white-gloved hand, which she offered to avert the risk of him smearing her matte-powdered cheek.

'*Ciao,* Maximus,' Sophie replied, politely cool. There were paparazzi everywhere, not to mention some guests who had slyly taken out their iPhones and, while pretending to check emails, were instead filming the stars. She didn't want to be seen as the spoilt prima donna everyone thought she was.

'More beeyootiful than ever, *cara* – how do you do it?'

'Make-up,' snapped the diva, then turning to the couple beside her said, 'Maximus Gobbi, may I introduce you to Count Nicanor Di Ponti and his lovely wife, Contessa Carlotta?'

'Charmed, charmed, I'm sure,' Maximus started to bow and then remembered he had buttoned his jacket to hide the rip in his shirt, and the button was already at breaking point. The bow turned into a sort of awkward head bend, which almost made Carlotta giggle. Maximus's Rolodex of a mind scanned through a bunch of names until he hit the jackpot. 'Of course, Count Di Ponti, delighted to meet you. You have a very beeyootiful wife, if I may say so.'

Nicanor, unimpressed by this old man in the wrinkled suit, nodded brusquely and turned to Carlotta. 'I'm going outside to watch the test runs – see you at lunch.' Then, with a disdainful glance at Max, added sarcastically, 'I'm sure he will entertain you.'

With that, Nicanor moved through the elegantly set tables to the outside terrace, where the Grand-Prix drivers were doing their warm-up lap through the streets of Monaco before the race.

Max turned to Carlotta with his most winning smile, 'Would you like to go outside to watch as well, my dear?' Carlotta shook her head shyly.

He sensed a vulnerability and nervousness in the lovely young woman, and also realised he had heard a lot about this famous Argentine family. Rumour had it that Nicanor was an avid womaniser who liked them very young and often beat them up. He was also a fanatical follower of the latest fashions in designer drugs, and there were rumours that he had caused the accidental death of a young girl. The marriage was no love match any more, Maximus had heard, but they stayed together for the sake of the Di Ponti family name and their daughter.

'Then would you like to sit down?' Maximus countered, noticing her wistful gaze towards her nonchalant husband, who was now leaning on the terrace balustrade, smoking a cigar and chatting animatedly with Sergei Litvak's gorgeous model wife, Lilly. Lilly was an ex-beauty queen and a model of exquisite perfection. From her tumbling blonde curls to her amazing body sheathed in skintight floral Dolce & Gabbana, she was the embodiment of gorgeous womanhood and she knew it.

Max clocked the couple's intimate body language, and stored it away in his mind for future reference, deciding to concentrate instead on this forlorn-looking but lovely flower of a young woman. Maximus, from years of practice, was an expert at reading people where others failed. He was able to penetrate the carapace of the public faces and see their real selves behind the masks, and he could sense palpable unhappiness emanating from Carlotta in the fleeting expressions and glances at her husband.

What she needs is a good roll in the hay, he thought, noticing Carlotta's eyes stray towards the strapping stud who had just sauntered into the room.

'Ah, Fabrizio, *caro*! Come here, I must introduce you,' he exclaimed to the young man.

Fabrizio Bricconni, at six foot three, oozed macho charm as well as devastating good looks. Black silky hair falling casually over one of his amethyst eyes, and a deep tan set off by a cream silk Brioni shirt and beautifully pressed cream trousers, made him a 'pussy magnet', as he charmingly referred to himself.

'Bingo,' thought Maximus. 'This could be a match made in heaven.' Although it was not common knowledge, Fabrizio was one of Maximus's exclusive stable of studs for hire – young men who dated older rich women and who often ended up either being kept by them or marrying them.

He noticed that Carlotta seemed amused by the guy, who had instantly turned on a trunk-load of his Italian charm and wit. As the three chatted, Sergei Litvak clapped his hands and announced, 'Ladies and gentlemen, please take your seats for lunch. The race is about to begin.'

Maximus excused himself, leaving Carlotta in the thrall of Fabrizio, and lumbered to the table plan at the door to find out where he was sitting. He managed to quickly exchange his place card so that he would be next to Carlotta then, returning to her side and taking her arm, he escorted her to one of the long white tables that, with their gleaming silverware and centrepieces of roses, lilies and hydrangeas, looked like an ad in *Architectural Digest*.

'Ah, what a coincidence!' Max smiled roguishly. 'We are lunch partners. I'm so happy.'

'So am I,' smiled Carlotta beatifically.

Lunch conversation was punctuated by explosive noises from the engines of the cars zooming around the track, but by the end of it, Carlotta felt she had found a new friend in Maximus Gobbi.

And Maximus Gobbi felt he had found a new patron.

Chapter Four

Buenos Aires, May 2015

After the death of her father, Flora had been begging her mother to send her to tennis camp in Connecticut in the summer and Carlotta had agreed. With the prospect of being unencumbered for two months, she decided to contact Maximus and tell him of her potential plans. 'I was thinking of coming to Monaco again,' she said tentatively. 'It's so beautiful and serene.'

'Serene? Yes, *cara*, serene like a graveyard,' Maximus cooed. 'It's really terribly boring for young people. You know what they say about it?'

'No, what?'

'A sunny place for shady people. No, no, my dear. Not Monaco for the summer season. It's far too dull and far too many old people. You must come to Saint-Tropez. You will adore it. If you will allow, I shall find you a suitable house to rent, and maybe even a suitable replacement for Nicanor?' He laughed a great rumbling bellow.

'Oh!' she exclaimed. 'I hadn't really thought of that. It's . . . it's much too soon – I haven't thought much about anything other than my Flora since her father died, but I would like to have some fun,' she added wistfully.

'Well, it is always a long, wonderful summer,' purred Maximus. 'And full of fun. Anything can happen in Saint-Tropez, and it usually does.'

'Perhaps that is exactly the kind of summer that I need after this . . . this terrible time. I'll think about it.'

'Yes, of course, my dear, but don't think too long. The best houses to rent are snapped up *très vite*. But do please come. I know you will love it. There is so much to do. Apart from a divine social life there are great beaches and restaurants, there is water skiing, paragliding and wonderful shopping.'

'Oh, I love shopping.'

'As far as shopping goes, the market every Tuesday and Saturday at the Place des Lices is a fabulous bustling bazaar. You can find everything there from antiques to artichokes and cheese to cheesecloths.' He bellowed with laughter at his own wit.

'That sounds amazing.'

'Oh, it is – it is indescribable. In the morning you can spend time browsing at the market, then have a slow, delicious lunch at one of the glamorous beaches.'

Carlotta sighed, 'That sounds wonderful.'

'Then, my dear, we now have every top brand shop – Dolce, Chanel, Vuitton, Gucci, Dior – not to mention dozens of tiny little boutiques selling one-of-a-kind outfits. It is a ladies' delight. I shall take you there, my dear. You will become addicted to Saint-Tropez, most people do.'

'It sounds too good to be true.'

'Oh, it is – it certainly is. My dear, it is unlike anywhere else in the world, so what do you think?'

'I will certainly try to come. I'll let you know as soon as possible.'

'Good, good. Don't wait too long or all the best houses will be gone,' he repeated.

'I'll let you know next week. My daughter wants to go to tennis camp for the summer so I will be free.'

'Wonderful, so I will make all the arrangements. I shall give a fabulous party for you to welcome you. I know everyone who matters in Saint-Tropez, and the rest of the Côte d'Azur too, for that matter.'

Indeed it was true. Maximus Gobbi knew everyone and everyone knew him. No matter that many would cross the road rather than acknowledge him, he was a party organiser *par excellence*, a mover and a shaker (in spite of his bulk), and he knew where many skeletons hid in the closets of the rich and famous.

After she hung up, Carlotta laughed for the first time in a month. Her hopes for a wonderful summer in Saint-Tropez and the possibility of finding true love, if such a thing actually existed, seemed to be coming true.

CHAPTER FIVE

30 Boulevard Suchet, Paris, May 2015

Maximus Gobbi had always been used to thinking on his feet. The youngest of a brood of eight hunky boys, he had been forced to wheedle, manipulate and even fight to get what he felt he deserved. Whether that was a small bowl of soup or the last crust of bread he would have to grab from his brothers, life had never been easy for young Maximus.

His elder brothers teased him mercilessly as he was a change-of-life baby born to a woman already worn out by motherhood and the slavery of running a home for nine males. She gave short shrift to little Maximus, who early on learned to live by his wits.

The family lived outside Naples in a tiny crumbling tenement apartment, which still bore the scars of the war that had ended the year Maximus entered the world. His brothers all worked in the dockyards with his increasingly ailing father, hauling enormous crates from the ships that crammed the flourishing post-war harbours. The ships and what they contained were supposed to bring prosperity to Naples and to Italy, but if they did bring it they brought it only to the wealthy, and the Gobbi family saw little of it. The men made enough to feed, clothe and pay the overpriced apartment rent, but there was none left over for the most minimum of necessities.

Since Maximus was fourteen years younger than his nearest brother, his hand-me-downs were always ludicrously too big, so to dress him half-decently his mother had to rely on the kindness of neighbours. A quiet and furtive boy, Max kept his head down and his thoughts to himself. He knew no one in his family would be remotely interested in anything he had to say in any case.

The one thing he had in his favour, however, was stunning good looks. Penetrating deep blue eyes fringed with thick black lashes, a mass of curly jet-black hair and a slim elegant physique were the attributes that attracted Federico Braganza, the celebrated movie director, one fine spring day in 1961. He was in Naples, on location in a café on the waterfront. He noticed the young Maximus, who had wangled a job as an extra in the background.

After a short, probing conversation, Federico discovered that sixteen-year-old Max was a) a virgin, having never been with either boy or girl, and b) bored – bored stiff by his life; he hated his family and he had no idea what to do with himself.

Federico soon sorted out both these problems. With the minimum of fuss, Maximus bade goodbye to his brothers, who couldn't have cared less about him, and to his parents, who were on their last legs in any case, and accompanied Braganza in his beautiful new Maserati to Rome – to the eternal city.

∞

In 1962 La Dolce Vita was in full swing. The sidewalks and cafés of the Via Veneto thronged with the international new jet setters and movie stars from the 1940s and 1950s, who were trying to revive waning careers. Masses of gorgeous young men and women, many on the make or on the lookout for a producer who might cast them in one of the many epics being filmed, also spent the afternoons drinking in the cafés and hitting the glamorous clubs at night.

Max was in heaven. Federico moved him into his luxurious apartment on the Via Condotti above the chic bustling shopping street, gave him a generous allowance and instructed him thoroughly in the art of homosexual Kama Sutra. Max was a fast learner, and with Federico busy at Cinecittà Studios all day, he started to practise his new-found amatory skills on a variety of handsome young bucks, not to mention older gentlemen, who often paid for the privilege.

After a few years, when Federico predictably tired of him, Maximus had managed to save enough *lira* to buy a tiny apartment in the chic Trastevere district of Rome. There he started to really enjoy the good life and live it to the hilt. He realised he had a knack of putting people together – particularly older, richer people who wanted to connect with famous people, and particularly young and good-looking ones. With his entrée into the show-business life, Maximus's address book was full of contacts – important, rich and influential people, dozens of hungry, handsome boys and gorgeous girls, and the occasional transexual for specialty tastes.

He soon saw the opportunity to have his business branch out across Europe, and took a small *pied-à-terre* in Paris, which doubled as an office. It suited his penchant for luxury to act like a jet setter.

Never having had enough to eat as a child, Maximus soon started to grow in girth at an alarming rate. His love of pasta, wine and rich desserts knew no bounds, and by the time he was forty, he tipped the scales at north of three hundred pounds.

Food and wine soon took the place of sex, and since his beauteous looks had long gone, he turned his talents to procuring young men for other men and women who would pay for the privilege. He collected a stable of hungry studs to suit every taste. But it was a perilous profession with no security and no state pension.

By the time he was pushing seventy, Max had become extremely worried about his financial future. Many of his young studs had found ways to circumvent him and go direct to the consumer; money was therefore extremely tight.

Maximus glared at his bank statement in a fury. '*Merde!* No-no-no-*nooooo! Non è posso!* Marie Christine!! *Viene qui!*' he yelled for his secretary, hoping she would come up with something – anything – to get him out of yet another ghastly financial situation. It seemed as soon as he solved one money problem, another one popped up.

'She's out to lunch.' Fabrizio Bricconni strolled in the door, shirt open to his navel, cigarette drooping à la Bogart from Cupid-bow lips. '*Ciao, caro, che è successo?* Why are you in such a state?'

Shit, thought Maximus, why is he here now? No matter, every encounter presents a possible solution.

'My dear boy,' he said unctuously, 'such a pleasure!' Maximus rearranged his features in order to beam at his prize protégé – definitely the most lucrative of his stable but a slippery piece of work. 'Fabrizio, *caro*, so good to see you. What are you doing in Paris?'

'I'm here meeting some producers from Kazakhstan. They're making an *X Factor* there and they're considering using me,' Fabrizio announced proudly.

'Really?' Maximus lowered his glasses and focused fully on Fabrizio, rapidly making calculations of possible financial outcomes. 'But, my dear boy, whoever told you you could sing?'

'I can sing, bitch,' Fabrizio replied sulkily. 'I've been taking lessons here in Paris . . . with Lara's blessing,' he added.

'Ahhh, so how *is* Madame Lara?' Max asked with bonhomie, then sharply spat, 'Did you make the deal yet?'

Maximus had been conspiring to make Fabrizio marry Lara Meyer since last summer. They both knew she had formed an inordinate obsession with Fabrizio (which even she admitted started and ended below the waist). But there was no denying her possessive adoration and Maximus mercilessly exploited that weakness. Maximus's objective was financial: Fabrizio's marriage to Lara Meyer would mean an increased monthly stipend, of which he would collect 20 per cent, plus an additional 20 per cent ownership of all of Lara's assets, which Fabrizio would share as soon as Lara convinced her controlling ex-husband to drop the intricate pre-nup his New York lawyers insisted on which stopped her from getting anything if she remarried.

But Fabrizio was becoming a real pain in the ass now. Content to draw on the already generous monthly allowance he was receiving from Lara, he was in no hurry to be pressured into wedlock. There were still too many female fish in the sea to sample – and what did he have to gain?

'All right, all right, all *right*,' Fabrizio drawled, *à la* Matthew McConaughey.

Maximus winced. He had tried to make Fabrizio stop attempting to emulate the American actor, but Fabrizio's harem thought it cute.

'Why are you still on about "the deal"? *Everythin's okay.*' Fabrizio continued, ramming home the caricature impression, which he knew irritated Maximus.

'Look, Fabrizio,' Maximus wheezed menacingly, 'you may be "okay", but Lara is not "okay" and I am *sicuramente* not "okay". I expect this deal to be made by the end of the summer or you will start not feeling "okay", *okay?*'

Fabrizio put on his 'little boy lost' bewildered look, which had served to diffuse many a difficult situation, but it had been over-used on Maximus. 'Chill. Everything's cool. Kazakhstan X *Factor*

41

definitely will go for me. I mean, I've seen some of the talentless nobodies – I'm a lock, bitch.'

'Don't call me bitch and don't give me your "everything's cool" shit! Kazakhstan is bullshit! It will never happen. Close the deal now before Lara finds out about CRAP!'

Fabrizio shuddered. CRAP – Carina, Raimunda, Alberto, Pietro – Fabrizio's two ex-lovers and their two children, was an acronym used between Maximus and Fabrizio. He was only able to maintain them through Lara's generosity. Maximus only mentioned CRAP when things became dire. Things must be very dire, thought Fabrizio, for it to be aired.

'If I can only get the bitch to sober up,' Fabrizio muttered. 'She's drunk morning, noon and night. Do you realise how hard it is for me to get . . . hard?'

'Think of someone else,' Max said dismissingly. 'It always worked for me – or get the blue pill.'

'Yeah, but you haven't had to get it up since the last century,' Fabrizio chortled, as Maximus's phone started ringing. Fabrizio, sensing advantage, sauntered to the door. 'See ya in Saint Trop, bitch. *Ciao* for now.'

'*Merde*,' snapped Maximus, picking up the phone. '*Ciao*, Maximus Gobbi.' He smiled as he heard the girlish voice.

'Oh, *ciao*, Maximus, it's Contessa Carlotta Di Ponti here. I've been thinking about your suggestion and I think it's a wonderful idea. I'd love to come to Saint-Tropez. It sounds divine for the summer. Do you think you could find me a house?'

'Of course, Contessa – *ne vous inquiétez de rien* – I'll take care of everything.' Maximus covered the receiver and hissed to Fabrizio, who had stopped in his tracks when he heard a young female voice and was lurking, ears hawk-like, 'Make the fucking Lara deal, now piss off!'

Maximus resumed his conversation after Fabrizio had strolled off. 'Sì, sì, Contessa, what a pleasure to speak to you.' He used his most honeyed tones. 'When do you hope to come?'

'Maybe early June would be good.'

As Max listened to Carlotta's hopes for a fun-filled life in Saint-Tropez, his mind started churning. If Fabrizio couldn't get Lara to commit to marry him, maybe he would look more enthusiastically towards the far younger and far more attractive Carlotta. He cast his mind back, visualising the petite raven-haired girl with the gypsy curls and innocent eyes. It would be a perfect match and one that Fabrizio surely couldn't resist. Besides, her net worth had to be larger than Lara's, and she had no pesky ex-husband to contend with.

Max chose his words carefully – he didn't want to scare off the prey. 'Now, there is just a tiny matter of my, eh, consideration?'

'Of course I understand.' Carlotta hadn't been around the Buenos Aires business world without wising up to their cunning ways. Besides, she had more money than she could ever use, and if a little extra would buy her some fun – why not? 'I will tell my secretary Amelia and she will take care of all your needs.'

'It's a pleasure, Contessa – an enormous pleasure. I promise I shall make your dreams come true. I am always at your service, and I shall take care of everything – absolutely everything!'

'Amelia! Please give Monsieur Gobbi your email,' Maximus heard her call. 'Goodbye, Monsieur Gobbi – see you in Saint-Tropez. I shall send you my arrival dates.'

'I shall meet you at Nice Airport,' he said with a great big smile on his great big face. Maximus leaned back and smiled. This could be what his American friends called a 'slam dunk', and it had come not a moment too soon.

CHAPTER SIX

Sénéquier Café and Bar, Saint-Tropez, May 2015

'Maximus, *Maximus!*' Lara Meyer blubbered down her cell phone. At eleven a.m. she was already on her third vodka-on-the-rocks with a slice of orange, telling anyone who asked that it was just water.

'Lara, *cara*, calm down. I spoke to Fabrizio. He is in Paris for the next few days, taking singing lessons . . . '

'Singing lessons? *Singing lessons?*' she shrieked into the receiver, making more than one head at the charming café turn. *'Who is she?'*

'He *told* you he was in Paris, with me.'

'Oh, yes . . . ' A faint memory emerged from her alcoholic mist.

'Go home now, Lara, get some rest. You need it.'

'I just got up, idiot.' Lara's voice was suddenly cold as ice. 'I'm not talking about his singing lessons, you moron. He's with another girl, I can sense it – I can feel it. The slut is kissing him, I can feel it,' she slurred, her fury subsiding as quickly as it rose. 'Besides, he doesn't want me, he only wants my money. I'm too . . . too . . . ' The word 'old' stuck in her throat, so she gulped another slug of Grey Goose and slid further down in her chair, revealing a beautifully manicured lady garden, thanks to the fact that she wore no underwear.

45

Lara was perched under the shaded part of the terrace of the Sénéquier Café and Bar on the front of the bustling port of Saint-Tropez. It was a perfect early summer day; the big white yachts were still being hosed down by the good-looking young deck hands to prepare for their voyages, and sloppily dressed tourists wandered by drinking in all the glamour and hoping some of it would rub off on them. A few glanced at the red-headed woman, wearing a short, unsuitable floral play-dress and comedy earrings, sprawled in a chair. Black shades could not hide the classic Slavic cheekbones of a world-famous celebrity and the notorious ex-wife of the infamous tycoon Jonathan Meyer.

Often known as the 'Siberian siren' (and, to some people, the 'Slavic slut'), Lara's glory days were far behind her. However, she still commanded attention in the Eurotrash set and with readers of celebrity magazines. But today she wasn't in the mood to take 'selfies' with her fans and brusquely got rid of a couple with a dismissive wave.

Aware of the tourists' curious glances, a young waiter threw a white napkin over her nether regions as Lara sank even further into her seat, holding the vodka glass up to shield her face. 'So,' she whispered, 'if he wasn't with someone else, where the hell was he?'

'Lara, calm down. He was just with me in Paris on his way to his singing lessons and I promise there was no slut, stupid or otherwise. I have a tail on him all the time.' Maximus had been getting an extra stipend from Lara for a private detective service, one so discreet it was like a phantom, which in fact it was.

'So, where are those photos you promised?'

'What? They didn't send them yet? *Merde*, those idiots! I will demand they send them immediately or else I promise you they will be fired!' Firing was Maximus's best expedient for getting out of a ruse – and he always knew how to end a con before it backfired. 'But, my dear, there is nothing incriminating in them.'

'Maximus, *Maximusssshh!*' Lara stared at her cell phone. 'Are you still there . . .? What was I saying?' Lara's short skirt was riding up to her waist now as she slid down almost horizontally.

Realising she was almost completely exposed, she pulled down her skirt, no mean feat holding a glass of vodka, and suddenly her vision gained a new perspective – she'd never noticed the ceiling at Sénéquier before. It was a nice ceiling, freshly painted white. She dropped her cell phone and gazed, in mesmerised admiration, at a fat bumblebee lazily circumventing the ceiling.

'Madame.' A waiter – whose pity had clearly overwhelmed his Gallic sensibility for *laissez faire* – sidled up, picked up her phone, and suggested maybe he could help hoist her back up to a sitting position.

'I'm just resting,' Lara replied curtly, then wailed piteously to the bumblebee on the ceiling, 'Oh, what am I to do?'

'Madame?' The waiter was confused that this famous socialite seemed to be engaging in conversation with him, although she wasn't looking at him. He bent closer, staring, fascinated by her artificially enhanced features. Face job, nose job, boob job, nail and hair extensions and, underneath the shades that had slipped halfway down her face, weird turquoise contact lenses . . . *which part of her was real?* he wondered.

His colleagues behind the bar sniggered. This had happened to all of them at one time or another – François, the rookie waiter, was about to get hooked into an endless conversation about Lara's love trouble with Fabrizio. An hour wasted just for taking pity on the poor creature. Tips would be lost due to the unenviable task of dragging Lara back to her flat on Rue des Ponches.

A deep voice from her phone suddenly boomed, 'LARA? LARA! ARE YOU STILL THERE?' Maximus's voice reverberated off the rafters of Sénéquier, chasing the bumblebee away and startling Lara out of her reverie. She pressed the 'end call' button in a daze and her focus was suddenly wrenched back to her phone, which started ringing almost immediately.

'Who on earth is calling me at this time of day?' she snapped at a surprised François. 'Don't they know it's impolite to call before noon? And what happened to Maximus? Wasn't I just talking to him?' Lara's eyes swam in and out of focus.

François picked up the phone and handed it to Lara. She mumbled, 'I'll call you back,' and then, overwhelmed, blacked out and almost fell to the floor. François caught her just in time.

∽

François wasn't as stupid as some people thought. He knew all the gossip about the trampy Lara Meyer: a rich bitch who drank like a fish and, when in her cups, stupid as a sheep about men, especially her gigolo, Fabrizio Bricconni.

'I'll take her home,' he insisted as the manager, Jean-Robert, came rushing over to see what was going on. 'I know where she lives.' He avoided the eyes of several British and German tourists gaping at this staple of the celebrity magazines passed out cold.

He took the spare key to Lara's third-floor apartment from a hook behind the restaurant's bar, then hoisted her none-too-slender frame further on to his young shoulders like a sack of coal and quickly jogged a few streets away to where she lived, while Lara's red head bounced up and down against his back. He entered the dark, stuffy apartment, strewn with the detritus of Lara and Fabrizio's chaotic existence – empty vodka bottles, magazines, clothes, shoes, underwear – and none too gently lowered her on to the unmade bed.

He stared at the stucco walls, where photographs and yellowing newspaper clippings were framed higgledy-piggledy. The tarnished silver frames cluttered every dusty surface. This poor cow was famous, thought François, but she had certainly seen better days. He was fascinated by the front page of a New York tabloid, which showed Lara, her then husband, Jonathan Meyer, and a beautiful teenaged blonde slugging it out on the slopes of Saint Moritz. 'Can Divorce Be Far Behind?' shrieked the tabloid. Another cover picture on *People* magazine, in colour, featured a much younger and more beautiful Lara in a gorgeous wedding gown, exchanging vows with Jonathan Meyer. 'Inside the Golden Couple's fabulous wedding', the banner headline shrieked. 'Tycoon Weds Glamour Model'.

'Ha, the jet set – bunch of losers,' muttered François. He surveyed the room, then returned to where Lara lay splayed out awkwardly. Looking down at her, he spied a key lying on the floor, half under a rug. Close inspection revealed it was a replica of Lara's door key.

Without hesitation, François pocketed the key, then opened one of the drawers next to the bed. Inside was a mess of bottles of pills, face creams, candy wrappers and some diamond earrings and gold bangles, all hopelessly mixed up with hairpins, lipstick and a couple of sex toys. 'What a slut,' he muttered, resisting the urge to pocket the earrings too. Then he walked silently to the door, leaving the snoring Lara to her slumbers.

CHAPTER SEVEN

The First Party of the Saint-Tropez Season, early June 2015

Carlotta had arrived in Saint-Tropez the previous day. Maximus had met her at the airport and driven her to a beautiful small house in the Parc de Californie, which he had rented for the season.

'One of the most prestigious addresses in Saint-Tropez,' he announced proudly. He introduced her to the staff – Lilliane, a housekeeper and cook, who was married to the gardener, Denis. 'And Denis will also drive you whenever you want to go somewhere.'

'Oh, but I love driving and I want to explore this beautiful part of Provence!'

'Excellent,' beamed Maximus. 'So, my dear, there is an amusing party tomorrow for Mina Corbain. Do you know her?'

'Of course, I met her with you last year at the Grand Prix. I mean – who doesn't know her? She has had a meteoric rise, hasn't she?'

'Yes, indeed she has. So you will you be my "plus one"?'

'Of course, I'd love to.'

'Well, my dear, then you should get some rest and I will pick you up at nine p.m. tomorrow.'

After he had left, Carlotta explored her new home with delight. It was charming, light and airy in the modern Provençal style – all white walls and furniture, cosy sofas and a brilliant azure pool that sparkled invitingly outside the sitting room, and a view of the Mediterranean that glittered and shone as hundreds of tiny yachts sailed gaily on the creamy waves.

I think I shall like it here, she thought as she lay on a sun lounger beside the pool, enjoying the hot, comforting sun on her body. *I think I shall like it a lot.*

∞

Carlotta was excited. She gripped Maximus's arm tightly as they sauntered into the spacious hallway of billionaire Harry Silver's palatial villa in Cap des Salins.

Harry Silver had made his fortune by selling arms to North Korea, but what the hell? Someone had to do it and this was, after all, Saint-Tropez, where for the most part you are only as good as your money, your youth, or your looks. Who cared where the money came from, as long as it was used to maximum effect and the procreation of pleasure?

Maximum effect had certainly been achieved on Harry's villa. It was an avant-garde vista of shining, whiter-than-white marble floors, with zebra-skin walls slotted between black mirrors, and fat black and white candles clustered on every surface.

It was a warm night and a full moon glimmered on the calm Mediterranean. A long table was set out on the terrace, thick with candles, orchids, Tiffany glasswear and gold cutlery. The sound of cicadas competed with the sound of South American sambas from Luigi the famous DJ, and the lights of Saint-Tropez twinkled across the water below.

'Ah, I see that the usual suspects are here,' confided Maximus to Carlotta. He loved nothing more than a good party, as did Charlie Chalk, the rotund and affable British TV personality who was the life and soul of every gathering. Next to Charlie stood his life-partner Spencer, an Australian 'trolley dolly' with Qantas Airlines, who spent more time faking illness to enjoy the Saint-Tropez high life than he did dispensing cocktails in the air.

Maximus introduced Carlotta and then pointed to a roguish middle-aged American movie star and whispered, 'There's Dirk Romano, aptly named "Dirk the dick". He loves dropping his pants and mooning the paparazzi while boating with his latest young fling, who is usually the age of his granddaughter.' Maximus laughed, wheezing as Carlotta followed his portly behind, wobbling in too-tight pink trousers, swaying over to greet their host.

Harry Silver was standing at the edge of the black onyx pool, a Havana cigar clenched between moustachioed lips, his slick, dyed-jet-black hair gleaming like a patent-leather helmet. Clutching at his legs, one on each, were his adopted twins, a pair of gorgeous three-year-old African infants, dressed in the latest blue denim diamanté-studded Saint-Tropez baby gear, their huge eyes gazing around with wonder.

'May I present the Contessa Carlotta Di Ponti?' Maximus said proudly. He loved a title, as did Harry, who bestowed a cigar-scented kiss on Carlotta's hand.

'I hope you'll enjoy the evening, Contessa. It's in honour of Mina Corbain as you know. Khris Kane is coming tonight and we will be the first to hear the new record he's produced with her,' bragged Silver.

Maximus was impressed. 'Khris Kane – he's the biggest record producer in the world now . . . And I hear Mina's out of rehab,' Maximus knew everything about everyone, thanks to TMZ, social media, and his gossipy acquaintances. Gossip was his currency and he used it to maximum advantage.

'This is the only party she will be coming to,' said Harry smugly, not mentioning that he was paying Mina a fortune to attend his soirée. This was just between him and her 'people', although Maximus suspected Harry had paid a whopping fee for the privilege. Superstars like Mina didn't attend parties of people they hardly knew, unless a lot of money changed hands. Mina was new and hot, a great coup to have at any event. Designers fawned over her and sent truckloads of clothes and handbags to her LA mansion, hoping she would choose to wear them and get their wares advertised for free in the media.

'Ah, here she comes now,' said Harry with forced nonchalance.

'*Mamma mia*, but she is gorgeous!' Maximus was awestruck. He was in social heaven. After money, parties and food, there was nothing that made his day more than meeting a real-life superstar.

'She's the biggest singer in the world now,' Harry had a self-satisfied grin on his face. 'And she's singing at *my* villa.'

'Hope she's off drugs,' said Charlie Chalk jovially as he watched Harry striding towards Mina to greet her.

Lara and Fabrizio were standing near Sophie Silvestri, her two acolytes propping her up as she tottered over to an inviting sofa. Fabrizio's face lit up as he saw the legendary actress. She had been his father's favourite and he admired her too. Lara was extremely jealous of the seventy-four-year-old icon and believed Fabrizio fancied her.

'Maybe when I was nine,' he had told her many times. 'Or maybe Papà did . . . when Papà was nine.' He laughed at his own joke.

Actually it suited Fabrizio for Lara to be jealous of Sophie. It allowed him to slip away for his alleged golf, tennis or gym sessions and let Lara's jealousy focus on Sophie when he was actually having matinées with some rich oligarch's trophy wife or a nubile young stranger from the beach.

'She's a witch,' hissed Lara, then stumbled over to embrace Harry with a vodka-scented air kiss. 'Darlink – we're so excited – tonight will be one to remember.'

'It will indeed,' replied Harry, and turned his back on her to continue talking to the ravishing Mina Corbain as the whole room gawked, basking in the glow of her celebrity.

Across the room, Sophie Silvestri glared at the young singer. So used was she to being the centre of attention at most Saint-Tropez parties that her nose was being put seriously out of joint.

But that didn't faze Mina who, seeing the legendary actress, hastened towards Sophie to greet her with a warm embrace and several air kisses. 'Oh, my God! They said you'd retired! I didn't know you STILL went out,' she said excitedly. 'Oh, I always admired you so much, my mom did too!'

Tight-lipped, Sophie allowed herself to be hugged and kissed, her nose wrinkling at the strong scent the girl wore.

Mina beamed, taking Sophie's expression of distaste for admiration. 'It's my new signature perfume: "Scallywag". Do you like it? I'll send you some.'

'It's – lovely – er – quite original.' Sophie tried to escape from the singer's embrace, conscious that the whole room was agog at the sight of these two divas, generations apart, face to face. She cast a 'help me' look towards Frick and Adolpho, but they were too awestruck by this amazing summit meeting to do anything but take pictures on their cell phones. Mina was hanging on to Sophie's arm, chattering away, and wouldn't let her go.

'I hear she got two hundred and fifty thousand euros just to show up tonight,' Maximus whispered to Carlotta, equally entranced by the tableau.

'What did Sophie get then?'

'Nothing,' he sneered. 'Everybody's seen her a million times. She's over. Yesterday's news.'

'I love your dress – it's so retro!' Mina gabbled to Sophie admiringly. 'My grandmother had one just like it in the 1960s! She loved your movies so much that she used to take me to all of them when I was a little girl.'

Sophie had had enough. Mumbling a brief, 'Oh, how sweet', she wrested herself from the singer's grip and toddled on her agonising stilettos over to Frick and Adolpho. She noticed Lara staring at her and recalled that fateful night twenty-five years ago at the Manhattan opening of her elegant new fashion line, when she was still a big star and a society hostess to be reckoned with. Lara and Jonathan Meyer, the darlings of New York society at the time, hosted the event. However, Sophie had been given the wrong address and was photographed by a gleeful paparazzo, who was inexplicably also at the empty restaurant when she entered triumphantly to be welcome by a bemused junior waiter with a tray full of dirty dishes.

The photos went viral and the papers ridiculed her mercilessly. Sophie was sure Lara had planned it on purpose to embarrass her and claim the number one spot in the Manhattan social world, which she soon did. Sophie had never forgiven her because – over the next fifteen years – young and beautiful Lara had become one of the top hostesses on the charity circuit in New York, while Sophie's star as an actress waned. Eventually, when the phone stopped ringing she decided to exile herself back to France again, where she was still an icon.

Sophie was a cunning creature who cared little for her fellow man, and she didn't particularly like women either. She lavished all her love and attention on the thirty cats and dogs that shared her grand dilapidated villa, high in the hills above

Saint-Tropez. They slept on her bed and left trails of droppings all over the house. Consequently, although Sophie managed to pull herself together in the glamour department when she went out, she never quite managed to erase the faint feline aroma that clung to her costumes. She had never married or had children, and had been famed for a constant stream of lovers, usually of the out-of-work musician, magician or bodybuilder variety. But recently there had been no young lovers and she relied on Frick and Adolpho to escort her to events like tonight's party.

'She's amazing for her age, isn't she?' Mina announced to her assembled admirers, but loud enough for Sophie to hear. Diplomacy was not the singer's forte, and she seemed unaware that being more than five decades younger than the actress, this was a terrible faux pas.

'Yes, amazing,' agreed Fabrizio, who had managed to ooze himself past Mina's hangers-on and admirers. Using his most seductive Italian stallion technique, he clasped both her hands in his and gazed into her big brown eyes. 'But *you* are so amazing. Incredible, you are incredible. No wonder they call you the most beautiful singer in the world.'

Mina accepted the compliment as her due, dismissing Fabrizio with a cursory smile. Yes, he was handsome, but handsome studs were a dime-a-dozen in LA, and she certainly had her plate full right now. She politely removed his hands and drifted over to Khris Kane, who was busily knocking back the vintage Cristal with property wunderkind Roberto LoBianco.

Roberto was enthralling Khris and a few other guests with the merits of the new luxury resort he was developing on an island 70 kilometres across the water from Saint-Tropez. 'Saint-Sébastien will make Saint-Tropez look like Bognor Beach,' he enthused. 'It has everything Saint-Tropez has but much more, and it's totally exclusive. You can only get there by boat so there won't be all that tourist riff-raff. I know we're going to get a lot of the rich folk who live here to buy there. It's hot, it's new and it's absolutely glamorous – it's really happening.'

'No one will give up Saint-Tropez,' said Khris Kane. 'It's an institution – it's legendary. There will never be a place to rival its uniqueness, its glamorous reputation and fame.'

'Ah, but remember the shit weather last season,' said Roberto. 'How many people upped sticks and went to Greece or Ibiza?'

'That is true,' agreed Charlie Chalk sadly.

'You could hardly get your yachts out of port,' scoffed Roberto. 'There was one mistral after another – it was tragic.'

'My God, but what will happen to the season in Saint-Tropez if people leave?' asked Charlie. 'So many locals depend on it for their living. We need the tourists and the high rollers to live here in their villas and give their dinners and parties here. Thousands of people rely on them.'

Roberto shrugged. 'Not my problem, Charlie,' he grinned, clapping the comedian on the back, 'and not yours either, dear boy. Just enjoy it while it lasts.'

At 10.30 p.m. the thirty guests sat down to a dinner of oysters on the half-shell, followed by bouillabaisse, the classic Côte d'Azur dish prepared by the owner of a small beach shack commonly regarded as making the most authentic example of this delectable fare. They dined on the moonlit terrace while Mina's surplus entourage was placed at another hastily cobbled-together table in the main salon.

A dozen white-clad waiters busied about, including François from the Sénéquier Café. He gave Lara a knowing, saucy smile as he set her oysters before her.

'What's with him?' asked Fabrizio, annoyed. Although a

championship flirt in his own right, it irritated him when any man put the moves on Lara.

'Nothing, *caro*,' she mollified. 'I have no idea who he is,' she added with sincere befuddlement, as she indeed had no memory of that May morning at Sénéquier. She put her hand soothingly on what Fabrizio often referred to as 'my noble tool'.

During the second course, a young magician entertained the guests at the table, because God forbid they'd have to rely on conversation. Brilliant bons mots at these parties usually consisted of celebrity gossip, scintillating questions such as, 'When did you get here?', 'How long are you staying?', and comments about the weather.

Carlotta was enthralled, Mina was bored, and Sophie was irritated. She hated magicians. Many years ago she had taken one as a lover and had had to watch over and over again as he practised his silly card tricks on her and the dogs. The dogs seemed far more interested in the tricks than she was, as he whisked playing cards from behind their ears and under their tails. Fed up one night, she rubbed his nether regions with bacon fat while he was sleeping and he woke up to find the entire menagerie fighting to get at his genitalia. Needless to say, she never saw him again.

The magician, aware of Sophie's basilisk stare that telegraphed unequivocally *get near me, kid, and I will have your balls for dinner*, and recalling the fate of the hapless magician who had shacked up with her, instead opted for Mina as his foil *pour la nuit* and was directing most of his magic to her.

Mina yawned behind her big fan, always a useful device to deflect attention and to swat away over-eager fans if her entourage failed to jump to it. She feigned interest. For 250,000 euros, she could feign anything, and watching the conjurer was preferable to engaging in small talk with Harry, the ghastly arms-dealer host, or the even more ghastly oligarch Sergei Litvak sitting on the other side of her. The conjurer was taking control of the table, asking people to choose a card, which would magically appear, half-covered in saliva from under his tongue. After masticating several cards and regurgitating them in this fashion, which was met with limited applause, he started doing disgusting things with balloons.

'*Regardez*,' beamed the magician proudly as he blew up a red balloon into a long sausage shape and swallowed the entire thing as the guests watched in shock and amazement.

'Revolting,' growled Sophie, sitting the other side of Harry, who was like a pig in clover sandwiched between the two divas.

'How does he do that?' asked Carlotta.

'Years of practice, my dear,' Maximus grinned knowingly. He knew this kid. The conjurer had been in his stable of cute rent boys several years ago. No wonder he was good at what he did with balloons.

Sophie shot her 'come near me at your peril' look at Maximus, whom she also loathed. She had overheard his earlier comment to Carlotta about Mina's vast fee. Last year, she had suggested that she might receive a little 'present' for attending an oligarch's party that Maximus was organising. He had practically laughed in her face and told her she was far too old to be interesting to the Russians. He was a pig. A fat, faggoty pig, and one day he'll get what's coming to him, thought Sophie darkly.

Sophie and Maximus went back a long way. Back, in fact, to when they were young and gorgeous in Rome in the 1960s. They were both living the good life. Rome was known as Hollywood on the Tiber and the bustling studios of Cinecittà and Scalera thronged with moviemakers, moguls and starlets, all waiting for a break. Sophie, at the height of her beauty and fame, could have any man she wanted, and one night at a party at the Grand Hotel what she wanted was young Maximus.

At dinner they flirted, chatted, and got along so well that Max was not at all surprised when she invited him back to her hotel for a nightcap. Soon they were in her bed, but in spite of Sophie's expert ministrations, Max was unable to perform, much to her chagrin.

He managed to escape from her clutches with some semblance of dignity, for she took it as a personal rejection and made spiteful comments to him as he slunk out of the door. Soon Sophie let slip to the gossipmongers of the Via Veneto that not only was Maximus Gobbi impotent, but that his equipment was no bigger than a child's. He had never forgotten that, so he had started a counter-rumour that Sophie was a lesbian who only pretended to like men and hated sex. They had been icy to each other ever since.

The magician finally retrieved the balloon from the depths of his throat and presented it to Mina with a tiny bow. With her fan she swatted it over to Harry with an offended squawk. The balloon burst in his face and the other guests giggled at his discomfort.

For his finale, the magician let off a series of tiny firecrackers behind several of the ladies' ears, which caused them all to shriek and hold on to their hairpieces.

'Enough!' thundered Khris finally to Harry. 'Isn't it time to hear Mina's new record?'

'Of course. Let's have dessert in the living room,' Harry said smoothly.

∞

They gathered in the huge open living room in which every surface was covered in glass and gold bric-a-brac and the soft furnishings were made from the skin of nearly extinct animals. Harry's sound system was state of the art and soon the CD of Mina's amazing voice echoed throughout the marble hall and carried down to the beaches. Her first ballad was a thinly disguised tale of her problems with an abusive husband, who got her hooked on coke. It brought tears to everyone's eyes, except Sophie, whose eyes were boring jealous holes into Mina's back.

Several classic standards performed in an innovative modern style were greeted with appreciative applause, and then an upbeat eighties disco-style song brought the normally blasé revellers to their feet; in classic Saint-Tropez style they started dancing and waving their arms in the air.

Maximus fancied himself as a cool mover and shaker, and in spite of his bulk, he shook his massive booty in front of a slightly embarrassed Carlotta.

Fabrizio reluctantly pranced with Lara, who always became a total exhibitionist on the dance floor, waving her disastrously bingo-winged arms above her head in a wild yet catastrophic facsimile of a teenybopper and flashing sun-damaged thighs in her sparkly red mini-dress. The seven vodkas she'd consumed added to her lunatic abandonment.

As the music became more frenzied, so did the dancing, and Mina's golden voice and her strong backing singers even drowned out the relentless sounds of the cicadas.

Then, almost as one, several of the dancing guests bent over, clutching their stomachs in agony. Some of them ran into the garden to vomit into the azaleas, while the other guests watched in horrified amazement.

'My God!' shrieked Sophie.

'It's the plague,' screamed Fabrizio, a total hypochondriac. Running to the onyx swimming pool, he threw up into it, then tumbled in.

Suddenly over half the guests were in paroxysms of pain; those who weren't tried to assist each other with the help of the waiters who seemed unaffected.

'Somebody call an ambulance,' yelled Harry.

'We need more than one!' gasped Maximus, through a paroxysm of pain.

Lying on the ground, face up, Britain's favourite comic, Charlie Chalk, his white face now matching his last name, lay completely still. His Australian lover Spencer cast himself, weeping, on to the vast expanse of his lover's inert body. 'Are you alright, darling?' he wailed. 'Please don't die, love.' As if to set his mind at rest, Charlie let out a loud burp and opened his eyes weakly. 'Thank God! I couldn't live without you!' Spencer started laughing and hugging Charlie's huge bulk, which made the comedian break some fierce wind.

Half an hour later, a phalanx of ambulances screeched to a halt as the retching and nausea reached a climax, coinciding with the final wailing soprano notes of Mina's CD.

At least everyone thought it was the final wailing notes of the CD, until Khris noticed that the music system had stopped and what could be heard was Mina herself, wailing in some undetermined location accompanied by a chorus of cicadas.

They started to search, but the young pop star's injured moans had stopped. Then a paramedic raised the alarm as he discovered Mina sprawled beside a lavender bush. He started frantically administering CPR as the stunned guests rushed down the incline to watch, then he shook his head gravely. 'I'm afraid she's gone.'

The assembled partygoers gasped in horror.

'Oh, my God!' shrieked Khris Kane. 'I'm ruined. What's going to happen to my tour?'

CHAPTER EIGHT

The day after the first party

Although Mina Corbain's death seemed like a straightforward case of severe food poisoning, under French law it immediately triggered an investigation.

When Captain Poulpe and his daughter Gabrielle arrived, they asked all the guests what they had eaten during the party.

Captain Poulpe was a short, stocky man of few words and many actions. He had been with the Saint-Tropez Gendarmerie for over thirty years and knew where the metaphorical bodies were buried. He had thinning black hair swept back from a broad intelligent brow and small brown eyes that seldom missed a trick. Invariably he wore a navy blue or grey three-piece suit even on the hottest of summer days. Everyone in town respected him because he never turned a blind eye whenever corrupt officials interfered with the small-business and beach-restaurant owners, who depended on making their money in the few precious months between April and September, which made them easy prey to coercion. He didn't tolerate the practice of *baksheesh* that seemed always to be prevalent in places that depended on tourism for their livelihood.

Gabrielle, his daughter, differed from him in that she was tall and lanky. She was a true tomboy, with flaming red hair that ran wild with curls and a sprinkle of freckles on her pretty, unmade-up face. But beneath the huckleberry exterior she was a good cop, and highly respected by those who knew her.

'There is no question that something poisonous in the food or drink has caused this mass outbreak. I note that none of the healthy guests has eaten the oysters,' Poulpe announced to the shaken guests, who had not been allowed to leave. 'There were plenty of other dishes that everyone had eaten but it seems that, of the unaffected guests, none had touched the oysters, so the source was unmistakable.'

He and Gabrielle then thoroughly queried each of the guests' activities on the day of the party to ascertain that none of them had anything to do with the preparation of the food. Having satisfied himself that none of them would fall under immediate suspicion, he allowed them to go home at four a.m., dazed and confused about the horrifying night. He even gallantly escorted Sophie to Adolpho and Frick's awaiting ministrations; much as he admired her, he had to place her on his list of suspects as well – now everyone was on it.

After the guests departed, Captain Poulpe returned to Harry Silver's staff waiting at the mansion. The chef told him that he had received the oysters from his regular party supplier the previous day.

'I thought they came from the Nice fish market, but I wasn't sure, so I kept them in ice for all that time,' he bleated. 'They couldn't possibly have gone bad.'

'Well, they did,' snapped Captain Poulpe. 'They most certainly did. Thirty people don't become extremely sick, with one dying, unless they've gone bad.'

The chef moaned, terrified of losing his job. 'It's not my fault,

I've never had a problem before and I've been serving oysters for Mr Silver for five years.'

'I know, I believe you.' Poulpe actually did believe the Algerian chef, a small, timid man, in France illegally. After all, he would be foolish to jeopardise his tenuous hold on residency.

'Understand that you are under suspicion – you'll be watched. If you as much as step out of the country, even out of this area, I will know about it,' he warned the chef, as he had all the other staff.

'I'm wondering whether someone tampered with the food,' Captain Poulpe told his daughter. 'It just seems odd that *so* many of the guests had such a violent reaction – so many, but not *all*. It would be understandable if one or two oysters had been contaminated, or one or two people were allergic; or indeed for everyone to fall ill if the whole batch was contaminated. But to have about half the guests falling sick – well, that seems really strange.' He would make sure the coroner checked all the possibilities at Mina's post-mortem.

Although the Mayor wanted this incident brushed under the carpet as quickly as possible to avoid the bad publicity that was sure to follow, Poulpe was certain this evening was far from accidental.

'No one is above suspicion,' he sighed to Gabrielle. 'Keep your eyes open for a very twisted mind.'

∞

It was the day after Mina's tragic death and Gabrielle had started the morning investigating the fishmongers who plied their trade in the ancient fish market situated behind the popular Sénéquier Café. The fishmongers displayed their wares beautifully, with every kind of fish laid out geometrically on marble slabs. The market was no more than a tiny alleyway from the main street leading to a small square where flowers, cheese and every kind of bread and pastry were sold. Work started at six a.m. and finished at two p.m., by which time the ground was awash with dirty, smelly water. Although the tradesmen cleaned the pavement, walls and surfaces of the alleyway assiduously with powerful lye, the odour of fish lingered in the aged tiled walls. At night the alley was dark and ominous, and few people fancied taking the stinking shortcut.

Gabrielle asked all the vendors to whom they had sold oysters within the past two days, but it appeared that the only bulk buyer had been a cook from a giant cruise ship that had departed before Harry Silver's party began. All other purchases had been small, but she logged them dutifully as her father had taught her.

Gabrielle finished her inquiries with each fishmonger and decided she merited a drink at Sénéquier. Everyone who was anyone – and plenty who weren't – visited the legendary Sénéquier Café. This area was truly the heart of the village, constantly bubbling with life. In the middle of the busy cobble-stoned street, and right in front of the port where the big white gin palaces lay at anchor, next to dozens of chic boutiques and restaurants, stood the Sénéquier, which had been feeding Saint-Tropez visitors since 1887.

She joined Charlie and his blond-headed lover Spencer, who sat at a table in the front of the Sénéquier sipping kirs and watching the world stroll by.

Cuddly Charlie Chalk, one of England's best-loved comedians, lived on a hill above Saint-Tropez, with his much younger civil partner Spencer Brown, in a small but beautifully decorated villa within walking distance of the town.

In the 1980s Charlie had made his money in England with a camp comedy sitcom called *Charlie's World*. He had invested shrewdly in that decade, a time when investments actually paid off, and now he and Spencer lived an idyllic life all year round, either in Saint-Tropez or travelling to exotic climes.

Gabrielle gently and casually started questioning Charlie and Spencer about the previous night as they sipped their kirs.

'It was a nightmare,' Charlie sighed, 'insane – I'm still feeling queasy. Poor, poor Mina! Such a great talent.' He sighed again, slightly more theatrically this time. 'But in spite of all the horror, the south of France is still the best place in the world to live. J'adore Saint-Tropez,' said Charlie, breaking out his execrable French accent.

'Oh, Lord, why don't you learn how to speak French properly?' sighed Spencer in exasperation. 'You've lived here long enough.'

Charlie was so popular that he spent his days accepting – and very occasionally declining – the myriad invitations he received. This also guaranteed that Spencer would always be around for the fun. Charlie was the life and soul of every lunch, cocktail soirée and dinner, and the confidant of many of Saint-Tropez's elite. When he wasn't socialising or travelling, he spent his time cultivating beautiful English roses, a difficult task in a Mediterranean climate, particularly since nests of wasps lived in the old stone walls of his garden.

'Don't you miss England then?' Gabrielle giggled, slightly forgetting the interrogation in her amusement. Charlie could make the most banal remarks entertaining with his theatrical delivery. Round and ruddy-faced, he was always beaming, and had a hearty laugh that announced his arrival at any gathering.

'Darling, I visit the cold and depressing UK only occasionally for medical or dental work. In fact, going there is exactly like having root canal treatment!' he guffawed.

'And for your charity work,' said Spencer loyally.

'Ah yes, of course.' Charlie smiled modestly, then wrinkled his nose. 'Join us for lunch now, darling. This smell is getting to me. It's all very fishy,' he quipped.

'I don't have time for lunch,' said Gabrielle. 'I still have to interrogate the caterers and the rest of the vendors that provided food for Harry Silver's dinner.'

'Phew! I can still smell the fish!' gasped Charlie, fanning himself with a copy of *Nice Matin*. 'Let's go to the Aqua Club.'

'Sorry, I can't.' Gabrielle stood up to leave, then blew him a kiss goodbye and walked away.

'Oh, I do love it here,' grinned Spencer, eyeing up the cute young waiter who was serving the table next to them. 'Oh look, here come the autograph hunters now, Charlie. Aren't you the lucky one?'

With that a portly mother and father from Yorkshire shyly shuffled up to Charlie with their two bored-looking children and asked if they could have their photo taken with him.

'Of course,' said Charlie benevolently, as he attempted to balance the rather overweight twins on his already overburdened knees. 'My pleasure,' he croaked.

'We love your show,' screeched the harridan mother, her stringy hair pulled back tightly into a 'Croydon facelift'. 'We watch all the re-runs.'

'Thank you, my dear, you're too kind,' Charlie gasped, trying to remove the children, who insisted on clinging to him while the father snapped frantically away on his mobile phone. Charlie was sweating hard, but the six-year-olds had attached themselves to him like leeches, mugging and grinning for their dad's camera.

A couple of local paparazzi magically appeared and started snapping the happy scene. Charlie attempted an avuncular grin while shifting the kids in front of him to try and hide his tummy.

Suddenly François, the young waiter, stepped in.

'*Excusez-moi*,' he snapped to the father, 'Monsieur Chalk is on holiday, so please respect his privacy.'

The children started to whimper as their mother pulled them off the puce-faced comedian, and in the struggle spilled his drink all over the front of his trousers. The eager snappers continued snapping furiously, to the amusement of the other habitués.

The waiter got busy with a napkin to mop Charlie up, which gave Charlie a burgeoning erection. The children began screaming with rage as the fat mother grabbed at their chubby little legs, trying to remove them from Charlie's ankles. The photographers loved it.

'I'll get five hundred quid for these from *OK!*,' grinned Pete the 'Brit-pap' as he was known locally. His red hair was sticking out of his weathered NY baseball cap and sweat was running down his freckled face.

'Forget them, I'm trying for the *Daily Mail* online with this one!' The older photographer, Jean-Pierre, had spotted the famous American actor Dirk Romano, descending from a yacht, with two gorgeous Russian hookers on his arm. He scooted over, scattering irate patrons on the way.

'Thank you so much, young man,' Spencer purred sweetly, as the waiter mopped up the spilled kir from Charlie's lap. Always aware of a pretty face he gushed, 'That's so considerate of you.'

'It's nothing,' said François, locking eyes with Spencer and virtually ignoring Charlie.

'These people are pests,' said Spencer, focusing all his charm on François.

'Your English is so good. What's your name?' asked Charlie, not taking kindly to being overlooked.

'François,' he replied, quickly pocketing the twenty-euro note

Spencer had slipped in the pouch of his apron. 'François Lardon, *à votre service.*' He gave a tiny bow and a secret smile: 'François Lardon, which in English translates to Francis Bacon.'

'Rather amusing,' Charlie said frostily, realising that Spencer seemed far too interested in the handsome waiter.

Gabrielle suddenly reappeared on her scooter and shooed the paparazzo away. François grinned at her. *Too pretty to be a cop,* he thought. *What a waste – those gorgeous auburn curls, those cute freckles, that hint of cleavage peeking out from her white uniform shirt. She is hot.*

Gabrielle stared back. This waiter looked familiar. Where had she seen him? Suddenly she remembered: Harry Silver's party – he had been one of the hired helps. She didn't remember interviewing him, though. She parked her bike and went over to the table.

'You were at Mr Silver's last night, during the party in which Mina Corbain died, right?'

François raised amused brows. '*Oui, mademoiselle,* I was there. In fact I helped many of the poor, sick guests. I believe I told your father everything I saw.'

'Dreadful, wasn't it, François?' Spencer was eager to get the sassy waiter's attention. 'My poor darling Charlie was so sick, weren't you, poppet?'

'I don't want to talk about it,' Charlie snapped, then with a winning smile turned to the waiter, 'François, dear boy, could you bring me another kir royale, please, and some of those yummy nuts?'

Spencer was glancing at François's nether regions with the sly grin that Charlie recognised only too well. He knew Spencer loved him, and he loved Spencer to death, but my goodness, the boy was a world-class flirt.

François gave another little bow after smiling seductively at

Gabrielle and left, leaving her staring after him as he zigzagged deftly around the crowded tables. He was certainly attractive, but something about him bothered her. She couldn't put a finger on it, but she would ask her father tonight what he thought about the waiter. He would know. There was just something a little too slick about him.

CHAPTER NINE

June 2015

Sophie Silvestri sat at her dressing table preparing for yet another grand soirée, even though it was only five o'clock. Frick and Adolpho buzzed around her like worker bees as the 'queen' studied her face in the pink-tinted mirror while her haggard features became transformed into a vision of gilded beauty. Frick was plaiting several tiny braids next to her hairline, which he then secured with a rubber band and pulled up as tightly as possible to be secured on a small bun of hair on her crown. This was the famous 'Hollywood lift' taught to Sophie by Marlene Dietrich long, long ago. Marlene had been very kind to the (then) young and beautiful Sophie, who had watched in wonder as the seventy-four-year-old diva had transformed herself into the ultimate glamour girl.

'One day you too will have to do this, my dear,' Marlene had drawled. 'Not yet, you're still young, but when that day comes, you will thank me for this.'

That had been forty years ago, and today Sophie was exceedingly grateful for the beauty techniques Marlene had taught her, which she had carefully instructed Frick and Adolpho to perform.

Sophie had been born in Saint-Tropez to a fisherman father. At sixteen she had won a talent contest in nearby Saint-Raphael, where a talent agent from LA, who was on vacation and looking for some fun, had spotted her. The nubile teenager was not averse to socialising with the powerful agent, and as things developed he dangled the prospect of fame and fortune in Hollywood before her beautiful blue eyes. Soon, with her parents' permission, the beautiful blonde was whisked off to Hollywood.

In the 1950s, Hollywood was still peopled with great and glamorous stars. The studio system reigned and they were constantly signing new young talent. Sophie's beauty soon gained her a contract at Paradigm Studio, where to get the roles she wanted she soon realised she had to 'be nice' to many of the old and odious studio executives.

Since one elderly executive looked much like the next one, Sophie became an expert in the art of fellatio, soon got the plum roles and found herself starring opposite some of Tinseltown's most glamorous leading men. Steve McQueen, Frank Sinatra and Anthony Quinn all fell for her exotic charms, as did the American public. They loved her quaint foreign accent, her mass of thick golden curls and her curvaceous killer body.

But, like all good things, in spite of her fame and beauty, it came to an end; the studio and the public eventually tired of Sophie Silvestri and she fled back to her native France, where luckily she was still worshipped. She took up residence in a grand but decaying villa on the outskirts of Saint-Tropez and lavished all her love and attention on her pack of dogs and litter of cats.

While Adolpho applied several layers of the thick theatrical foundation only available at Ray's, the Broadway cosmetic boutique, Sophie thought about tonight's big event. She didn't really want to go; she disliked parties now – she'd been to enough and would far rather loll around on her vast canopied bed surrounded by her dogs, eating chocolate croissants and surfing the TV. Most people bored her, but tonight she was interested in meeting the Hollywood producer in whose honour the party was being thrown. Marvin Rheingold was a maker of hits and he was about to produce a remake of *Suddenly, Last Summer*.

Although she didn't need the money, Sophie coveted the role of the mother, a part played by Katharine Hepburn in the original. She had discovered that Angelina Jolie was tipped for the daughter role that Elizabeth Taylor had played in the original, and Miss Jolie was the only current actress Sophie actually admired. Besides, it would be interesting to see Hollywood again. She hadn't set foot in 'Sodom and Gomorrah', as she disparagingly referred to it, for over thirty years, and she was curious to see if all the changes she'd heard about were true. Her signature perfume, Garden of Gardenias, was doing reasonably well in Europe, but the sales needed pumping up and a trip to LA and the subsequent publicity could be of enormous benefit. So said her agent Jake Moreno, the slimiest bastard in Hollywood but one of the most cunning. Besides, although Sophie wouldn't admit it, the tedium of old age was getting to her and she had suddenly become horribly aware of her own mortality.

As Frick settled a blonde bouffant wig on Sophie's head, the doorbell rang.

'Who the fuck is that?' she growled. Her face, now looking a good fifteen years younger than its actual seventy-four, glowed in the mirror.

'I don't know, but at least you're ready to receive!' beamed Frick as three barking dogs scampered ferociously down the stairs. 'You look gorgeous!'

'It's the fuzz . . . for you.' Adolpho was out of breath. His morning love of chocolate croissants had recently added several kilos to his normally slender frame.

'Captain Poulpe? What does he want now?' Sophie was stepping into a fetching off-the-shoulder peignoir. 'I already spoke to him.'

'It's not a him, it's a her!'

'A who?'

'A her! It's Gabrielle Poulpe, the daughter of the Captain. She's on the murder case too.'

'What murder case?'

Adolpho sighed. Was his mistress immune to everything but herself? She'd been at Harry's party and seen the chaos – or maybe this was the onset of early dementia?

'Well, I suppose I'd better see her.'

Sophie disappeared into her dressing room and returned in a black velour dressing gown encrusted with dog hairs. No sense in looking sexy for a woman. She walked cautiously down the stairs, Frick holding fast to her elbow.

Gabrielle was admiring numerous gold- and silver-framed photographs of Sophie, artfully arranged on the grand piano. Beside them were a pile of books on aerobic exercises and several videos all starring Sophie. They were not, she noted, of recent vintage.

Indeed, as the great star limped into the room, Gabrielle could see a faint expression of pain in her lovely azure eyes. Obviously she had overexercised in her youth, and it had finally caught up with her.

'Sit down!' barked the star. 'What can I do for you?'

'We're investigating the death of Mina Corbain and I wondered if you knew of anyone who would wish her harm? We think it could be murder and Interpol has been summoned.'

Sophie frowned and sat down heavily.

'Oh that . . .' Sophie lit a slim brown cigarette and blew some smoke into her favourite pug's face. 'I forgot about that.'

Frick and Adolpho exchanged glances. They knew their boss was a trifle forgetful, but this was strange behaviour. Mina's death had not only been the talk of Saint-Tropez for the past four days, but half the news media of America, Britain, Europe and Japan were camped around the village desperate for titbits; anything to cast a clue on the death of one of America's most shining stars.

Gabrielle was slightly in awe of this icon. She had only been in the Saint-Tropez police force for five years and this was her first murder investigation. Murders were few and far between in this golden community, although adultery, larceny and immorality were rife.

'My father, Captain Jacques Poulpe, and I strongly believe the circumstances surrounding Miss Corbain's death are suspicious, even though several of the other guests were ill as well. However, there seems to be no clear motive, so we wondered if you knew of anyone who had a grudge against her?'

Sophie thought for a moment then said, 'Mina was a performer . . . a great star. Everyone hates stars, you know.'

'Really? Why is that?' Gabrielle was fascinated by this piece of information.

'Jealousy . . . they're all jealous.'

'Why?' asked Gabrielle, seemingly nonplussed. Sophie stared at her disdainfully and started explaining as if to a five-year-old. 'Most people envy the life of a star because they think they have it so easy. It's not true, you know. Stars get where they are through hard work, dedication and talent . . . I should know!' she finished bitterly.

'I see. But most of the other guests were wealthy. Why do you think anyone there want would to kill Mina?'

'Oh, really?' Sophie gave a hollow laugh. 'Take Madame Lara – the famous ex-wife of that Yankee industrialist? She's always on talk shows. She's publicity crazy, giving lectures all over the place and posing for the magazines – she'd love to be a top society hostess again, or even a reality star,' she sneered. 'Or take that stupid gigolo of hers – Fabergé . . . or whatever his name is. Maybe Lara thought Mina was after him.'

Adolpho chimed in, 'We've heard Lara has been secretly studying singing. Wants to make a record with him – can you believe it at her age? And Lara is jealous of Sophie.'

Sophie bristled at the word 'age', and Adolpho and Frick snickered until Gabrielle shot them a stern look. Useful information was often garnered through gossip, but these two weren't being helpful.

'I see, but I think we're missing the point here.' She made a few notes on her iPhone and then asked casually, 'Anyone else you can think of who might bear a grudge?'

'Well, Maximus Gobbi – he would be jealous of Mina's success too. He's jealous of everyone with any talent – since he has none himself,' said Sophie scornfully. 'He probably resented the fact that she made two hundred and fifty thousand euros that night and he didn't get a cut, which is how he makes his pathetic living.'

'Hardly enough reason to kill her,' said Gabrielle flatly.

'I have no idea – you're the detective – so detect. Why don't you talk to the cook, or the caterer?' Sophie snidely inquired. 'And what makes you think she was murdered?'

'Thank you. I will be in touch with you again. You've been most helpful . . .' she fibbed as she opened the door.

. . . *Not*, Gabrielle thought, closing the door as the hot summer dusk enveloped her. *No help whatsoever*.

But then no one she had interviewed in Saint-Tropez about that night had been helpful at all.

Fabrizio was admiring himself in the mirror in the cramped bedroom of the third-floor flat he shared with Lara.

It was a tiny place in one of the back streets of St Tropez, but since Lara liked to spend most of her days on her boat or at the beach, she considered too much living space unnecessary.

This was just perfect for Fabrizio, who had a habit of disappearing every morning. Between nine a.m. and two p.m. he was unavailable. He told Lara that he was at the gym or playing tennis, but he was usually having extracurricular trysts with some of the rich widows and divorcées often supplied by Maximus, who supplemented their combined income in this way. The mutual need and the commercial aspect of the assignations assured complete discretion.

Although some considered Fabrizio a gold-digging gigolo, he never thought of himself in such a crass light. 'Necessity knows no law,' he would mutter to himself as he stripped off to parade his buffed body before servicing some lonely, grateful rich woman. He had a fertile imagination, an overly active libido and a limitless supply of Viagra. He also basked in the admiration of his prowess in the sack and his unusually large cock. But he and Maximus were careful only to accept engagements with ladies who were passing through and not staying too long. 'You don't want to shit where you eat,' Maximus had warned him. 'We must be careful.'

Today Fabrizio could hardly contain his excitement. French TV company TF1 had come to the nearby town of Saint-Maxime to audition attractive young men and girls to be the professional dancers in a version of *Dancing with the Stars*. Fabrizio had auditioned and, unknown to Lara or Max, had been chosen as one of the twenty-four potential contestants. The show was due to start rehearsing at the end of June, but the producers insisted that everything must be done with the utmost security, which suited Fabrizio just fine: if Max found out, he'd want his cut.

Fabrizio was also in the running for the Kazakhstan version of *The X Factor*, so he was busy taking singing and dance lessons from a cute British beauty called Betty, who lived in the hills above Saint-Tropez in the quaint village of Ramatuelle. At least twice a week he managed to slip away to polish his dance steps, work on his voice, and occasionally give a willing Betty a taste of paradise.

On top of everything else, Fabrizio also needed to continue to hit the social scene with Lara, so by two thirty in the afternoon he tended to be at Club 55 or Nikki Beach, suave in his regular uniform of black shirt and white pants, satiated after sex. He usually had to have a 'matinée' with Lara after lunch around six, while she was still sober enough to participate, and for that he would have to pop another blue pill.

In the evening the couple normally attended dinners and small parties, since Lara hated staying at home. Often she had to be carted home and poured into bed by Fabrizio, who then hit the clubs. Night-time was his time, and he would often pull a beautiful girl and go back to her place or a small hotel room, where he had a convenient arrangement. His capacity for sex was endless and it often amazed even him.

Fabrizio was playing a DVD of *Saturday Night Fever* and busily mirroring John Travolta's sexy moves as he primped and sang along with the Bee Gees. Tonight he had even decided to dress like Travolta. He figured the white suit and tight black shirt showed off his Saint-Tropez tan to perfection. He struck a few Travolta poses – one arm up, the other stretched downwards, framing his tightly encased derrière – and grinned at his reflection. 'Handsome devil,' he thought. 'How can that stupid bitch refuse to marry me?' Tonight he would show them all. He had persuaded Monty Goldman, the host of tonight's party, to let him sing a couple of numbers. He was extremely excited and quite nervous.

Just then the bitch walked in, attempting to clasp a vast parure of emeralds and diamonds around her scrawny neck. 'Darling, you're no Travolta,' Lara sneered. 'Give it up and do this up.'

'Just you wait.' He bragged, refusing to rise to the bait, 'Tonight's the night I'm gonna show 'em.'

'I suppose you think Khris Kane's going to sign you up to make a record now that he doesn't have Mina Corbain,' she sneered.

Lara's high-pitched, tinkly laugh irritated the crap out of Fabrizio, who merely smiled mysteriously as he fiddled with the clasp of her necklace.

While he fiddled with that, Lara fiddled with his zipper. God, this woman was insatiable. He'd serviced her twice already today: once in the morning, which was relatively easy as he had a morning 'woody', and Lara being half asleep liked the 'wham, bam, thank you, ma'am', and then after a liquid lunch on her boat when she'd dragged him to her cabin, not even giving him time to top up his tan on deck. She'd beckoned to him imperiously and he had followed her into the cool sanctuary of her stateroom, where she coaxed his reluctant member into suitable tumescence with a relatively reasonable blow job. Now she was hot for him again. Fabrizio felt like a male whore, but what choice did he have? Every time he complained to Maximus the fat man brought up the ogre of the money he owed to CRAP – the ex-girlfriends and the brats.

Lara had just started pulling down his pants when the doorbell rang. 'Who the hell is that?' she said crossly.

'I'll get it,' Fabrizio said, extremely relieved, while hurriedly doing up his trousers. 'Saved by the bell,' he thought as he vaulted down the stairs.

A very pretty woman stood on the doorstep. Never mind that she wore a police uniform; she had tumbling red-gold curls, wide-apart green eyes, and a sprinkling of freckles on her pale un-tanned and un-Botoxed face. She was as different from all the women in the Eurotrash set he mixed with as Snow White is to the Wicked Stepmother.

'I'm Lieutenant Gabrielle Poulpe,' smiled the vision. 'May I come in?'

Fabrizio bestowed on her one of his most dazzling smiles, and opened the door wider. 'Of course, I recognised you from the other night, mademoiselle.'

'Lieutenant,' Gabrielle said quietly. 'I'll just take a few minutes of your time.'

Lara appeared, introductions were made, and Gabrielle asked if there was anyone they thought might have wished Mina Corbain any harm.

While Lara attempted to answer her question by insisting she had no idea, Fabrizio couldn't help comparing the two women. They were both red-haired and green-eyed, but there the comparison stopped. While Lara was the wrong side of fifty, Gabrielle was the right side of thirty. Lara's hair was tinted a vivid shade of bright ginger and back-combed to within an inch of its brittle life. Gabrielle's natural auburn curls caught the dying rays of the sun and framed her pretty little face perfectly. She also seemed intelligent and totally without airs and affectations, while Lara constantly waved her hands in the air dramatically and spoke in that fake Euro accent.

Why must I try to make this woman marry me? thought Fabrizio. *I could be happy with the simple life and a simple girl like this Gabriella . . . Gabrielle. Who are you kidding?* said his inner voice. *You just want to get a leg over cop-girl. In fact, you usually want to do that with every good-looking girl you meet.*

'True,' said Fabrizio out loud, as both women looked at him in surprise. 'Oh, I mean true that neither of us had ever met Mina before "that night".'

'Well, if you think of anything, anything at all, please don't hesitate to call me day or night.' Gabrielle handed Fabrizio her card, which Lara promptly snatched.

She wasn't about to let Fabrizio have this one's number, even if she was a cop. She knew her boy too well. He was a walking sex machine. She tried to slake his enormous sexual appetite by making herself available as often as she could, but she knew that he was ruled by his cock and that three or four times a day was not too difficult for a twenty-nine-year-old to achieve. As the front door closed, Lara pulled Fabrizio on to the sofa to score a hat trick.

Chapter Ten

The Second Party of the Season

Ostensibly the occasion was a party in honour of 'Hollywood royalty' hosted by Monty Goldman for the legendary producer Marvin Rheingold during his annual break in Saint-Tropez. Marvin, now in his early seventies, had been a major player in Tinseltown since he had made his name in Rome in the 1960s. He had imported American stars who had passed their sell-by date and featured them in a series of cheap but successful movies. Rome was known as 'Hollywood on the Tiber' then, and Marvin's fortunes had flourished; shortly afterwards he had returned to his roots in Hollywood and churned out block-buster after blockbuster, each one surpassing the last in revenue.

Barrel-chested and bald, always wearing his signature Saint-Tropez look of a loudly patterned Versace shirt open halfway down his chest and creased white linen pants, Marvin was now intent on making serious movies. He had just finished an artsy black and white film of *Richard the Third* starring Sir Kenneth Branagh, and was now in pre-production for a new version of *Suddenly, Last Summer*, the Tennessee Williams classic.

There were a few celebrities at Monty Goldman's soirée, as

well as several skimpily clad teenage Russian hookers and the usual Saint-Tropez party people.

The good-looking waiters and waitresses – none older than twenty-five and mostly out-of-work actors, actresses and singers – were attired in Greek-themed white togas in which their lithe bodies were displayed to full advantage for the delectation of the guests.

They passed Mediterranean delicacies of tiny tomatoes stuffed with foie gras and massive bowls of Beluga caviar while the throng idly watched a dozen gorgeous showgirls, imported from Paris, gyrate around silver poles that had been installed over the glass dance floor that covered the pool. Underneath, thousands of silver stars shimmered in the turquoise water, and six expert swimmers dressed as mermaids complete with tails gyrated like Esther Williams.

'So tacky,' remarked Lara as she and Fabrizio entered the enormous, stiffly formal white and silver art-deco living room. 'This is completely inappropriate for the Saint-Tropez lifestyle.' She looked irritably around as they stood in line to greet their host, Monty Goldman. A self-made British billionaire and ex-barrow boy, he had worked his way up from selling fruit from a stand on Church Street to the largely Muslim population of Edgware Road and its environs, to running a secondhand clothes boutique in Marylebone High Street. As several down-on-their-luck actresses lived nearby, he started bringing in some of their finery from their glory days in the 1940s, fifties and sixties. Monty paid them a pittance for these beautifully constructed clothes and elegant costume jewellery, then managed to sell them for a hefty profit to an upmarket vintage boutique in Notting Hill, often featured in *Vogue* and *Tatler* and frequented by young trendsetters of the 1970s and eighties.

By the late 1980s there was a huge market for the elegant

clothes of past eras, and with well-placed ads in *The Lady* and the back pages of fashion magazines, Monty's business boomed. Every young model and actress worth her salt shopped there, as did the stylists, a new phenomenon that no young starlet could live without.

Monty sold his business for a fortune in 1994, then joined forces with one of the canniest top retailers of the day, Nate Kowalski. Nate the Greek, so known because of his Peloponnesian heritage, had a fantastically successful string of shops and boutiques throughout the UK and US. Looking to branch out into Asia and the Middle East, Monty seemed the top man for the job, and within a few years the two partners had become bosom buddies and regularly featured in the *Sunday Times* Rich List.

Monty stood in his mirror-covered foyer to greet his guests, stocky and mahogany-faced, his thinning thatch artfully combed to cover an incipient bald patch. By his side stood his faithful trophy wife of twelve years, Chantelle.

Impossibly thin after four children, she spent three hours a day honing her taut, tummy-tucked body in the vain expectation that Monty wouldn't dump her for a younger model, as he had done to wives number one and two. But Monty already had his eye on wife number four as he surveyed the throng of expensively dressed and bejewelled guests who were clustering around and admiring his novelty bars. In two clear acrylic coffins, young girls wearing fishnets, suspender belts, corsets, masks and jewelled nipple guards writhed in simulated ecstasy, while the shirtless bartenders nonchalantly mixed exotic drinks and poured vintage wines and champagne on the mirrored bar tops.

Carlotta had gone shopping with Maximus, who had taken her to Dior on the Rue François Sibilli, the main shopping street in Saint-Tropez. He had insisted that she buy a spectacular full-length gown for the evening.

'A bargain at twenty-five thousand euros,' he persisted, winking at the manager, who would have to turn over 10 per cent to him, 'and because it's couture and fresh from the A/W collection, no one will have anything like it.' It was indeed a fairy-tale dress that, despite having seven inches cropped off the length, fitted Carlotta's petite figure to perfection.

'I wish I wasn't so short,' she said.

'You are deliciously petite,' said Max, as Carlotta twirled in front of the three-way mirror, while the seamstress struggled to pin up the hem. 'The models today are all beanstalks, some even quite ugly. You are a divine package.'

'You don't think it's a bit too brash?' she asked.

'My dear, you are gorgeous. It is a "look at me" dress, so everyone will look at you tonight, and so they should.'

'Well . . .' Carlotta surveyed the deep, somewhat revealing décolleté on the pale pink chiffon, which was sprinkled with a million glittering paillettes. 'I hope I won't be too overdressed.'

Max snorted with laughter, 'My dear, just you wait to see what Lara will be wearing, and that old crone Sophie will pull out all the stops for this party – mark my words.'

'Oh, I don't think Sophie's a crone. She's beautiful and actually very nice, and has been sweet to me.'

Max snorted again but decided not to bad-mouth Sophie to Carlotta. He had made a couple of attempts to get Fabrizio and Carlotta together, but each time his plans had been thwarted by Lara, who could immediately smell a rat if it came anywhere near what she perceived to be her property. And her property was Fabrizio, even though he was out of her sight in the early mornings and late at night. But when they were home or in public, he belonged to her and her only.

When Carlotta entered Monty Goldman's villa on the proud arm of Maximus Gobbi, the blasé crowd stared slightly longer than the usual millisecond. Her dress made her look like a modern-day 'Cinderella at the Ball', and with her jet-black hair framing her oval face in cascading ringlets, and a stunning seventy-carat diamond necklace from the Di Ponti estate around her neck, she was as beautiful, if not more so, than any of the models and starlets in the room.

Everyone looked up as the model *du jour* Zarina Jacobs arrived with her pop-star girlfriend Sin in tow. They called each other 'wifey', although Zarina claimed in publicity to still be a virgin. Nineteen-year-old Zarina was chatty and full of coke. She demanded 'cuddlezzz!' in a high-pitched shriek from all who came into her orbit or, if she didn't like them, stuck her tongue in their ears. She threw her arms around Monty Goldman, almost losing her beaded halterneck-top in the process.

'Uncle Monty!' she screamed. 'Can I borrow your heli to get to the airport tomorrow?'

'Of course, sweetie,' said Monty smoothly. 'Anything for you, babes.' Then he bent down to whisper in her ear, 'Tell me, sweetie – she's your latest girlfriend, right?'

Zarina nodded enthusiastically, then wrapped her lips around Sin's half-exposed breast, her tongue darting like a small adder.

Even Monty was staggered by this show of affection. He recovered and asked, 'So what are you? Bisexual? Homosexual?'

'No, babes, I'm trisexual . . .' She paused a moment, letting it sink in. 'I'll *try* anything! Maybe even you one day, Uncle Monty!' She bit his earlobe and he blushed while she screamed with laughter.

Monty could never resist a celebrity, and Zarina was the hottest cover girl in the world right now. Who cared if she had a little cocaine problem and preferred girls? She was young – she'd get over it.

One who had got over it was Chloe Kensington, the supermodel of yesterday. Still on top form in spite of the young upstarts trying to kick her off her throne, at thirty-eight she still had the cheekbones and the cheeky charm that had been entrancing snappers since she was discovered in a supermarket at age four-teen. Although she'd been nicknamed Chloe Cokehead, she was now clean and happily married to a plastic surgeon. It was rumoured that it was he who kept those famous cheekbones look-ing razor sharp and the full, kissable lips plumped to perfection, but Chloe always denied ever having any 'work' done.

'I eat whatever I want, whenever I want!' both Zarina and Chloe told the press, although in truth their basic diet was ciga-rettes, champagne and coke, with the occasional low-carb, gluten-free organic rice and prawn dish, or a large kale or mâche salad without dressing.

Suddenly there was a fanfare of trumpets and the MC for the night – beloved Charlie Chalk – called for the guests to make their way to their tables. Charlie attempted to shush the throng, who were too busy talking to sit down.

'Ladies and gentlemen – *mesdames et messieurs* – as the opening act for tonight I have the greatest pleasure in introducing to you a new young singer who I know you will take to your hearts and adore. Please – give it up for . . . Fabrizio Bricconni!'

'Young!' Khris the record producer snorted. 'He could be Justin Bieber's father!'

'He's twenty-nine,' Maximus answered smoothly. 'He has a big future; he just needs a little bit of training.'

A smattering of applause led by Lara followed Fabrizio as he strolled on to the stage and started crooning '*Volare*' in his special Dean Martin voice. The audience, still milling about and drink-ing, was singularly unimpressed.

'I don't think Michael Bublé has to worry,' Frick sneered to Sophie, who sneered right back. 'Six bucks and my right nut bets he never even makes it to Moldova, much less Kazakhstan.'

Sophie was delighted to see Lara's trumped-up gigolo making a fool of himself. 'He's a real horn-dog,' she hissed to Frick. 'You know, he even made a pass at me!'

'Do tell, *cherie*,' said Frick, expectantly.

'Oh, it was a long time ago,' Sophie said vaguely. 'It was in Rome, twenty years ago.'

'But, *cherie*, he would have been only nine years old then!' Frick was usually careful not to upset his mistress, but this had knocked him for six.

'Oh, well, it was someone who *looked* like him then,' she snapped irritably. 'All those Italian stallions look alike, you know,' she shrugged.

As Fabrizio segued none too smoothly into a standard that had recently been re-popularised by Rod Stewart, Frick, Adolpho and Sophie started giggling and whispering amongst themselves as Lara hissed an angry, '*Shhhh*!' from the next table.

Maximus was sitting between Carlotta and Lara, but he needn't have worried about Carlotta, for, although she had mixed with the aristocracy of Buenos Aires, she was wide-eyed with wonder at the opulence of the flowers and the setting and the seemingly enormous combined wealth of the guests.

'So many millionaires and magnates,' she whispered to Max.

'My dear, only a few millionaires here tonight. The majority of these capitalist pigs . . . ooh, I'm so sorry!' he hiccoughed, realising that his pre-prandial cognac at his hotel and the two glasses of champagne at the terrace had made him a tad tipsy. 'Most here tonight are billionaires, even a few multibillionaires.'

Lara was pulling at Maximus's arm, annoyed that he was paying so much attention to the new girl in town, and by the fact that the dinner partner she had drawn on her left was an ancient billionaire wearing a bad brown toupee and too much orange Saint-Tropez tan on his wrinkled face. He had tried to engage

Lara in conversation, but all she could see when she turned to him were several long black hairs cascading from his nostrils, not to mention the mat of grey chest hair peering out from his half-open Gieves & Hawkes silk shirt.

'Isn't Fabrizio absolutely fantastic?' she whined at Maximus. 'Don't you just adore his voice? All those lessons were worth it! What do you think? Do you think he could have a shot at *The X Factor* in Kazakhstan?'

Maximus was now gently holding her hand, anxious to prevent her from picking up her fifth vodka.

'He's not bad, not bad at all,' Max lied. If there was any time to sort out the pre-nup situation with the feisty Russian socialite, this was a perfect opportunity. 'I think he has a good shot.'

Max was well aware that Fabrizio's show-business sights were set a good deal higher than a gig in Kazakhstan. He had found out about the French TV show that had been secretly interviewing and auditioning Fabrizio for the Gallic version of *Dancing with the Stars*, which would be far more prestigious. Fabrizio had also been taking singing lessons in Paris and was trying to wheedle enough money from Lara to make a record.

'I'm *so* glad you encourage him, Lara, my dear. You are so unselfish.'

'Unselfish? What do you mean?'

'Well, don't you see? He is so good – I think he's almost as good as Harry Connick, Jr.'

'What do you mean "almost"? He's younger, better-looking, and much sexier than Connick! He could be a star.' She smiled dreamily, remembering the early evening sexathon with Fabrizio. He never failed to turn her on, even if she was angry with him.

Max noticed the dreamy look and leaned in for the kill.

'Yes, much sexier than Connick. You are so right. As usual you have a sharp eye for talent. Who knows what fame and success he might achieve?'

He almost could read the rest of his unspoken sentence writing itself on Lara's face. It dawned on her that, if Fabrizio found fame and fortune, she would be left far behind.

Maximus decided to administer the *coup de grâce*. 'How about marrying him now, Lara, darling? Forget about that silly pre-nup – no? I don't believe that Mr Meyer cares *that* much whether you agree to that stupid rule to never marry again – don't you agree, my dear? You deserve happiness, darling. Let's have a wedding next week!'

Max released her hand so she could down another vodka, then he simultaneously signalled the waiter for another, and to Fabrizio, who was by now doing his strolling troubadour act around the room. Fabrizio swaggered over to Lara's table and crooned softly into her ear: 'You're just too marvellous, too marvellous for words.' His hand caressed her bare shoulders, and she shivered in anticipation of tonight's delights if she could remain sober, and not get angry about watching other women lust after her property.

'Like glorious . . .' Lara preened. 'Glamorous . . .' Lara smiled. 'And that old standby, amorous . . .' Lara cast her 'cat got the cream' look towards the crowd, unaware that they were talking amongst themselves and not paying the least bit of attention to Fabrizio's crooning.

Fabrizio finished his set, planted a tender kiss on Lara's Botoxed lips, glanced at Carlotta, who seemed not to notice him, then took a bow to a smattering of giggles and applause – but Maximus was jubilant. As Lara tottered off to the Ladies' room to repair her lipstick, Max clapped Fabrizio on the shoulders. '*Mio caro*, I think we've got it!' he crowed. 'The way you sang to her she was practically coming in her seat. She's gonna forget about the pre-nup now, I know it! When I suggested you get married next week she didn't disagree . . .'

'Yeah, I guess,' Fabrizio said gloomily. 'But you know, Max, I still wanna live the dream. I have aspirations. I wanna become a great singer.'

'Forget it,' said Maximus brusquely, 'you're never going to live *that* dream. You got Lara now, for Christ's sake – be happy, Fabrizio!' He clapped the younger man on the shoulder and grinned. 'You'll be Mr Lara Meyer, and all the rest of my . . . er . . . boys for hire will be green with envy.'

∞

In the Ladies' room, Lara reapplied her cyclamen lipstick. Since she was short-sighted, she leaned forward towards the mirror, then to her dismay saw Vanessa Meyer standing behind her, Jonathan's third and youngest trophy wife. Vanessa was hanging on to her marriage to Jonathan, whose roving eye was legendary, by the skin of her Hollywood-whitened teeth, which she bared now with a disingenuous smile.

'*Daahling*, you look *maahvellous!*' Vanessa lied, taking in the overtanned skin and last season's too-tight Hervé Léger. They exchanged an indifferent *mwah-mwah* as Lara checked the younger woman's almost flawless skin and the latest Dolce & Gabbana couture dress, which her Pilates-toned curves enhanced.

'I didn't know you were in town,' Lara trilled.

'We just managed to get a mooring in the port. Jonathan has business here; we arrived last night.'

'So Jonathan is here?' In spite of herself, Lara's heart started to thump. She couldn't help but still harbour a longing to be back with him, queening it up in his gorgeous duplex on Park Avenue and being invited to all the best social events in Manhattan and The Hamptons. Mrs Jonathan Meyer had a great deal more cachet about it than plain Lara Meyer. In spite of her sexual obsession with Fabrizio, Lara still longed for those days when she was the undisputed queen of New York society; when she was on the boards of all the best charity events, and photographs of the fabulous couple frequently appeared in *Woman's Wear Daily* and the *New York Post*, while layouts of their Connecticut and Palm Beach mansions were featured in *Town and Country*, *Vogue* and *Bazaar*. Shot by the likes of Mario Testino and Terry Richardson they caused envy amongst the super-rich. She'd even made *Vanity Fair*'s best-dressed list for two years in a row. Not bad for a poor little chorus cutie from Minsk.

How could I have thrown it all away just because of my stupid jealousy? thought Lara, applying another coat of gloss. She remembered that day on the slopes of Gstaad too well. She had been skiing with Valentino, having celebrated New Year's Eve the previous night at his chalet, when they had decided to take a hot chocolate at an out-of-the-way inn off one of the pistes. She'd spotted Jonathan's distinctive black parka with its yellow lining immediately. He was standing at the bottom of the piste, his parka open and his arms enclosing a lissom blonde, his lips locked with hers. Without further ado, Lara had marched over to them, spewing a stream of abuse in Russian. The girl, no more than eighteen and one of the contestants in the Miss Teen USA contest that Jonathan sponsored on TV, had turned around, shocked. Lara had grabbed her long blonde hair and punched her hard on the face, breaking her pretty little nose. As if by magic a photographer appeared, eagerly snapping pictures of the melee. The teenager began screaming as blood dropped from her nose on to her baby pink ski jacket, and Jonathan started yelling at Lara. She screamed and began pummelling her husband, 'I *vant* a divorce – I *vant* a divorce, you cheating bastard!'

'Well, you can have one!' he bellowed, rushing her away. 'It's time I got you out of my life, you nagging Russian bitch!'

This caused Lara to explode even more. She stopped hitting him and grabbed at Jonathan's shiny black toupee, whipping it off his bald pate and waving it in front of a bemused Valentino and a crowd of interested onlookers while crowing, 'Now you know he has no hair! Ha ha ha!'

The photographer was gleeful. 'I'm in pap heaven!' he thought as he continued snapping away until a security guard came and escorted an incandescent Lara away.

Jonathan attempted to replace his wig – another photograph that hit all the papers and went viral. The girl sued, her hopes of becoming Miss Teen America shattered like her nose, and Lara's apologies and entreaties to remain Mrs Meyer fell upon Jonathan's deaf ears. The divorce was a quickie; a few months later Jonathan married the Honourable Vanessa Anstruther-Formby, the twenty-one-year-old daughter of an English aristocrat whom he had been banging for the past four months. Six months later, Vanessa gave birth to the apple of Jonathan Meyer's eye, his first child, a son whom they named Jonathan Junior. Lara never got over it. She hid her sorrows in the vodka bottle and latched on to a selection of gigolos, the latest of whom was Fabrizio.

'Nice to see you again,' Lara muttered to Vanessa, and stalked out of the powder room with her head held high.

∞

Carlotta had been surreptitiously watching the two women and noting their obvious dislike of one another with interest. In San Miguel she had had one loyal girlfriend and she had never really been aware of the animosity and jealousy that seemed to fuel these jet setters' lives. They all had so much *stuff*, she thought as she nodded a greeting towards Vanessa and started touching up her make-up.

Yes, Nicanor had been profligate, but they had only owned one home, the villa in San Miguel, and just two or three cars. These people had multiples of everything. They all owned at least *five* homes, some of which they hardly visited, even though they kept them fully staffed. They all had yachts and the men competed each year to see who could acquire the biggest one. Carlotta smiled to herself as she remembered what Maximus had told her.

'The guys who insist on having the biggest boat are the ones with the smallest willy!'

The sad thing, thought Carlotta as she snapped shut her compact, was that so many of these transient Saint-Tropeziennes seemed so miserable. The old cliché 'Money doesn't buy happiness' sprang to mind.

But I wonder if it can buy me love, she thought fleetingly, and just as quickly dismissed it.

Some of the young scions of wealthy families in town had approached her for a date, but they all seemed spoilt and callow. She sighed and began to walk out of the door. *Maybe Saint-Tropez isn't the right place to meet the love of my life.*

∞

Returning to her table, Lara grabbed Fabrizio's hand and, looking into his eyes, said, 'Darling, I will marry you. Fuck the pre-nup and fuck Jonathan Meyer – I don't care anymore. I love you – I do, I do!'

Embracing Lara with joy mixed with a sense of impending doom, Fabrizio high-fived Maximus, then quickly refilled her vodka glass as he asked, 'When shall we do it, *cara?*'

'Oh, er . . . next June, I want to be a June bride,' she simpered.

Oh God, thought Fabrizio, no way, a year to wait. I'd better try to make that record or get that gig in Kazakhstan, or *Dancing with the Stars* in France.

Maximus leaned over to whisper in Fabrizio's ear, 'It's too long to wait, dear boy. CRAP are giving me problems,' he hissed, evoking Fabrizio's ex-lovers, Carina and Raimunda, and their children. 'You'd better start working on her again – this time try harder.'

Maximus was distracted; he wished he could overhear what property wunderkind Roberto LoBianco at the next table over was saying to Carlotta, who was sitting next to him. She seemed to like what he was saying as her eyes sparkled and she nodded her head in agreement several times. As Maximus passed her table he bent down to whisper, 'Don't forget about lunch at the beach tomorrow, *cara*.'

'Of course not,' Carlotta smiled. 'I can't wait.'

∽

The following day Maximus sat at the table at Eden Beach with Carlotta and three handsome young men from his stable whom he thought would amuse her. The DJ was playing a popular track of a French chanteuse warbling about trying to '*trouver mon souvenir*'. His iPhone beeped every five minutes with one or other of his hostesses bombarding him with questions about the table plans for their soirées, or how many house guests the invitees were bringing. The competition for the best dates for the upcoming mid-July party week was fierce, and Maximus was a mine of information and advice about what the best dates available were and how to navigate the tricky social waters of Saint-Tropez. He also collected favours, and more than the occasional 'consideration' from a grateful hostess when he unravelled a knotty problem.

Vast mirrors on the beach wall reflected the sparkling sea and, in the middle of the wooden dance floor, a small old-fashioned bathtub sat incongruously. After the group had consumed their starters, four dancers came out to perform an energetic can-can. The girls wore tight corsets, frilly petticoats and lacy knickers, and the boys were chiselled and bronzed. They enthusiastically splashed the bath water on some of the nearby patrons, who squealed with laughter, while the girls danced between the tables, flashing their undies at the men.

It was a hot and humid day but Carlotta was enjoying the open-air atmosphere and the sun glittering on the white-capped waves. After the cabaret, the sounds of Michael Jackson and Justin Timberlake's song 'Love Never Felt So Good' radiated from loud-speakers hanging from the wooden rafters. The warm breeze ruffled Carlotta's hair as she glanced up to where several heads had swivelled as Fabrizio and Lara entered and stood looking around for a table.

'Come, join us!' Maximus waved eagerly. 'Move up, boys!' He shooed his three young studs along to the far end of the table and put Lara in a wicker chair next to him and Fabrizio at the far end of the table.

Lara stared at the dancers in a hung-over daze, while Fabrizio couldn't stop staring at Carlotta in her white cotton sundress and straw hat from the market. *God, she is pretty*, he thought. And when she flicked a glance at him through her Ray-Bans, he could almost imagine her voluptuous body lying next to him. He adjusted his black cargo shorts then, when the dancers left, mouthed to the DJ, 'Play "Happy".' Obediently the DJ changed his track and launched into the hit of the summer. *Go get her!* he said to himself.

All three of the studs bounced on to the floor, pulling Carlotta with them. Fabrizio closely followed and all of them hit the wooden dance floor. Soon the whole beach club was rocking to the sound of Pharrell Williams. Fabrizio had filled Lara's wine glass copiously so she was feeling no pain as she lay back, closing her eyes and listening to the music.

I've never felt so happy and so free, thought Carlotta, as she clapped along and whirled with Fabrizio, who was showing off his coolest moves in front of her and Susie and Warner, two of the best dancers in Saint-Tropez.

'This is so much fun!' Carlotta was breathless as she finished dancing two more sets then plopped on to her chair next to Fabrizio. 'I love it here!'

'I'm so glad, *cara*.' Max frowned at Fabrizio. He looked like he was doing far too well with the young Contessa – a positively 'cat and canary' scenario. Through half-closed eyes, Lara also observed Fabrizio looking and laughing with Carlotta. She felt a pang of jealousy but then Maximus refilled her glass and she nodded off again.

As the afternoon wore on, the customers became more raucous and the music became louder. Soon most of the patrons had lost their inhibitions, thanks to the copious amounts of Pétale de Rose they had all consumed. Maximus's three studs whirled Carlotta around again and again till she was flushed and giddy. They then performed a mock fight for her benefit, which ended with one of them being thrown into the bathtub. One of them tried to grab Carlotta and pull her into it, but Maximus took hold of her elbow. With a firm, 'Time to leave, *cara*,' he ushered her out towards the back.

'Oh, but I'm having such a good time.' Her eyes were bright and glowing. 'I don't want to leave.'

'Yes, my dear, but when I see paparazzi on the beach trying to get an undignified snap of you, that's when I must pull the plug.'

'Oh well, in that case, thanks,' she laughed. 'Actually I'm quite exhausted now.'

∞

Back at their poky apartment, Lara started screaming at Fabrizio as soon as the door closed.

'How dare you disrespect me!' she pointed a scarlet-tipped claw at his face while advancing on him screaming insults. 'You *bastard* – you flirt with that slut, you embarrass me in front of the whole beach – you bum! You piece of shit!'

'What have I done?' wailed the hapless Fabrizio. God, this woman was unbelievable; she was becoming more psychotic each day and yesterday she had said she wanted to marry him. Talk about unpredictable. He backed off towards the tiny window that faced the bustling port.

'For God's sake, Lara, stop it!' he yelled, but she was wallowing unrelentingly in her fury, her make-up running down her face, her ginger hair a mess.

'Bastard, you're nothing but a spineless, cock-sucking cunt!' she screamed, throwing her sunglasses at him.

'What have I done? What the fuck have I done, Lara? You're not making any sense.'

'You flirt with that foreign slut . . . I saw you dancing – oh, so close – and loving it!'

'We were all dancing, you idiot.'

'Don't call me an idiot!' She looked around for something else to throw and, grabbing Fabrizio's iPad, hurled it at his head with all her might. In a save worthy of Fabien Barthez, he grabbed the device with one hand while trying to control the raving Lara with the other.

'I was not flirting with Carlotta. It's you I love,' he lied, then screamed as she bit his arm. He tried to hold her back and propelled her, kicking and screaming, to her bed. There was only one way to calm Lara when she was like this. Throwing her on to the bed, he summoned thoughts of Carlotta into his mind and proceeded to stem the flow of her fury in the only way he knew how.

Chapter Eleven

Gabrielle had been on the Saint-Tropez police force since leaving college at the age of nineteen. Her father had been with the gendarmerie practically all his life, and although he didn't actively discourage his only child from becoming a gendarme, he didn't encourage her either.

Jacques Poulpe had brought Gabrielle up almost single-handedly. His beloved wife and ten-year-old son had been killed in a car accident on the Moyenne Corniche in Nice, and broken-hearted, he had taken over sole custody of his eight-year-old girl. Sadly, Jacques had been unable to give the child the nurturing and motherly love and understanding that Madame Poulpe would have supplied in abundance. Not to mention instructing her in the facts of life – and how to buy tampons.

Jacques was a good man, a strong and stoic member of the police force, but he was often away all day and into the night. An ancient aunt, Greta, came in to cook and help out, but she spent her days watching endless soaps on TV and paying scant attention to Gabrielle.

But Gabrielle adored her tough, hard-working papa. Completely dedicated to his work, he knew everyone in Saint-Tropez and was much respected. He had hoped his son would follow in his footsteps and was devastated by his death. He loved his daughter but didn't really know how to show it. Wanting to spend more time with him, as a child Gabrielle became a tomboy, excelling at sports and accompanying her papa to the many sports events he liked. She took karate and boxing lessons, had little time for boys, and by dint of complete application and slog was, in spite of her papa's lack of enthusiasm, eventually accepted into the Saint-Tropez gendarmerie.

But Gabrielle was still an innocent girl of nineteen – too innocent – when an incident occurred that changed her life.

She was just starting out at the gendarmerie in Saint-Tropez when he walked in. She was completely dazzled. Seldom had she seen such a handsome man. It wasn't so much his looks, although nature had been very kind, but he dressed in a way no one did in Saint-Tropez, at least not during the daytime. He wore an impeccable cream linen suit accessorised by a pale blue cotton shirt and a yellow tie with tiny butterflies on it.

'I'm here to report a break-in,' he smiled charmingly.

'Of course.' Gabrielle felt herself blushing as the stranger's curiously light green eyes connected intensely with hers.

'How do you do? I'm Jeremy Anstruther-Formby and my shop was broken into last night.' He held out a beautifully manicured hand, which Gabrielle shook.

'I'm Gabrielle Poulpe. I'm just helping out here today, but I most certainly can take your report and pass it on to a detective.'

She helped Jeremy fill out the reports and, later, when Gabrielle's father took over, she couldn't tear herself away from him. She listened eagerly, pretending to be taking notes. She loved the way Jeremy talked. His French was impeccable but she thought his English accent was so cute.

After work, Gabrielle went to Le Gorille, a little restaurant on the port where she often met with her old school friends to watch the boats dock in the late afternoon. That day there were no friends to meet, but sitting at the next table was Jeremy Anstruther-Formby. She pretended not to see him – she didn't want him to think she was stalking him, but he noticed her immediately.

'May I join you?' he asked in his cut-glass voice. 'Unless you're expecting someone?'

'No, no, I'm just winding down after work. I only started at the gendarmerie last month and sometimes it gets quite difficult. So many things to remember and they are all so important!'

'So much red tape and bureaucracy. How ghastly for you,' he laughed, but she looked bemused so he quickly added, 'I'm sorry, that's just my British sense of humour.'

'Oh, but I agree,' said Gabrielle. 'Far too much red tape. My father gets swamped. He has to fill things in triplicate and write down the tiniest of details, otherwise his cases may be thrown out.'

'Well, I hope you were very thorough with my case then and that you will find the culprit,' Jeremy smiled at Gabrielle so entrancingly that her heart did a somersault.

They talked and talked and she discovered that he was from an aristocratic family in England, that he was one of three children with a life-long passion for collecting antiques, and that he had opened a small shop in one of the quaint back streets of Saint-Tropez just a few months ago, after selling his shop in London.

He was twenty-nine to Gabrielle's nineteen, but that did not stop her falling head over heels in love with him. After their third date, in his shop late one night, he looked surprised at her confession, but then he held her gently and told her how much she meant to him. She had hoped – no, expected – that he would want to make love to her. All of her girlfriends had had boyfriends, lovers, some even had husbands now, but she had never been interested in any of the local Saint-Tropez boys. They seemed gauche and unworldly, particularly next to Jeremy, who was a man of the world, much travelled and extremely knowledgeable. He enthralled Gabrielle with exciting tales of far-away places he had been to and the glamorous and famous people he had met.

The more they saw each other, the more Gabrielle wanted – she needed Jeremy to make love to her. When she haltingly broached the subject after months of meeting, he told her that he didn't feel she was ready yet.

'You're so young, my dear. I want to educate you before we make love,' he said, sipping a vintage claret at Maxim's the next night.

He had contrived to take her on a trip to Paris, where he had booked a suite at Le Bristol. The room had two bedrooms and the first night, although he came into her bed and cuddled up to her, they did not make love, contrary to her fervent desire. Gabrielle started to feel inadequate. At nineteen her hormones were in full flow and she listened to tales of her girlfriends' lovers and liaisons with frustration and a little jealously.

'Be patient,' Jeremy had said to her often. 'Be patient, *cherie*, and when you are ready I will love you more than you can ever imagine.'

So she continued to worship at Jeremy's shrine and to hope that one day he would feel she was ready for love. He taught her a lot – about art and music and the theatre – but he never taught her what she most wanted to know about: the art of making love.

One day, after having solved a rather complicated case of cheque fraud and bursting with pride, she decided to surprise him by popping over to his shop. She couldn't wait to tell Jeremy about how she had cracked it and she hoped he would congratulate her, and then, maybe . . .

They were supposed to celebrate her twentieth birthday that

night at Chez Madeleine, a quiet restaurant on the Route de Tahiti in Ramatuelle that specialised in fresh lobster. But Gabrielle was too excited to wait until then. They could always have a lovely afternoon and drive there together in his beautiful open-top vintage Bentley. Perhaps now he would no longer see her as a teenager, and he would feel this was the right time.

She arrived at the antique shop where he worked just after one o'clock, but the front door was firmly locked. Then she realised it was lunchtime, when every self-respecting French shopkeeper closed for at least two hours.

Undeterred, Gabrielle walked round to the back of the shop. Although she had only been there a few times, she remembered the narrow back alley where deliveries were made.

A sleepy ginger cat lay in a small patch of sunlight outside the back door. Gabrielle shooed it away with the toe of her boot. Its hackles rose and it hissed at her fiercely, arched its back, then stalked off with dignity. She pushed the back door, which to her surprise opened, and found herself in a short dark passageway, at the end of which was another door.

Some instinct told her not to call out Jeremy's name. It was quiet in the shop, except for the light hum of traffic and the ticking of an ancient clock. Slowly she opened the door at the end of the passage and walked into what was obviously a storeroom. Finding herself flanked by a pair of massive ormolu candelabra and some imposing bronze and marble statues of golden youths, she stopped dead beside a stack of folded Aubusson rugs. She could hear something. Behind an elaborate black lacquer screen she could hear sounds of breathing – harsh, masculine breathing – and whispers too faint to be properly heard.

She could smell the potent cologne that Jeremy always wore, his signature scent, musky and strong.

The rubber soles of her espadrilles muffled her footsteps as she approached the screen. There were panels of glass running along the top of it, and standing on tiptoe she now peered through one of them.

What she saw made her almost scream. Behind the screen, Jeremy was lolling back in a huge velvet armchair, naked except for his pink silk shirt. His eyes were closed, his mouth hung open, and at his feet knelt a short young man. Both men were oblivious to everything around them, as the boy's head bobbed up and down rhythmically between Jeremy's suntanned legs.

The revolting spectacle of the two men – so totally engrossed in each other and with such obvious disregard to the fact that anyone could have walked in and caught them – completely paralysed Gabrielle. As if hypnotised, she watched Jeremy shudder, his whole body convulse, as he thrust himself into the other man's eager mouth. This couldn't be happening – it couldn't be real. It was like a horribly degenerate peep show; she was hallucinating; this must surely be a dream – a nightmare. She shook her head to try to rid herself of the shocking image and took a step backwards, knocking into a pile of porcelain plates.

'Who's there?' she heard Jeremy's voice. 'Who is it?'

Stifling the sob in her throat, Gabrielle turned and ran. Stumbling over ornate carved side tables, side-stepping umbrella stands and stuffed deer heads, she ran as fast as she could, away from the dim musty shop into the bright October sunshine.

That had been over four years ago. After that Gabrielle threw herself into work, determined to become the best policewoman she could. All thoughts of boys and men were banished so, at almost twenty-five, Gabrielle Poulpe was still a virgin.

∽

Captain Poulpe sat at his kitchen table reviewing his copious notes about Mina Corbain's curious death.

Gabrielle was busying about, fixing him his favourite beef bourguignon and waiting for her father to speak. She knew well enough not to interrupt him when he was thinking and, by the way he was slowly sipping his red wine, she knew theories were bubbling.

'You know what I think, Gaby?' he finally announced.

'What, Papa?' She set the steaming plate of food before him. An excellent cook, Aunt Greta had taught her well.

'I don't think it was just food poisoning. I believe the murderer put poison in the oysters.'

'How could he do that?'

'Let us say the murderer buys a dozen oysters. He invites thirty people for dinner. Before this he'd bought another twelve oysters from another source and left them somewhere to go bad. He brings in the deadly oysters, mixes them with the fresh oysters that are being served. He injects a tiny bit of botulism from the poisoned oysters into two of them. All the guests will get some sort of food poisoning from the oysters, but the victim, in this case, Mina, served with the bad oysters with the poison will die.'

'But why Mina? She was so adored, so young and talented. Why would the killer choose her?'

'I don't know.' Her father sipped his wine and gazed into the fire. 'I have no idea, but the more we question all the people who were at the party, the closer we may get to an answer.'

'But the Mayor has closed the case; he said it was an accident.'

'Maybe, maybe not – but we must keep our eyes and ears open, Gabrielle.'

∞

Later that night, Gabrielle and Captain Poulpe stood outside the massive white yacht *Hedonist*, moored on the quay on the far outskirts of the port, watching yet another party. The vessel, owned by the Russian oligarch Sergei Litvak, was too big to get a berth inside the main part of the port, so two hundred of Saint-Tropez's social butterflies, ranging in age from twenty to decrepitude, plus another two hundred good-looking scrapings from the beach, had to trudge down the cobbled wharf to get to the party. Before they could board, they had to remove their designer shoes and park them in one of the canvas hampers guarded by one of the *Hedonist*'s sailors; only then were they allowed to clamber up to the decks. Everyone was dressed in white, as instructed on the invitation. Sergei Litvak was throwing the party in honour of his friend, the mega-rich tycoon Jonathan Meyer. Litvak stood on the top deck in a flowing white kaftan, surrounded by several lithe teenagers posturing in white sequinned bikinis and pearl chokers. His tame photographer stood nearby, recording Sergei's every move. Like most denizens of Saint-Tropez, Litvak adored publicity and had his every move recorded for posterity by his personal team.

Jonathan stood beside him in a crisp white silk suit, his gorgeous young wife Vanessa clinging to his arm.

Maximus Gobbi, in a creased white linen jacket, was down on the wharf checking to see if there was any more new action. He badly needed to replenish his stud stable. The three guys he had invited to the beach with Carlotta were not for sale, as they had recently been taken; Fabrizio was becoming too difficult and too busy and he still seemed to be unable to seal the marriage deal with Lara. He was also spreading himself too thin with other liaisons, one of whom Maximus suspected was Betty, his dance instructor.

Two of Maximus's stable of boys had recently scored big with rich divorcées and left for Miami and New York respectively. They had paid him the commission on the monetary gifts they had received, but not on the cufflinks, leather jackets or cashmere sweaters, so there was little hope now of him collecting any more of anything. 'Ungrateful bastards,' he thought as he idly watched the famous elderly English racing driver Henry Phillips walk carefully up the gangplank, followed by his shrill American wife, Blanche.

Henry had won the Monaco Grand Prix forty years ago and, to celebrate this anniversary, he was being feted by the British ex-pats and the visiting Americans all along the Riviera. But at seventy he was partied out and felt far too old for endless festivities and fun, unlike Blanche. For her, there were never enough parties to attend, and even this early in the season she had schlepped Henry all over London, Madrid and the Côte d'Azur relentlessly socialising. The social crowd tolerated her because Henry was a folk hero, but Blanche gave new meaning to the words 'crashing bore'. Many a matron had exchanged place cards at a dinner table to save their husbands from her inane chit-chat.

Blanche always carried with her a bald, snappy, midget dog, and as she reached the top deck, heavily out of breath, she parked herself as close to the Mayor of Saint-Tropez as she could manage.

'Oh, he's so cute,' cooed Chantelle, Monty Goldman's wife, a blonde, Britney Spears lookalike, as she stroked the mutt's liver-coloured head.

'Careful!' warned Blanche, 'Pixie hates to be touched.' But the warning came too late. With a low growl the dog clamped its tiny gnashers on to Chantelle's acrylic neon nails and succeeded in biting one of them off, then chewed on it contentedly. Blanche berated the unfortunate Chantelle.

'Never touch Pixie,' she screamed furiously, straightening the pooch's faux-diamond collar. 'She hates being stroked by strangers, don't you, sweetie?'

Chantelle was dumbstruck, her over-filled lips parted to suck on her bleeding finger, tears running down her cheeks. Blanche ignored her and quickly whisked herself off to the top deck in search of someone famous, one arm cradling Pixie, the other pulling a recalcitrant Henry behind her.

Watching in amusement, Gabrielle Poulpe followed her. The insane lives of the Eurotrash and American social climbers never failed to interest her. She smiled at Contessa Carlotta, who looked angelic in a short white Grecian gown, which showed off her lovely legs. Gabrielle's brief questioning of Carlotta had given no clues as to Mina's death, but she hadn't really expected anything. Carlotta was new in town and she seemed sweetly innocent, not yet tarnished with the blasé attitude of the Saint-Tropez majority. As she walked around the packed throng, Gabrielle noticed many of the men eyeing Carlotta, but Fabrizio was bold enough to approach her.

Never one to let the grass grow beneath his size elevens, he had strolled over to the party early looking for fresh fields to furrow. Lara, still being tended by half the hairdressers and *visagistes* of Saint-Tropez, had told him she would meet him on the boat, so he knew he had a little time. And there she was, the newest object of his desire, standing at the bar alone.

'You're looking ravishing tonight, Contessa,' he purred, his dancing eyes never leaving hers.

'Thanks, you are sweet, but you told me that at the beach on Sunday.' She tried to move away but there was too much of a crush at the bar, and in her bare feet she felt dwarfed by Fabrizio's height.

'Ah yes, but your beauty grows like . . . like . . .' He searched for an appropriate metaphor.

'Weeds?' Carlotta smiled blithely.

'No, no, no, Contessa. Your beauty grows like . . .' He bent to whisper in her ear lasciviously. Carlotta flushed.

'I think you're rather crude!' she said.

'Sorry, sorry, it was a joke!' Fabrizio realised he'd made a big mistake. Likening Carlotta's beauty to the size of his cock was probably not the coolest attempt at a chat-up line, although it had sometimes worked for him on previous occasions. One thing Fabrizio did not have, in spite of his looks, charm, and prowess in bed, was a way with words. He watched as Carlotta walked over to another group, then he slouched over to the bar. Ah well, '*que sera, sera*'; there was always another time.

Maximus suddenly appeared by his side, having heard their dialogue. 'If you don't stop fucking around the Contessa and get your wedding date to Lara sorted, I'll wash my hands of you,' he hissed in Fabrizio's ear. 'And I'll tell CRAP,' he finished darkly.

'Oh, shit, where are they?' asked Fabrizio despairingly. 'Why can't those bitches leave me alone?'

'They will when you come up with enough money for the two of them and your poor starving infants. Get married pronto; don't wait a year. You're not getting any younger. Make Lara a bride *now*! Then you can pay off CRAP – get rid of them for good.'

'Fuck you, I'm only twenty-nine! Do I really need to marry a fifty-year-old drunk?'

'Yes,' Maximus said gravely. 'You know she's addicted to you.'

'And to vodka and to dope as well,' snapped Fabrizio. 'I'm trying to get the Contessa interested in me. She's rich and young and beautiful. We'd make a great couple.'

'Forget Carlotta, she's much too good for the likes of you. Go for the Russian broad – get her pregnant.'

'*Pregnant?* You're joking! She's fifty-three, for Christ's sake! It's a bit too fucking late! Christ, what a life I've got myself into! It's hard, Maximus, I don't even like Lara any more. She's a total bitch. I could really make it with Carlotta.'

'No way,' said Maximus. 'I'm too fond of her to let her get involved with a bum like you.'

'C'mon, give me a chance to work on her – okay?'

Maximus remained silent, but levelled a cold, hard stare at Fabrizio who, realising he was defeated, wandered gloomily over to the bar. Maximus stared after him. He started to think about the possibility of a liaison between Fabrizio and Carlotta. Why not? If Lara's ex-husband Jonathan was so obdurate about cutting off her alimony if she remarried, then maybe Fabrizio and Carlotta *would* be a better match, and he could get a significant finder's fee. Maybe he should encourage it.

∞

Carlotta managed to escape to the top deck, where Henry and Blanche were deep in conversation with the Mayor, Sophie, and Frick and Adolpho.

'Carlotta, darling, darling *cara*! Welcome to Saint-Tropez! I'm so thrilled to see you. You look gorgeous!' shrieked Blanche, cranking herself up to give Carlotta an effusive hug, then pulling her down to sit between her and Sophie. 'I haven't seen you since the Grand Prix in Monaco last year. You were with your poor husband . . . I'm so sorry, darling.' Blanche arranged her face in what she thought was a sincere expression of sympathy but which, thanks to multiple facelifts, just came off looking comical.

'Thank you, Blanche,' said Carlotta. 'Yes, it was very sad.'

'And so young! And so handsome!' Blanche was in full flow now, which made Carlotta feel a little uncomfortable. She had had to play the grieving widow in Buenos Aires for four months and she had hoped that in new environs most people would grasp that the mourning period was over. Luckily Blanche skipped to another subject.

'Oh, and remember that lunch we had the next day when we saw Prince Harry on the beach with his girlfriend? Poor guy, he was trying so hard not to be noticed, but we saw him, didn't we, Carlotta?' Carlotta nodded. She tolerated Blanche because she found the pushy socialite rather pitiable, and Carlotta tried never to be rude to anyone.

Blanche pulled Carlotta down beside her on to the banquette, but Sophie was not best pleased by Carlotta's inclusion in the group. She liked Carlotta but never took kindly to younger, prettier women sitting next to her, and Carlotta's exotic natural beauty and sweet nature seemed to be making her popular with the Saint-Tropez social set.

Suddenly Blanche's dog, which was the size of a rat and having regurgitated the plastic fingernail, decided to pounce on one of Carlotta's dangling emerald earrings. For a tiny pooch Pixie had simian strength, and Carlotta shook her head violently to try to dislodge the animal. But Pixie seemed determined to swallow her Harry Winston bauble. Carlotta tried pushing the dog away, but it hung on, tiny teeth attached to the emerald earring and growling as menacingly as a toy pooch could.

Blanche seemed unaware of what her pet was up to yet again as she continued to recount to a bored Sophie the saga of her recent breast reduction.

'That Beverly Hills doctor is magic, just magic,' she confided. 'I was a 38DD and he cut everything out and made me a 34B – look!' She proudly pulled down her loose chiffon top to reveal six-month-old breasts on a sixty-nine-year-old chest.

Frick and Adolpho, totally taken aback to see this elderly American flashing her fresh boobs, turned away, giggling uncontrollably. Carlotta looked as embarrassed as she was able with a snarling puppy attached to her ear.

Sophie, grinning devilishly, purred, 'They're lovely, darling, simply divine. Hollywood starlets would be jealous of those – er – breasts.'

117

'Ya think?' Blanche looked extremely pleased, then finally noticed Carlotta trying to wrestle her earring from Pixie's fangs.

A young man, who had been leaning on the handrail watching the scene with amusement, came to Carlotta's rescue. He gently removed the earring from the yapping dog's mouth and returned it to Carlotta with an enigmatic smile. *My God, but she is lovely,* he thought. *So much more refined and beautiful than the over-Botoxed and over-tanned females in this town.*

Carlotta smiled shyly back at him. 'Thank you so much. I'm not quite ready to be dog meat yet.'

He laughed and held out his hand. 'Nick Stevens – and that dog has great taste in snacks.'

She laughed and shook his hand, 'Carlotta Di Ponti. I'm glad to meet you.'

Nick Stevens was nothing like the blasé two-faced partygoers who would stab you in the back while saying, 'Darling, you look amazing!' Dressed in simple chinos and a plain white shirt, he was medium height with sandy-blond hair, cut unfashionably short. His deep tan was not the kind one gets from lounging on the beach or a yacht covered in suntan lotion. It was the dark almost chestnut brown acquired from being out in the open air with no beauty aids. The crinkles around his pale, almost translucent blue eyes attested to an outdoor life. His handshake was firm but not bone crushing, and he held it for a fraction longer than necessary, looking into Carlotta's eyes.

'Do you want to help me stargaze?' he asked.

'Of course,' Carlotta stood up, glad to get away from the mad dog and the hysterical Blanche, and followed Nick over to the handrail. 'You don't look like you really belong here,' she said, then hastily added, 'I mean, I'm sorry to sound rude.'

'Not at all, Contessa.' He smiled and she realised he knew who she was. 'I don't belong, you are right. But if you don't mind my saying so, you don't seem to be like these people at all.'

'Oh, I'm the new gal in town. Please, call me Carlotta.'

'You're a widow, are you not?'

She nodded. His questions should have put her on her guard, but Nick was not only good-looking in a non-threatening way, but also had a down-to-earth, relaxed attitude that she really liked.

'Another drink?' he asked.

'Why not?' Carlotta smiled as he signalled to the waiter, then they leaned on the railing watching the stars and listening with amusement to the cacophony behind them.

Having heard the story about Blanche revealing her boobs, Fabrizio bounded up like a big puppy and plonked himself down next to Blanche and joked in his little-boy voice, which many women found adorable, 'Can I have a look at your boobies too?'

He winked at Carlotta, who was at the handrail staring down at the dark, diamond-encrusted waves but had heard his remark. *He had some nerve, that boy. Good-looking as he was, he never knew when to quit and his jokes weren't funny.*

But Blanche, delighted to have such a handsome audience, obligingly pulled down her top again for Fabrizio's and everyone else's delectation.

Pixie was feeling left out, and having been denied her emerald earring, decided to get some attention by taking a nip at Blanche's left nipple.

Blanche's screams were so loud that they echoed through the ancient back streets of the village and started all the dogs barking madly. Carlotta turned, startled, then rushed to comfort her. Fabrizio, ever the hero, tried to cover Blanche's breasts with a cocktail napkin that was far too small for the job.

Lara heard Blanche's manic cries as she minced up the steps in search of Fabrizio. Her white Lurex Hervé Léger was too short, too tight and too low-cut but, having heard how fabulous she looked from her 'wrecking crew', she oozed confidence. But when Lara saw Fabrizio, one hand on Blanche's chest and looking at Carlotta with a buffoon-like smile, she went ballistic. '*STRONZO BASTARDO!*' she screamed, yanking him away by the collar of his white Dolce shirt. 'What are you doing with her?'

'Nothing,' he yelled, adjusting his shirt, uncomfortably aware that all the guests were watching with great amusement.

'I'll show you nothing,' yelled Lara, slapping his face for the second time that night with a be-ringed hand.

Galvanised into action, Maximus rushed up the stairs and watched helplessly as Fabrizio attempted to defend himself from the onslaught of ten pointed acrylic nails.

François, the waiter from Sénéquier, in the process of serving Sophie a glass of wine, grinned. He liked nothing more than to see the so-called 'beautiful people' making fools of themselves and each other, and he thought Lara was a 'Grade I' bitch. Another incident had occurred with Lara just that morning. As François had manoeuvred around the overcrowded tables of Sénéquier Café and Bar, she had accused him of spilling water down her sun-ravaged décolletage. He'd attempted to deny it, but she had threatened to have him fired. To placate her he had signalled to another waiter to bring her another vodka.

'On the house,' he smiled. She was a nasty piece of work and he wasn't about to let her get away with her endless bullying. Her time would come.

Lara was still hissing at Fabrizio, who looked like a cowering dog. François felt a touch of pity for the poor gigolo. What a way to earn a living – banging raddled old bags, waiting for hand-outs and singing horribly.

François would never lower himself to that, even though rich women had propositioned him many a time. Yes, he was good-looking, but he had a lot better and bigger fish to fry right now, and he was getting quite a kick out of it, not to mention a ton of cash.

Suddenly the Captain appeared in the crowded main salon below the top deck. Clapping his hands he announced with all the gravitas of a lifetime of maritime experience, '*Silencio*. Ladies and gentlemen, please evacuate the boat immediately and in an orderly fashion. We have just been informed that there is a bomb on board.'

CHAPTER TWELVE

'A bomb!' Ignoring the Captain's calm command to leave the boat quietly, and shrieking with fear instead, four hundred movers-and-shakers, socialites and members of the Eurotrash set began to shove each other out of the way in their frantic quest to escape being blown to smithereens.

Henry and Blanche were first down the narrow stairs, Pixie perched terrified on her mistress's shoulder, her shrill barking adding to the cacophony. Behind them lumbered Maximus, sweating and cursing profusely. Suddenly he missed his footing on the slippery steps and, with a bellow of alarm, fell forwards, his huge body propelled on to Blanche's wizened frame. With a squeal she jumped out of his way but dropped Pixie. The puppy fell to the ground, and then Maximus's massive bulk landed on Pixie with a sickening crunch.

'Oh, my God! My *dawg!*' screamed Blanche, frantically scooping up the tiny mutt's remains. 'My baby – my Pixie poo.' Black tears ran down her rouged cheeks as Maximus struggled up on his feet to face her barrage of fury. 'You killed Pixie, you murderer, you . . . FAT . . . *murderer*. You killed my darling little doggie.' She held the puppy's body closer, sobbing into its squashed and bloodied fur.

'Madame, I am so sorry, I did not see your dog. I mean it is so tiny . . . and in the rush . . . I apologise, *madame*, but, but . . . she had a painless death. So sorry.'

'She was the most precious thing in my life. You're a monster,' Blanche sobbed. 'I demand an arrest now. Monsieur Le Mayor – listen, listen to me, please . . .'

She grabbed the Mayor's sleeve as he awkwardly clambered down the steps, but as he was only concerned with getting off the ship himself, he brushed her arm off and jumped on to the steps down to the quay to join the gawking throng.

'Madame, I will buy you another dog,' Maximus blustered as the stewards started herding everyone – including Blanche and the dead dog – off the vessel. 'A proper dog, one that is fully grown.'

'How *dare* you! Pixie was fully grown; she had the finest pedigree; she was special. She was my *baby* . . .' Weeping piteously, Blanche staggered on to the wharf, where she collapsed into her husband's arms.

Camera phones started clicking all over the quay as everyone rushed from the local cafés to capture the scene.

Lara stomped down on to the quay and started rummaging through the basket of shoes.

'My shoes? Where are my Louboutins?' she yelled to one of the sailors, who ignored her. 'Where're my jewelled sandals? They were brand new from Neiman's,' she demanded of Maximus, who sat hunched over on a concrete slab, wheezing horribly. 'And where's Fabrizio?'

Maximus's asthma was playing up so badly he could only point weakly back up at the boat, then had a coughing fit.

'He's still with *her*?' Lara's collagen-ed lips drew back into a snarl. 'How could you let this happen, you idiot?'

Maximus, unable to speak, shook his head and wheezed some more.

Suddenly there was another loud proclamation from the Captain. 'Man overboard. *Attenzione* everyone. *Attenzione!* Two men overboard! No – no, there's a *woman!* Oh, *mio Dio!* Woman overboard too.'

∞

When the frenzied, terrified throng started to abandon ship, Carlotta, who was still chatting to Nick, pressed herself against the ship's railing to avoid being crushed by the crowd rushing to safety. Fabrizio, still hot for her in spite of Lara's jealousy, had manoeuvred himself nearer to tell her a few more bad jokes. Before he had the chance to even start, all hell broke loose.

The handrail, which had recently undergone inept repair work, collapsed, and Carlotta and the two men had tumbled head over heels into the poisonous, polluted waters of the Saint-Tropez port. This part of the Mediterranean, so close to the giant yachts, was extremely dirty, as the crews of the floating gin palaces thought nothing of disposing of their detritus into the sea. Carlotta tried to swim to the quay but her mouth was full of the foul filth in the water and she was almost choking on it.

Nick put his arms out to Carlotta to help her, and managed to pull her to the edge of the slipway. Dripping and filthy, they were manhandled out unceremoniously on to the jetty. Carlotta, Nick and Fabrizio were covered in muck and slime as they lay panting on the concrete dock. Somebody passed around bottles of water and Carlotta gratefully rinsed out her mouth.

Nick gave the impression of latent strength as he helped Carlotta to sit. His sinewy muscles supported her and she leaned against his chest gratefully. A feeling of safety enveloped her. In spite of the shock of falling and the maelstrom around her, Nick Stevens felt good, solid and safe.

'I guess they scrimped on repairs,' he grinned. 'But hey, it could have been worse. We could've drowned in that crap.'

The paparazzi were having a field day, feverishly jumping up and down and pushing people out of the way to get the best shots of everyone shivering on the quay.

'They look like drowned rats!' crowed Pete the Brit-pap, 'This summer is a real money-maker!'

'The tabloids and the celeb mags are going to eat these up!' gloated Jean-Pierre, the French paparazzo. 'You know how the public loves seeing celebrities looking terrible.'

'This is the sorriest-looking bunch I've ever seen,' said Pete, in his element, stoked by the prospect of dollar signs dancing before his eyes.

Jonathan Meyer's white suit was covered in red wine spilled on him by his wife Vanessa. As they struggled down the boat's steep step, her dress rose above her thighs; in an attempt to pull it down, she put her hand on her husband's head to steady herself and dislodged his toupee, which slid over one eye. With his black eyes and moustache, he looked like a passable imitation of Hitler. Some of the onlookers, noting the resemblance, excitedly snapped pictures on their phones.

Blanche was 'papped' weeping, clutching a small dead dog to her half-naked breasts. The videos went viral the following day.

Sophie Silvestri, who hated the paparazzi, was photographed adjusting her blonde bouffant wig while being comforted by the Mayor who, having always fancied her, was feeling rather excited.

Lying flat out on the concrete quay and choking on slime, was Fabrizio Bricconni. A barefoot Lara Meyer, bloodshot eyes burning with rage, was standing over him and she had resumed her verbal flagellation as he coughed and spluttered.

'That's a great shot!' panted Pete, hot-footing it over to them.

Ignoring the assembled snappers, barely managing to contain her fury, she screamed abuse at him as flashbulbs exploded in front of them like 4 July fireworks. Suddenly, when the realisation of what was happening hit Lara, she hissed through gritted teeth, 'Come, Fabrizio, let us go home. I'm gonna take care of you, *darling*,' as she grabbed him by the collar of his sodden silk shirt.

Fabrizio, shivering with cold, felt his knees turn to jelly. God knows what was in store for him now. Lara's ominous 'I'm gonna take care of you, *darling*' could mean anything. He would never put it past her to threaten suicide, then cut up his suits and throw them out of the window. Whatever it was, he knew tonight he was in for a bumpy ride, yet again.

'What you do with that woman?' she hissed, pointing to Carlotta.

'I wasn't with her. I wasn't doing anything. She was talking to that guy next to her.' He stumbled to his feet, glancing over to where Nick was helping Carlotta to sit up.

'We'll talk about it later, *caro*. Come, let's go.' The furious socialite attempted to throw a rictus grin towards the panting paparazzi as she hustled her lover away by the neck of his ripped shirt.

'This is just like what she did to her husband when he was banging that teenager,' said Pete the Brit-pap to Jean-Pierre.

'Lara Meyer's a goldmine when she's pissed off,' grinned Jean-Pierre. 'These photos are gonna make us a mint!'

∞

Gabrielle and her father took notes while they and a dozen local gendarmes attempted to interview everyone who was on the boat, who in turn were attempting to escape both the amateur and professional paparazzi.

The Bomb Squad, in full body armour, arrived by speedboat from Saint Maxime. They cautiously searched every inch of the vessel, but after several hours the Captain of the squad informed Captain Poulpe: 'It must have been a false alarm or a hoax. There is no trace of bombs or explosives of any kind. We do, however, have this note that was delivered to Captain Boursin. It came with a bouquet of red and white carnations.'

He handed it to Captain Poulpe, who shared it with his daughter. Simply printed in childish handwriting it said, 'There is a bomb on this boat and unless everyone leaves by midnight the vessel will explode.'

'Death,' Gabrielle whispered. 'Red and white flowers mean death, Papa.'

Amazingly, not one of the thirty staff and fifteen crew members had any recollection of the bouquet being delivered to the Captain, who admitted that he had only noticed them an hour earlier in his wheelhouse when he had first read the attached note.

'I wonder if whoever played this sick trick could be the same person who killed Mina?' said Captain Poulpe. 'But was it a sort of warning or a practical joke in very bad taste? I think, Gabrielle, we have not heard the last of this individual.'

∞

The shadowy figure lurking behind the gawping crowds grinned. *What a great joke, how the mighty fall*, he smiled to himself. *These people are going to get sick to death of being in this place after what I have planned for them.*

∞

Carlotta sat shivering on the quay next to Nick. He was also soaking wet and covered in filth, and even though his blond hair was plastered flat to his head as he tried to pick a strand of seaweed out of it, she thought he still looked attractive.

'I think it's about time we got out of Dodge,' he smiled.

'We can't – here comes the Sheriff to string us up,' she laughed.

Captain Poulpe marched over to the couple and, after briefly questioning them, released them with the warning that they might be more extensively interviewed at a later date.

In the police car taking her back to her villa, Carlotta told Nick that she had definitely felt somebody push her from behind.

'Did you see who it was?' he asked.

'No – I have no idea. Maybe it was a passing waiter but I'm sure they didn't mean it.'

She shivered and Nick tentatively put his arm around her. She liked the comforting feel of his body so close to hers – it made her feel warm and safe, and it had been a long time since she'd had that feeling.

'Let's try and forget all this. Why don't we get to know each other a little bit better? How about lunch tomorrow?'

'That would be nice. Why don't you call me?' She smiled up into his eyes and gently moved away from his embrace. 'I'd love to go somewhere quiet, away from the Saint-Tropez razzmatazz.'

'I know the perfect place,' he said.

∞

After the crowds finally dispersed, Gabrielle sat on the edge of the quay, making notes on her cell phone. François, the waiter, came to sit beside her.

'Hi,' he said. 'Has anybody ever told you you're too pretty to be a cop?'

Oh, please, she thought – *from what clichéd movie had he stolen that line?*

129

She coolly appraised him. He certainly had a boyish charm and good looks in abundance, and his alibis for Mina's death had checked out after the interrogations, as did his credentials. François Lardon's profile stated that he came from a good bourgeois family in Marseille and had been working as a waiter there until he became employed at Sénéquier the previous year.

As they chatted, Gabrielle started to realise she enjoyed talking to this young man. She had had no boyfriends since the terrible night when she had discovered the truth about Jeremy. Because her mother had died when she was so young, she had become the woman of the house. She had devoted herself to her father, ran their *ménage* and was determined to be the best she could at her job in the gendarmerie. What little spare time she had was taken up by working out diligently in the gym, honing her strength with karate lessons and T'ai Chi. There had been little time for dating, but she was only twenty-four and her hormones were rampant, so when François Lardon asked her to a concert in Ramatuelle with him the following week, she decided to accept.

∽

The next day, Nick took Carlotta to L'Auberge de la Môle, a small family-run restaurant in the picturesque town of La Môle – a good half-hour away from Saint-Tropez. The owner Clothilde came bustling up and hugged Nick, who was obviously a regular and valued customer, and escorted them to a table in the corner of the forecourt, next to the wall where the bougainvillea bloomed in abundance.

'You will love the food here. I hope you have a good appetite.'

'I certainly do,' said Carlotta. 'I'm ravenous.'

Clothilde brought them five fabulous courses and Carlotta enjoyed every single one of them, particularly the large terrines of assorted pâtés like mousse de canard and pâté de campagne, which she devoured with large hunks of buttered grilled rustic bread and a big jar of assorted *cornichons* and other pickled delicacies.

They talked as if they had known each other for years. He told her about his life as a journalist working on a range of stories, including being in the frontlines of hotspots all over the world. Carlotta wasn't ready to tell him too much about her miserable life with Nicanor, however. At the end of the dinner, he drove her home, and at her front door said, 'Goodnight, Contessa. This has been very special.'

'For me too,' she replied tenderly. Reaching up she kissed him softly, and he gently pulled her closer to him. He felt so safe and strong – a world apart from the way Nicanor had held her, even in his tenderest moments. The thought made her shudder involuntarily.

As if reading her thoughts, he whispered, 'So special that whatever happens between us should start slowly.'

'I agree,' said Carlotta. Although she was still eager for the sensual feel of his mouth on hers, she gently pulled away.

'I have to go away tomorrow on an assignment – just a day or two – and when I return I want to see a lot more of you, Carlotta.'

'And I want to see a lot more of you too,' she said softly.

CHAPTER THIRTEEN

After a screaming row, which only ended when Fabrizio reluctantly calmed Lara down in the way she liked best, she gave him the silent treatment over the next few days. Any attempts by him at conversation were met with monosyllabic replies or sarcastic grunts.

Feeling totally pussy-whipped, he expunged his anger by fierce games of tennis and even fiercer bedroom games with Betty, the pretty Brit who was teaching him how to dance. He tried to call Carlotta and she sweetly but firmly refused his attempts to ask her out.

But life goes on in Saint-Tropez, and its denizens wouldn't let a little thing like Mina's murder or a bomb threat deter them from having the time of their lives. As the big party month of July grew closer, every day dozens of humongous yachts pulled into the tiny port of Saint-Tropez. Those that couldn't fit, or couldn't afford the unbelievably high mooring charges, parked their massive gin palaces in the choppy waters outside the beaches of Pampelonne.

∞

Lara loved her jewellery. All of it had sentimental value for her. She had received most of it when she was the queen of Manhattan society, and she kept it all under her bed in a big leather jewel case from Asprey's. Fabrizio had often told her she was foolish to keep so many goodies in their flat and not in the bank, but she always told him to 'Shut the fuck up – I always keep it locked, *stupido!*'

Stumbling home from a boozy boat lunch with Maximus and some of his young studs one afternoon, where she had fallen asleep sunbathing without her make-up, Lara collapsed drunkenly into her bed. Staring down, she was vexed to see her beautiful jewel case on the floor, smashed to pieces, which sobered her up immediately.

'My jewels!' she screamed, and fell to the ground attempting to pick up the few remaining trinkets that the thief hadn't bothered to take. 'Oh, my God, I've been robbed! Help, help, somebody help me!'

She staggered to the window, where a couple of passing tourists looked up curiously. 'Oh, look, Mags, isn't it that Lara something or other?' said the English holidaymaker, whipping out his iPhone and snapping the dishevelled socialite as she waved her arms frantically, shouting for help in such a slurred voice that no one understood her.

Lara's red hairpiece was slipping down her forehead and getting in the way of her pleas for help. She ripped it from her head, leaving her looking, without her massive beehive hairdo and her unmade-up face, like a pink boiled egg.

'Cor, Barry, she looks bloody awful! Can't be 'er,' said Mags, rolls of junk-food flesh oozing out from above her tight Lycra mini-dress.

'It is,' said Barry, snapping more photos, his brawny tattoo-encrusted arms holding up the phone as high as possible to get the best shot. 'Wot's 'at she's holding in 'er hands, eh?'

'Her syrup,' replied the woman with practised knowledge.

'Aw, yeah – syrup of fig – wig – got it,' Barry smirked. 'Hullo, Lara, darlin'. 'Ow'r you doin'?'

'Help me – please get the police,' cried Lara piteously, only it sounded more like 'Heppe plis get 'e please.'

'Yes, heppy, darlin'. Pleased yer happy, darlin',' laughed Barry, snapping more photos on his iPhone.

'*Nooooo! Hep-hep-Heeeeeppppe me*,' raged Lara in frustration. 'Paleeze – *Paleeeeeeze!*'

'Wot's that she's sayin'? Sumpthing about the palace?' Mags was still smiling and waving at Lara. 'I think she's well "hit and missed".'

'Yeah, as a newt,' said Barry. 'The *Sun* will pay a bundle for these pics, I bet.'

'Just wave and smile,' said Mags, and they slowly walked away, leaving Lara so distraught that she fainted, her body half-hanging out of the window. Her hairpiece fell to the ground, where minutes later a stray mongrel found it, sniffed it cautiously, cocked its leg and urinated on it.

When Fabrizio returned he found her sprawled on the floor, her face swollen and tear-stained, and buried in what remained of the Asprey box.

∞

In an effort to cheer herself up after the robbery, Lara had decided they absolutely must attend a charity gala at the Sporting Club in Monaco. 'Shirley Bassey's singing,' she snapped. 'We'll take the helicopter!'

'I hate helicopters,' he whined.

'Fuck you,' she retorted. She was still in a foul mood – jealous of Fabrizio's apparent interest in Carlotta, distraught about her missing jewels and furious about the photo of her that had appeared in the papers.

Fabrizio, in full black-tie regalia, sat nervously in a tiny, chartered helicopter with Lara, who wore a skimpy purple dress. Lara, who had been drinking all day, took out a silver flask for another swig of Grey Goose.

'Don't you think it's a bit early?' he enquired.

'Don't you think you should shut the fuck up?' she spat back.

'I think you should cool it with the drinking, *cara*.' Fabrizio tried his soothing voice and held out his hand. 'It's not good for you. Give me the flask, darling.'

Ignoring him, Lara pulled the flask away then stared down at the glorious Mediterranean glistening in the late afternoon sun. Tiny speedboats sped across the waves and children frolicked at the water's edge, but she barely recognised anything as her Botoxed lips sucked at her flask like an infant at its mother's breast.

Fabrizio sighed and turned to look out of the window. This was becoming too much of a chore. Did he really have to marry this drunken, jealous shrew? Was all the money in the world worth the ignominy, insults and abuse he had been putting up with for nearly two years? He had crept away earlier to call Maximus to tell him he couldn't and wouldn't close the deal to marry Lara, but Maximus had been adamant.

'You owe me, *ragazzo*, and you owe those two little bastards you carelessly sired. If you renege, you know what will happen to you.'

Fabrizio shuddered. He certainly did know. Maximus had powerful connections, not only on the Côte d'Azur but also with some of the crime bosses in Sicily. Two of his handsome young studs had disappeared without trace four years ago. Their bodies were never recovered, but the rumours of what had happened to them were too horrific to dwell on.

He was also worried that time was running out and the producer of *The X Factor* Kazakhstan had not returned his calls, and the record deal he was hoping for had suddenly fallen through.

∞

The producer, Derek Flukle, was an infamous and much-disliked English spiv. He called himself a manager and a 'star builder' but he was known to be the biggest sleaze-bag and crook in showbiz. At sixty-plus, having successfully bilked several singers and actresses out of vast amounts of money by crooked scams, he had turned his meagre talent to managing a Kazakhstani pop star. When that failed he managed, by lying through his teeth, to get a job as line producer on *The X Factor* Kazakhstan. He was not a man to be trusted and had no scruples about trampling people under his feet.

Fabrizio didn't really trust him, but he had to go along with his false promises of stardom, hoping against hope that something would come of it. He had met Derek and his fat ugly wife at a B-list celebrity party in London the previous year. Derek had chatted him up, telling him he had great potential and that he would love to represent him.

'I've got a contact list as long as my arm,' he boasted. 'I know everyone from Andrew Lloyd Webber to Beyoncé. You sign with me and I'll make you a star as big as Enrique Iglesias,' he added with a viperish grin.

Without telling Lara or Max, the guileless Fabrizio had agreed and paid Derek 20 per cent of all his income, despite the fact that he had come up with exactly nothing for him. When he complained, Derek threatened him with a lawsuit and finally persuaded Fabrizio that it would be in his best interests to keep quiet and take the potential gig on *The X Factor* in Kazakhstan. Fabrizio, disgusted but powerless against Derek and his slimy West End law firm, gullibly agreed.

When he casually checked Derek's credentials one day with Maximus, who actually did know everyone, Maximus scoffed. 'Oh, *Dio mio* – that *puto* is a total swindler. He conned the English singer Helen Bookham out of a fortune when he managed her, and I heard he grabbed another 20 per cent from Joan Collins for some clothing deal that he had nothing to do with.'

'How did he manage that?'

'Who knows? He bullies people into paying him. I wish I had his balls,' he laughed.

∽

'Life's a bitch,' Fabrizio thought as he looked mournfully out of the helicopter window, 'and I'm lumbered with two of them – Derek Flukle and Lara Meyer.'

There was one silver lining, though. The producers of the French *Dancing with the Stars* had come to watch him in rehearsal with Betty yesterday and they seemed quite impressed. All he had to do now was get into the final twelve. After that all he had to do was win it. He sighed, that could be a big hurdle, but he was going to give it his best shot.

Lara greedily drained the last dregs from her flask, then asked the pilot if he had any vodka.

The American pilot laughed. 'Sorry, ma'am, it's a short trip and we don't carry supplies on board, especially booze.' He snorted with laughter again, then said something incomprehensible into his mouthpiece.

This infuriated Lara, who snapped, 'Don't you dare laugh at me, young man. I'm paying a lot of money for this ride.'

'Sorry, ma'am,' the pilot became even more sarcastic, 'but you're not paying me, I'm just the airline's hired help.'

This made Lara completely insane and she started screaming obscenities at the pilot. Before Fabrizio could stop her, she began hitting him on his shoulders and back with the latest 'it' bag.

'For God's sake, lady, are you fuckin' crazy?'

The desperate pilot tried to keep the chopper on course while Fabrizio attempted to hold Lara down, but she was like a woman possessed. As the pilot made valiant efforts to stop her, she continued to attack him. Then a particularly vicious blow with the Fendi clasp – aimed at his head but which he managed to duck – hit the instrument panel. With a terrifying noise the helicopter started zigzagging across the sky, shaking and turning violently.

'Mayday! Mayday!' gasped the hapless pilot as Lara let out a series of deafening screams. 'Mayday! We're going down!'

CHAPTER FOURTEEN

Carlotta couldn't sleep. She tossed and turned in the vast bed, haunted by horrible dreams. She had never been able to forget the last time Nicanor had tried to make love to her. He had been as brutally violent as ever. Since he had been having regular sex with prostitutes who didn't mind being tied up, sodomised and raped with objects, he had decided to do the same thing with his wife. To Carlotta's horror he had woken her up in the middle of the night so stoned he could barely talk. He had bound her to the bedposts with his silk cravat and forced a hideous hard object inside her with such force that it ruptured her. Blood soaked the sheets and an ambulance was called. Carlotta, whimpering in agony, was escorted to the local hospital. It was announced that the Contessa had suffered a miscarriage of a longed-for baby boy – which was a lie – and then the truth emerged: that she would never be able to have children again.

Along with the strong mistral winds that shook the shuttered windows until they shuddered and made the palm trees bend almost to the ground, this was the image that woke Carlotta. The horrible whistling noise of the wind terrified her even more. She sat up in bed to turn the bedside light on but nothing happened. Thick darkness enveloped her and she started to shiver. She fumbled for the flashlight she kept in the bedside drawer but it wasn't there; then she remembered she had taken it to the kitchen the day before for a fresh battery and had left it here. She scrabbled around in the drawer until shaking fingers found a book of matches and she managed to light a small candle. She picked up the landline but it too was dead.

Carlotta felt cold with fear. The whistling noise of the mistral seemed to have die down but it was replaced by another sound – was it moaning? Was it breathing?

The hairs on the back of her neck bristled. She was alone in the house, having given Lilliane and Denis time off to celebrate their daughter's wedding in San Raphael.

She felt her way carefully to the bedroom door, which by habit she always kept locked. Holding the candle close to the door handle she saw with horror that it was slowly turning. Someone was in her house; someone had come up the stairs; someone had obviously cut the phone line and the electricity.

'Who's there?' she whispered, her voice a terrified croak.

There was no answer, only heavy breathing, almost as though whoever was outside had some sort of asthmatic problem.

'I-I've called the police,' she lied. 'They'll be here in a minute.'

The mistral suddenly resumed with a loud whoosh and the shutters began rattling again. Was it her imagination, or was that a low-pitched laugh she heard outside her door? Then the handle shook violently, and with a shriek of fear she saw that the key in the lock started coming loose.

'Oh, God – oh, my God, please go away!' she screamed so loud that her breath blew out the candle. Now she was in total darkness.

But the darkness allowed her to see the tiny light of her mobile phone where she had left it on the bed. She remembered that the battery was low, but maybe there was enough juice to call someone – but who? The mobile face said three a.m. Who could she call? Who was on her speed-dial who could help? Maximus had gone to Paris for a few days and she hadn't bothered to enter the numbers of most of the people she had met in the past few weeks . . . except for Nick's. He'd been on a short assignment but he'd rung to tell her he'd be back some time that evening.

Nick, Nick, please be at home, she pleaded in a tsunami of terror as she fumbled in her unlock code, messing it up twice.

Her eyes had become accustomed to the gloom so she rammed a heavy chair up under the moving door handle and twisted the key in the lock firmly. She heard an angry grunt on the other side of the door, then soft, maniacal laughter.

Desperately Carlotta dialled Nick's number. The phone rang four times while she prayed that the key would hold, and if not that the chair would keep whoever was on the other side at bay. The voicemail connected with Nick's pleasant, laid-back voice asking to leave a message.

'Shit!' she wailed, as the scraping at the door became more frantic. She hung up and redialled immediately. The phone rang once, twice . . .

'H-hullo?' Nick's voice, thick with sleep, answered the phone.

'Nick!' she screamed, 'help! Someone's trying to break into my room – they're in my house!'

A second went by before Nick registered what was going on, then he calmly commanded, 'Put me on speakerphone and turn up the volume to full!'

She fumbled for the right button and immediately Nick's firm but reassuring tones filled the room. 'Whoever you are, I've called the police and they are on their way, so leave now.'

The door handle had stopped shaking, so had the key.

'Can you hear me? Stop now and leave immediately.' Nick's voice was strong and assertive but his question was met by stony silence. Even the mistral had died down abruptly, and all Carlotta could hear was her own panicked breathing.

When the lights went on in her bedroom, Carlotta screamed.

'Carlotta? Darling, what's happened? Is someone still there?' Nick's urgent voice could be heard through the din.

'Oh, God, Nick – there was a man outside – oh, God, I almost died of fright,' she laughed and cried simultaneously in a hysterical fit. 'He's gone – the lights went out – it was so dark – the lights . . .'

'Carlotta, Carlotta, are you okay?' he insisted. 'Are you sure he's gone?'

Looking down on to her terrace and garden, Carlotta saw only waving palm trees and the swimming pool ablaze with light.

'Y-yes, yes, Nick. I'm fine. Thank you. Oh, God, thank you,' she sobbed.

The sound of police sirens racing up her driveway filled the night air, and shortly afterwards she heard the banging on the front door and the harsh voices of the police announcing their presence. She raced down the stairs to let them in.

∽

They didn't believe her. Captain Poulpe and Gabrielle asked her many questions, but they had found absolutely no evidence of an intruder. Even when Carlotta showed them the door, they found no sign of force nor the slightest trace of evidence that the lock had been picked. Gabrielle was extremely sympathetic to Carlotta's story and wanted to believe her, but her father told her she was being foolish.

'Imagination,' he said curtly. 'You know better than anyone what the mistral does to people's minds – they get illusions, they see things, and they hear things.'

Gabrielle nodded, remembering the oft-told tale of the

man who had killed his wife during a four-day mistral, but who had been let free because of what the judge called 'mistral madness'.

'This is what happened to the Contessa's mind,' he said. 'A classic example of the mistral madness.'

Nick had raced over to comfort Carlotta and arrived as she finished her interrogation. He insisted on staying the night with her.

'Don't worry – I'll sleep in the guest room next door,' he said.

'I-I would love you to sleep with me – I want to sleep with you, Nick, but I can't right now – not yet – soon, I promise. I really like you so much but I just *can't* – please understand, Nick, my love. Please, please, be patient with me.'

'Of course,' Nick said soothingly.

Captain Poulpe, who had just been leaving discreetly, overheard them and arched his eyebrows at Gabrielle as if to say: *See? That is how to get a man.* Gabrielle just raised her eyes to the heavens and stalked off.

The police left Carlotta and Nick together on the sofa. *He is so comforting, so understanding,* thought Carlotta as she nestled in his arms. Why couldn't she sleep with him? Why couldn't she allow him to make love to her? She wanted to, that much she knew, but every time they started to kiss and caress each other, something made her stop and she was unable to go through with it.

'I'll wait,' he reassured her, kissing the top of her head. 'I'm good at waiting. I've waited a long time to meet the love of my life, and you, my darling, are definitely worth waiting for.'

145

Chapter Fifteen

The residents of Saint-Tropez couldn't go outside their homes without some stringer from a tabloid newspaper asking questions about Mina Corbain's death, the bomb hoax and Lara Meyer's robbery. They were becoming unsettled and upset, and some residents started talking about selling up and moving to Mykonos or Ibiza. The weather had also been temperamental, with a series of mistral winds, which everyone hated.

Charlie Chalk disliked seeing his little slice of paradise overrun by the media types and curiosity seekers, eager for a quick sound bite or snap. Every time he ventured into the village, he found himself caught by some doltish journalist cross-questioning him.

'As if I knew,' he snapped.

Since there were no important parties for a few days, Charlie decided to take himself and Spencer off to London and accept several of the charitable engagements his agents were pressing him to do.

'I'll be glad to get away,' he said to Spencer, pulling his battered Vuitton down from the attic. 'It'll be good for the two of us to have a few days in good old London. See some shows, catch up with a few mates.'

'Oh, I don't think I can come.' Spencer was examining a tiny pimple on his chin with studied indifference.

'Why ever not, sweetie? We always go everywhere together – unless you're working. Have you got a job?'

'Yeah, I've just heard Qantas have got me on stand-by for the Friday trip to Melbourne.'

'But you can stand-by in London, can't you?'

'Not really. I'll have to take the Nice flight to Paris then connect on from there. It'll be tricky and I gotta be ready to go at short notice.'

It was a lie, of course. Spencer didn't want to go to London. As fond as he was of Charlie (and fond was the operative word as love didn't come into it), he had developed a tiny crush on the cute waiter at Sénéquier. Having visited there for coffee and aperitifs in the past couple of days, he was determined to work his magic on the young man.

There was nothing that turned Spencer on more than seducing a straight guy, and his 'gaydar' signalled to him that François Lardon was 100 per cent straight. Being blond, thirtyish and reasonably pretty, Spencer was still able to 'pull', and he took full advantage of every opportunity in his stopovers on the long-haul flights to Australia.

If big-hearted Charlie knew or even suspected, he didn't let on. Spencer was his legal 'wife'. They had performed a civil ceremony in England two years previously. He'd had to do it as Spencer, being Australian, was running out of excuses with the immigration department to stay not only in England but in France also.

'Well, okay then, I'll be back at the end of the week. Don't forget to get Henri to feed my roses and for God's sake watch out for those bloody wasps! I got stung on the bum last week and it wasn't funny.'

'Don't worry, darling, I know, I'll be careful – I hate those little buggers.'

With 'mwaw' kisses and hugs, Charlie left for Nice Airport and Spencer breathed a sigh of relief. 'Alone at last.' He smiled at his reflection as he finally disposed of the annoying pimple.

'Watch out, Monsieur Lardon, here I come.'

∞

François was amused by Spencer's somewhat amateur attempts to flirt with him. Having spent his formative years in some of the toughest streets in Marseille, he was wise to the tricks of the seducer and could see it coming a mile away. He saw Spencer arriving at the Sénéquier immediately. It was hard to miss the twenty-nine-year-old in a neon yellow windbreaker with a famous logo on the chest, tight white jeans, his blond hair tweaked into fashionable spikes.

Spencer took a table at the back of the café and surveyed the scene. The usual suspects were already at their kirs and their beers, preparing for another evening's pleasures.

Sophie Silvestri, resplendent in the latest Oscar de la Renta cruise wear, sat straight-backed in the middle of the room, her flunkeys Frick and Adolpho either side of her. She glanced around the crowded café, as regal as a queen, graciously accepting the obsequious attentions of her two escorts and the occasional fawning fan.

All of a sudden there was a flurry of activity at the door. Cell phones were furtively raised to snap photos and waiters quickly moved tables aside so that Lara Meyer and Fabrizio Bricconni could be seated. Lara was on crutches with one arm heavily bandaged, while Fabrizio, apart from a few cuts and scratches, looked more or less as good as new.

François leapt to attention and went to arrange a cushion solicitously behind Lara's chair. As usual she had no idea who he was.

'My God, what happened?' Spencer moved his chair closer to his friends.

'You haven't heard?' Fabrizio signalled to François to bring cocktails. 'We were in a terrible helicopter accident over the water.'

'Stupid fucking pilot!' Lara came out of her trance and lit a cigarette. 'He couldn't control the fucking machine, he let it plummet all over the place. We were terrified. What an idiot! We're suing the heli-company.' She blew smoke into Spencer's face then posed for a couple of passing tourists.

'Actually, it wasn't the pilot's fault,' said Fabrizio sotto voce to Spencer, 'but he handled the whole thing magnificently. I thought we were goners, but just as we almost hit the ocean, he managed to get control of the helicopter again and we made an emergency landing on the Carlton Beach at Cannes. You should have seen the sunbathers running like hell! It was pretty bumpy, I can tell you. That's when boss lady got hurt.' He gestured towards Lara, who was enjoying the attentions of her fans.

'He must have been a superb pilot,' gasped Spencer. 'I wonder if he ever worked for Qantas – they're the best, y'know.'

'He told us he'd been watching Captain "Sully" Sullenberger land that jet in the Hudson a few years ago, and he was just taking a leaf from his book. Praying, thinking positive, all that stuff – he was terrific.'

Lara turned to sneer, then posed for another photo. 'Amazing,' said Spencer, 'what a great escape! You're lucky.'

Lara shot Spencer a withering glance as François placed her drink in front of her. It more than telegraphed, 'Fuck off now, you're boring me.'

Spencer took the hint and returned to his table as François placed his Martini in front of him. Spencer gave the boy a bold smile. He was so pretty, so very pretty. He looked like Alain Delon in his youth. 'I've got some stuff for you again,' he mouthed, pretending to fumble for his wallet.

François cocked an interested eyebrow but said nothing.

'When do you get off?' asked Spencer.

'Ten o'clock,' the waiter replied.

'Right, shall we meet in the back of the fish market at ten fifteen – is that good for you?'

François nodded, aware that no one had noticed their exchange, and moved obsequiously to Madame Silvestri to refill her glass of champagne.

Spencer sat for a while admiring Sergei Litvak's massive gin palace as it backed into its place in the port.

A dozen young sailors, in white T-shirts with HEDONIST stencilled on them and tiny white shorts accentuating their tanned limbs, eased the great ship into its home base, careful not to bump it into either of the massive vessels each side of it.

The sailors lowered the gangplank to the quay, then some even better-looking stewardesses started lighting candles and arranging flowers and drinks on the table on the port side. This was watched by dozens of gawping tourists standing on the quay and snapping wildly.

Suddenly several news crews appeared, calling out to the sailors to summon Mr Litvak to get a quote about Mina's tragic death and the recent bomb scare on his boat. When Litvak finally appeared, barrel-chested and brown, silk shirt open to the waist and wearing short shorts, totally unsuitable for a man of his age and girth, Spencer decided to leave.

He strolled along the waterfront for a while, studying the menus posted outside the restaurants, then went into Chez Joseph for his last meal.

Chapter Sixteen

At approximately the same time as Spencer was dining at Chez Joseph, Carlotta and Nick were having their second dinner date.

They had spoken several times while he'd been away, and of course he had come to her rescue the night she'd heard the intruder. She was more than interested in him, but when she mentioned to Maximus Gobbi that she was having dinner with Nick Stevens, he went berserk.

'Why you want to go out with that penniless boy?' he spat.

'He's not a boy. He's thirty-eight.'

'Okay, okay, but when I give my masked ball next week I have someone wonderful for you to meet. A prince – very rich—'

'You know that I don't care about rich,' she interrupted. 'I'm rich enough.'

'My dear, as Wallis Simpson, the Duchess of Windsor, so rightly said, "You can never be too rich or too thin".'

'Oh, what nonsense! I'm sorry, I have to go.' Carlotta hung up, slightly annoyed with Maximus. He had promised her a wonderful romantic summer in Saint-Tropez, and now that she was finally becoming involved with somebody, he seemed to be trying to prevent it happening. Never mind. She was thirty years old; she would do what she wanted.

∞

Nick took her to Nioulargo, which couldn't have been more romantic. Perched on the sands on one of the most secluded beaches of Pampelonne, it was surrounded by trailing vines and waving palm trees. The heavy scent of jasmine, which climbed the outside walls, hung in the air. Candles dimly lit the interior, the music was soft and mellow, and the other diners were mostly French as tourists weren't encouraged.

They dined on delicious food, and made inroads into two bottles of the excellent rosé wine, a specialty of Provence.

It was a mild, moonlit night and after dinner they took a walk along the shoreline. The sand was warm beneath their bare feet and a faint breeze ruffled Carlotta's black curls.

They didn't speak much. Nick took her hand tentatively, which felt small and soft in his. He loved the feeling of it. After a while they sat on the sand, the water lapping at their feet.

When Nick took Carlotta's pashmina, laid it on the sand, then tenderly lowered her on to it, she did not protest, and when he kissed her so gently her heart pounded, she felt an emotion she had not experienced in a very long time. As his kisses became more ardent she wanted to succumb.

'I've never felt like this before,' she whispered. 'Oh God, what a cliché that is!' All the feelings she had stored up inside her went flooding through her whole body.

Nick smiled. 'I think you have had a hard life, Carlotta.'

'How do you know?' She wanted to break the spell he was creating with his embrace, but at the same time she didn't want his kisses to stop. His lips were warm and soft, so unlike Nicanor's, who was the first and last man who had ever kissed her.

'What do you know of my life?' she whispered.

'I know you were married very young and had a little girl quite quickly. I know your husband was . . .' Nick paused, not wanting to hurt her feelings.

'Go on, say it . . . He was a devil,' said Carlotta bitterly.

'I didn't think I should say, but there were rumours . . .'

Carlotta sat up, feeling the bitterness engulf her that she had tried so hard to suppress.

'Sometimes the nightmares frighten me. That's why I woke up that night. Nicanor hurt me, you know. He . . . he . . . hurt me so much that I can't have any more children.' She stopped, feeling she had said too much. Her cheeks were flushed and she felt giddy.

Nick stroked her cheek, his eyes never leaving hers. 'You already have a child. I believe kids aren't so important if two people love each other.'

'That's what I've always wanted, Nick – to love and to be in love and to have someone love me. Is that naïve?'

'No, it's what everyone wants deep down, if they'd only admit it.'

'And you? What about you, Nick? You're thirty-eight, so you must have a history – wives, girlfriends, children . . .'

'Oh, I do,' he grinned boyishly, which made him look younger. 'There have been a few relationships. No kids, though. As you know, I'm a journalist . . . I went to Bosnia to cover stories for my newspaper.'

'Your newspaper? You owned it?'

'No, of course not. It was only a local paper in Ohio, but they were hot to get all the news live – I was young and ambitious so I went to Bosnia. I saw some sights there, my God . . .' His eyes became cloudy. 'You'd never believe some of the things those bastards did.'

'I'm sorry,' Carlotta stroked his forehead. 'You never wanted a wife? Just girlfriends?'

'Never had a wife,' he smiled. 'Girlfriend, yes – college

sweetheart. Talk about clichés. We were going to get married when I returned from Bosnia but it didn't happen.'

'Why not?'

'She met another guy. Happens a million times,' he grinned wryly. 'I mean, we'd been together a long time and she got sick of waiting, I guess.'

'And then?'

'And then and then . . . Well, what do you think? I was still in my early twenties and the news services like my stuff so I decided to base myself in Europe as a freelance to cover all the crap that was happening at the beginning of the millennium. You know, the riots in France, the Kosovan crisis, the usual Middle East problems; I travelled a lot and yes, there were girls of course, women, but nothing serious. Not until I met you.'

'But you hardly know me,' she whispered.

'Ah, but I do know you, Contessa Carlotta. I think I know you well, and one of these days I think I shall ask you to marry me.'

Chapter Seventeen

The following day, Lara Meyer limped into a beauty salon on the Place des Lices for a facial and a full 'Brazilian' bikini wax. Lying on the bed, her face covered in a mask of thick clay and cucumber slices on her eyes, she heard the attendant Blandine, who did the waxing, enter the room.

'Gently, Blandine, gently; you know I'm delicate down there,' she said, opening her legs as the therapist pulled down the towel on her waist.

'*Oui*,' replied a deep voice, 'I know.'

Lara screamed as a pan of boiling wax was poured on to her delicate female anatomy. Shrieking to raise the roof, she struggled to pull off her eye mask. There was no one in the cubicle. The staff came running, but no one recalled having seen any men other than those who worked there.

The police were called and some of them were unable to contain their amusement at what had happened to Lara, but there were simply no clues. Even the fingerprints on the waxing bowl only matched those of the female workers.

Unable to walk for several days, Lara suffered horribly. She lay in bed nursing a scalded vulva and a hurt ankle from the helicopter crash, spending her days watching DVDs of *Desperate Housewives* and drinking straight vodka until she fell into a stupor. She tried to make Fabrizio stay in to watch TV with her, but after some desultory attempts at cooking and tidying up, he became so restless that she dismissed him as totally useless and brought in a woman from the village to cook and be her slave.

After escaping from the third day of Lara's cranky behaviour, Fabrizio and Maximus lunched at a quiet corner table at Club 55, still the most popular beach restaurant in Saint-Tropez.

'It's not working with her. She won't set a date to get married any sooner. She even says she doesn't want to now – in fact she says she hates me.' Fabrizio was becoming seriously worried about his future.

'She hates everyone, don't worry.' Maximus swallowed the last of his oysters and signalled to the waiter to refill his wine glass. 'So would you if you had a wounded pussy,' he grinned.

'I'm going to be thirty in six months, I think I'm losing my hair, and I'm becoming sick and tired of her. Apart from everything else, she's an absolute fucking bore.'

'Well, maybe you're a boring fuck,' hooted Maximus as Fabrizio shot him a look.

'That I'm not,' huffed Fabrizio.

'Too bad,' Max continued. 'That's the deal, sport.'

'I want to end this ridiculous relationship with Lara. I've decided that – whether you like it or not, Max – Carlotta's the one for me. Every time I see her, I feel a connection,' Fabrizio said firmly, eyeing up a smiling young beauty at the next table. He continued his sentence, albeit slightly more distracted. 'Not only is she beautiful and nice, but she's also goddamn rich.'

He smiled back at the young beauty. Well, maybe . . . why not? His afternoon was free and he'd been celibate now for four days – a record for him.

His eyes roamed around Club 55. It was packed with people, many of them celebrities who liked to pretend they were just

158

plain folk, many of them rich not famous, yet too grand and sophisticated to acknowledge the sprinkling of actual celebrities in their midst. There was a snobbery about the higher-echelon millionaires and oligarchs. Most of them considered themselves far above mere movie stars, even though they covertly eyed them, whispering amongst themselves, 'There's Puff Daddy – that's his yacht; it cost thirty million euros', and, 'Oh, look – it's Simon Cowell and his girlfriend.'

Johnny Depp sat at a long table, with a group of American agents and producers. With his hat pulled low over his eyes, he seemed inconspicuous except to a stream of young children who lined up respectfully for 'Captain Jack Sparrow's' autograph. Liam Neeson and his sister-in-law Joely Richardson were seated at a quiet table in the far corner next to the bar and, unmistakable in spite of dark shades and a battered baseball cap, Leonardo DiCaprio sat in the middle of the room, surrounded by acolytes and pretty girls, whom he entertained so well that raucous laughter shook their table. The young model Zarina and her girlfriend Sin were at the centre of a group of young and obviously wealthy young men and they were all screaming with laughter and taking countless selfies.

It was a hot day and Patrice, the owner, had switched on the 'air conditioning', which consisted of fine sprays of cool water emanating from small pipes attached to the wooden slats above.

Several white super-yachts were berthed at sea beyond the jetty, and small tenders zoomed back and forth across the waves to pick up passengers and bring them to the club. They picked their way through the oiled sunbathers lying supine on striped mattresses on the sand up to the packed beach bar.

Maximus glanced over to the bar, which was crowded with young men and girls, all wearing the most minimum of designer beach wear and bikinis, talking animatedly as they waited for their table. Max spotted a couple of his 'stable' and wondered why they were chatting up nubile young flesh, obviously without money, instead of older prey – divorcées and widows with wealth. There were plenty of those around. He frowned. He'd have to see about that. He'd obviously been concentrating too hard on the Fabrizio/Lara deal and on Contessa Carlotta too.

'So, where is she?' asked Fabrizio. 'I've called her every day now for a week. The damn housekeeper blows me off. If I could have some time with Carlotta, I know I could make her fall for me – I just need time. You know I could.'

Max turned to study Fabrizio. 'You know you're looking a bit rough around the edges. You need more rest – stop screwing around. I think Carlotta is a lost cause for you, Fabrizio.'

'Why?' he asked. 'I'm handsome, I'm funny, I'm great in the sack and I have a huge dick. Why can't you talk her into at least *seeing* me?'

'Fabrizio, you aren't the only stud on the beach, nor the youngest,' said Maximus.

'Yeah, but I'm the best looking and the most amusing one.'

'To tell the truth, you're not any more – you're fast approaching your sell-by date. You've *got* to close the deal with Lara,' said Maximus. 'I've told you a million times. Spend more time thinking how you are going to persuade her to marry you. Get the money, honey. She's been divorced for ten years now, for God's sake.'

'She told me after that ridiculous accident in the salon she will only marry me if *I* agree to a pre-nup, which means if we split I get fuck-all. I've gotta get out of this deal, Max. Help me, please,' pleaded Fabrizio.

Max chewed slowly on a carrot from the exquisite arrangement of fresh vegetables in the middle of the table.

'The problem is, my boy, I promised Carlotta a romantic time in Saint-Tropez. I'm sorry to tell you this, and she told me in confidence, mind you, but she seems to have fallen for this American, this journalist, Nick something or other. Pah – a penniless writer.'

'*What?*' Fabrizio choked on his celery stick. 'Fuck . . . Why the hell did you let her get away? I thought you were in charge?'

'I thought so too, but now I do not know where she is,' said Max, truthfully. 'All I know is that she told me she likes this guy very much and they're going away for a weekend to get to know each other better.'

'What the fuck? . . . Where? Where have they gone?'

'If I knew I'd tell you, but I don't. Forget Carlotta – work on Lara. Hey, look, there's Ivana Trump. I must go and say hello.' Still chewing his carrot, he lumbered off to greet the vivacious socialite who was lunching with the newest mayoral candidate for London, the boyishly good-looking Ivan Massow.

Fabrizio sat fuming, wishing his life would turn into the fairy tale his wonderful mamma had always told him it would. But he wasn't alone for long. Zarina and Sin, dressed in skimpy bikini tops and shorts that exposed most of the cheeks of their firm young bottoms, came bounding up, clutching each other's hands and each holding a cigar in their free hand.

'You look sad, Fab,' Sin laughed at her unintentional rhyme. 'Wanna come play with us?' she asked.

'Sure, sit down, girls, let me buy you a drink.'

'No, this'll do,' Zarina said as she poured some of the rosé wine into the glass Max had left, took a swig and passed it to Sin. 'We like a loving cup,' she grinned. 'Wanna hang out with us at our pad . . . Fab? We're all by ourselves this afternoon.'

They all laughed at the rhyme now, as they stroked each other's shoulders then started on Fabrizio.

'Hey, that's an offer that's hard to refuse, ladies!' Fabrizio checked the neighbouring tables to see if any of Lara's intimate friends were lunching, but all he could see was Roberto LoBianco hosting a table of rich Russian oligarchs with their overly tall and overly dressed hookers, none of whom Fabrizio recognised.

Roberto looked over at Fabrizio, happily sandwiched between the two gorgeous girls, and gave him the thumbs-up and a wink, which made Fabrizio nervous. LoBianco had a big mouth and could easily spill the beans to Lara or to any of the other Saint-Tropez gossipmongers.

'Let's get out of here,' said Fabrizio.

'No problem, we can't wait.' Sin handed her cigar to Fabrizio, 'Wanna drag?'

'No way,' he said, ushering them to the main entrance. Lara would have a fit if he came home stinking of cigars. She was always suspicious of everything he did and questioned him exhaustively about his day; even though he was an expert in the art of deception, cigar breath was impossible to conceal.

As they reached the entrance to Club 55 and waited for Chris the valet to bring Fabrizio's car round, an open-top red Tesla zoomed to a halt in front of them and Jonathan Meyer got out, adjusting his black toupee. He nodded approvingly when he saw Fabrizio between the two youngest, prettiest and craziest girls in Saint-Tropez.

'Good lunch, old sport?' he grinned, then waited for a very elegant Vanessa to emerge.

'Hello, Fabrizio,' she said, smiling coolly. 'How are you?'

Fabrizio always loved a cut-glass English accent, and Vanessa not only had that in spades but she was a totally classy piece of work. 'A lady broad,' he had confided to Maximus some time ago. 'I would fuck her in a second!'

'You'd better lay off her,' commanded Maximus. 'Don't even

think about it. Jonathan Meyer is a very powerful and extremely jealous man. No one fucks with him in business and certainly no one would ever dare to fuck his wife, especially no one who is already fucking his ex-wife!'

'The grapevine says she fools around when he's away,' Fabrizio retorted.

'Maybe . . . maybe with a married movie star who would be utterly discreet, but Fabrizio, my dear deluded boy, she would never fool around with you – she's not an idiot.'

As Vanessa passed Fabrizio, leaving a delicious scent in her wake, she gave him a sidelong glance, which he interpreted as interest.

But right now it looked as if he had two insatiable teenagers to satisfy, and he spent the rest of the afternoon in their hotel room doing just that.

∞

Fabrizio had led a charmed life until ten years ago. The only child of a well-off bourgeois Roman family, his childhood had been idyllic. Spoiled rotten by a doting Italian mamma, he had been popular and adored by girls and women. Men were jealous of his looks and charm, but that didn't bother young Fabrizio. His father indulged him and allowed him to become the hand-some playboy his hard-working father had always secretly wished he could be.

Fabrizio cut a sexual swathe through the young girls and women of the Trastevere suburb of Rome, most of whom fell for the dark-haired, handsome boy. Then, when he was eighteen, one of his casual lovers became pregnant. Papa Marcello forked out enough to keep her and the baby quiet, until a year later another teenager also fell into the same trap. Marcello reluctantly coughed up again, but this time he gave his nineteen-year-old son a warning.

'Don't get any more girls knocked up, son, because next time I won't bail you out.'

But sadly there was no time for that. Within the space of a year, Fabrizio's adored mother and then his father both developed cancer. By the time they died, within months of each other, the medical bills and death duties finished off what was left of the Bricconni family's money. Young Fabrizio was on his own – twenty years old, penniless and with two illegitimate infants and two teenage baby-mammas to support. That's when he met Maximus, and his fortunes started to reverse.

CHAPTER EIGHTEEN

Charlie and Spencer usually spoke to each other by phone at least once or twice a day, but when Charlie arrived in London on a sunny afternoon, he was immediately bombarded with phone calls from friends all wanting a piece of him. Charlie loved the fact that he was so popular with everyone, fans and friends alike, and he spread himself thinly.

He revelled even more in the attention he had received the night he arrived at a chic dinner party in Eaton Square given for him by the notorious Dowager Mariella von Hapsburg. Charlie loved a title and there were many British aristocrats at the soirée in Mariella's elegant drawing room; there was even a rumour that Prince Charles's wife Camilla, Duchess of Cornwall – a good friend of Mariella's – might pop by for a drink after dinner.

Charlie regaled everyone with hot gossip from Saint-Tropez, and attempted to give them the inside track on Mina Corbain's death, which was rumoured to be murder, and the bomb threat on board Sergei Litvak's yacht. He really knew little more than anyone else did, but he was a great wit and embellished his anecdotes beautifully.

After having imbibed more than his share of fine wine, Charlie toddled off back to The Dorchester, his preferred home from home. With the time change in France he realised that it was probably too late to call Spencer and, forgetting to set an alarm, he fell into a deep, dreamless sleep.

Charlie was awakened by the concierge telling him the chauffeur was waiting to take him to Cardiff, where he was due to host a charity lunch. In the car he tried ringing Spencer but there was no answer. 'Probably at the gym,' he told his agent Peter, who was sitting beside him.

'There are so many golden opportunities for work here, Charlie,' Peter said persuasively. 'They love you here in the UK, we can get you a series – why don't you move back?'

'Why? Because I have a beautiful villa and my gorgeous roses. I have my darling wife Spencer. I live a glorious, fulfilled life in Saint-Tropez. I'm sixty years old and reasonably rich, so why do I want to schlep back here to this pocket of misery that used to be called Great Britain?' He looked out of the window at the grey winding motorway, slick with rain, and the bleak, monotonous houses that lined the route. Shabbily dressed, forlorn-looking people shuffled along the streets. 'They all look suicidal,' Charlie observed. 'I don't see one happy face. In Saint-Tropez everyone is happy.' *Or pretends to be*, he thought.

'That's what happens to happiness if you live in today's UK.' Peter sounded mournful. 'Even if you make a decent living, you're taxed to death. And most of it goes to the layabouts and the immigrants.'

'That's *why* I'll never leave the south of France. This isn't the country I was brought up in; I could never live in this place again,' Charlie observed sadly.

'You had fun last night, didn't you?' asked Peter.

'Well, of course, darling, I was with the rich. The rich are different from everyone else, particularly in England. They live an insulated life of wealth and entitlement, even if they don't have a title.'

'But in Saint-Tropez – aren't the rich different from the hoi polloi?' asked Peter.

'You have no idea how different this group of nouveau riche is. They have brought their boats and their egos to Saint-Tropez; they live in a parallel universe from the rest of the world. They are obsessed with money and it doesn't matter how much they have, they always want more.'

'Sounds like your average theatrical agent,' laughed Peter.

'Oh, no, darling, to the super-rich, money is God; they worship it and they worship those who possess it. Their lives are a ridiculous competition with their peers – who made the most money last year, and we are not talking millions here, we're talking billions.'

'Yeah, I read the *Sunday Times* Rich List; they can make fortunes in a year.'

'And lose them,' said Charlie. 'And none of them are really happy unless they're making a deal that trumps their competitor.'

'Sounds just like Hollywood,' smiled Peter.

'Yes, and they just love to be on the Rich List, even though they pretend they don't. They must always save face in front of their competitors who are also their best friends, although they love to see them fail.'

'Yes, that's really like Hollywood – those actors and actresses who are nominated for Oscars and have to pretend they don't care if they've lost. You can see the envy and hatred underneath their make-up.'

'My God, I'll never forget the look on Burt Reynolds's face when he lost fifteen years ago to Robin Williams,' laughed Charlie. 'I thought he was going to kill someone!'

'Yeah, that clip's still on YouTube,' said Peter.

'But the super-rich oligarchs are the most ambitious lot in the world. They are obsessed with themselves and their contemporaries. They are rarely content with what they've got. Why do you think they have to change their wives so often and fuck hookers in between?'

'I would if I could,' grinned Peter, 'Some of those Russian sluts are pretty damn juicy.'

'And their yachts and cars and planes! They say that the smaller a rich man's dick, the bigger the boat!' laughed Charlie.

'In that case my boat would be tiny!' Peter grinned.

'Bragger,' winked Charlie.

'But on the other hand, everyone is happy in Saint-Tropez, or they seem to be. The sun shines, shopkeepers take pride in their shiny shops, restaurateurs take pride in their restaurants and waiters enjoy being waiters. Maybe it's just my opinion, but it's a gilded, glorious life down there and I love it.'

Charlie clicked the speed-dial on his iPhone again, but Spencer still didn't answer. 'He's probably in the pool, toning his torso. Sometimes he does three hundred laps, he's such a jock,' he smiled fondly. 'And you should see his muscles!' The men laughed affably as the limo arrived at the venue in Cardiff.

Charlie had great success at the charity lunch in which he raised nearly £100,000 for the children's hospice Shooting Star Chase, and he was again inundated with gushing fans and friends. As soon as he got into the car to be driven to an evening event at another hotel in Birmingham, he fell into an exhausted sleep.

Charlie raised even more money in Birmingham; in the car back to London, he realised his cell had run out of battery so he couldn't call Spencer and, back at The Dorchester, he again realised it was too late to ring him. He went to bed, well satisfied with his day's work.

The harsh ringing of the hotel telephone awoke Charlie abruptly.

'Charlie, I'm afraid I've got some news for you and it's not good,' said Peter. 'I'm down in the lobby but I'm coming right up.'

∽

The pool man had discovered Spencer's corpse in the morning. He was lying naked and splayed out beside the bed of roses Charlie had so carefully cultivated, which was situated next to a crumbling old stone wall, home to nests of wasps. His body was covered in wasp bites; many of them were still buzzing furiously around.

Captain Poulpe and Gabrielle were quickly on the scene with the Saint-Tropez gendarmerie. As well as the wasps, there were many flies buzzing around the body. 'He's obviously been dead for at least twenty-four hours,' said the Captain.

'Somebody disturbed these wasps – look . . .' said Gabrielle. 'Someone poked this stick into the crevices and made the wasps really angry.'

The body was taken to the morgue.

'*Regardez*,' said the pathologist, who had been examining Spencer's body. 'In his throat there is a dead wasp. It stung in his larynx, which caused it to swell up so he could no longer breathe.'

'But why?' asked Gabrielle. 'Why on earth was he down there, poking a stick into the wasps' nest? He knew they were dangerous.'

'I do not know,' said the pathologist, carefully removing the dead wasp from Spencer's swollen throat, 'but there is no question that this little insect is what killed him.'

'But this is murder then, isn't it?' Gabrielle whispered to her father. 'There's no other way that this could have happened. Who would want to kill Spencer? Everyone liked him – and they love Charlie.'

'Who would want to kill Mina? Who would want to cause such chaos on Litvak's boat the night of his party? Who would pour hot wax on Lara Meyer's . . .' Captain Poulpe stumbled over the word.

'Vagina?' added Gabrielle helpfully.

'Erm, yes, of course,' replied Captain Poulpe, regarding his daughter with raised eyebrows. 'Exactly what I was going to say.'

Chapter Nineteen

Roberto LoBianco was holding court in the corner of the room during a small dinner party he was throwing to celebrate the summer season. Several of the most seriously rich Saint-Tropeziennes, plus Monty Goldman, Khris Kane and Nate Kowalski were glued to his every word as he expounded on his favourite subject: the decline of Saint-Tropez and the glory of his brand-new resort. 'Saint-Sébastien is going to be the *crème de la crème* of glamour resorts. We've already built a small airport, for private use only, of course, because never the twain shall meet.' He laughed and blew the smoke from his Havana into the warm night air. 'But if you come commercial, you'll go to Toulon Airport, and Saint-Sébastien will supply an Augusta Westland helicopter, the same type the president uses, to get you down there – it'll take less than fifteen minutes.'

'Will it be that exclusive?' asked Monty.

'Absolutely, old man – top of the line. No other resort will be able to touch it.'

'Sounds too good to be true.' Khris Kane was ever cynical.

'Yeah, it's gonna be gigantic, but we need a few more investors. You all know that to get back millions you have to invest millions. Private resorts are the future, boys, you'd better believe it.' The men all nodded. 'Saint-Tropez is a dinosaur. Look at the dreck that shows up here in their crap buses and their motorbikes every day. They bring *nothing* to this place – nothing but trash.'

Monty, who never pulled his punches, agreed angrily, 'Yeah, and what about the fucking burglars? They come here every summer – I don't know where the fuck from; Latvia, Romania, you name it. They're all gypsies who don't give a fuck, here for the loot. They shit in the doorways of my shops, sometimes, and they often sleep there too; they're bloody vagrants, for Christ's sake, and they doss down outside my shops and scare the customers away. They even robbed Lara Meyer. Frankly I'll be glad to explore new venues – this place is old hat and getting tired.'

'Yeah, yeah, yeah, it's tough at the top,' said Roberto dismissively. 'We don't get the bums on our island. What we do get, to quote you English – ' he grinned at Nate and Khris, who kept the stony expressions of true gamblers on their faces – 'is bums on seats in our casino.' He grinned broadly, 'Get it?'

'Casino? Are you kidding? What about permits and gaming licences – all that stuff? We've been trying to get a casino in Saint-Tropez for decades without success!' said Monty.

'Listen, if they can gamble in Monte-Carlo, they can gamble on my island. I've been in the casino business for twenty-five years and, if it's done properly, it's a licence to print money.'

'Just a casino? What about great restaurants, beaches, fabulous shopping – are you gonna have these?' asked Monty.

'You bet,' said LoBianco. 'Everything that Saint-Tropez has we will have – except more, better, more beautiful and trendier. I've already got interest from Gucci, Fendi and Prada.'

'Sounds too good to be true,' said Khris Kane. 'What about nightlife?'

'Sure, we'll have great nightlife, but the day life's gonna be hot too.'

'Sounds too good to be true,' echoed Monty.

'It's all good. It's more than good, and it's ready to roll. All I need now is you gentlemen to put up a little collateral. You put ten million euros each in my bank as seed money and Saint-Sébastien will be set to open by spring 2016. We're selling the villas and apartments now. There's huge interest, and there's been even more since these horrific events,' said LoBianco. 'Mina Corbain's death was the beginning of a terrible cycle. The bomb scare at the Litvak boat, and now the queer guy found with a wasp shoved down his throat – it's given half the residents here the wind up.'

The other men looked cynical, but LoBianco continued persuasively: 'Some of them have been quietly putting their homes on the market and looking at our properties for the past month.'

'I've been thinking about it,' said Monty. 'But people love Saint-Tropez too much to leave.'

'Gentlemen, this is an investment opportunity that comes along once in a lifetime. Within five years I can guarantee you'll get your money back. It can't miss – a perfect place for perfect people; no tourists, no vagrants, no gypsies and *no* murderers – because that's what's freakin' everyone out here.'

'Well, sometimes you gotta let something die before you let something live,' said Khris philosophically.

'If we have to pay a few people off, we will,' said LoBianco.

'Like who?' asked Monty.

'Like the villagers that live there now. We've started construction already – we have three hotels almost finished and soon we can afford to buy off the fifty or so villagers who still are in their little hovels on what will be prime real-estate. *Prime*, gentlemen. Within a few years you'll have doubled – no, *tripled* your investment. I'll tell you one thing,' LoBianco continued, 'this spate of incidents has helped me no end! So many people are fed up with Saint-Tropez now and want to get out.

'So, gentlemen, do you want to take a trip to Saint-Sébastien island with me?'

∽

Roberto LoBianco had invited just a few select guests for a trip to Saint-Sébastien. They set off on a vintage Riva from Le Lavandou, a charming village twenty kilometres from Saint-Tropez.

'We could have left from Saint-Tropez port,' Roberto announced as the horizon melted into the background. 'But I wanted you guys to see how easy it is to get to the island from Toulon Airport.'

They nodded in agreement. It was a perfect June morning. The sky was the pure azure that gave the Côte d'Azur its name, and the irritating mistral had calmed the sea down so the boat glided on it as if it was glass. Roberto had chosen his guests carefully. They were people whom he thought were becoming bored of Saint-Tropez or, in the case of the lovely Contessa Di Ponti and Henry and Blanche Phillips, would be open to the suggestion of buying a home. The speedboat was one of the largest of its kind. It sat twenty people easily, and it sped over the crystal water without causing the passengers any irritable bounces.

The wind whipped Carlotta's hair into tight curls as she lay back and allowed the sun to warm her. This was the life. How different from the stifling years she had spent in San Miguel. She could live here happily with the sun, the sea and the relaxing and calming atmosphere. Why not? There were good schools close by and Flora would thrive here. If only she had someone to share her life. She had loved getting to know Nick, but a client had suddenly called him away on assignment to cover an ISIS crisis in Iraq. They had tried to keep in touch by cell phone, but it was extremely difficult, so the odd email had to suffice. Although Carlotta didn't want to admit it, she was a little lonely and she missed Nick. In fact, she thought she might be falling in love with him.

As if reading her thoughts, Fabrizio, who had accepted Roberto's invitation on Lara's behalf and then conveniently omitted to relay it to her, came to sit next to Carlotta. He had decided to play it much cooler with her, having realised what an ass he had made of himself at the disastrous party on the boat. Lara was safely tucked away at home, a bottle of vodka next to a large bottle of painkillers and several DVDs of *Sex and the City* waiting to be viewed. But, knowing Lara as he did, Fabrizio was secure in the knowledge that the vodka and pills would keep her in a drugged deep slumber for the rest of the afternoon.

Roberto had informed the group that there would be no cell-phone reception or internet access on this trip. 'But it's only temporary, guys,' he announced. 'My technicians are working on getting everything sorted out, so by the time Saint-Sébastien is ready to roll, everything that the modern world can provide will be at your disposal.'

Harry Silver, Khris Kane, Monty Goldman and Nate Kowalski were all sitting together in the prow of the speeding boat. All mega-rich and long part of this 'masters of the universe' boys' club, they were eager to see if this project had the possibility of yielding them even more mega-bucks.

'Those guys have more money and property and toys than they could ever use in a million years, but they still need more, more and more,' Fabrizio grinned at Carlotta.

'Oh, I know the type,' Carlotta replied. 'Buenos Aires was full of them. I wonder why they're so driven to make more?'

Fabrizio wanted to say, 'It's because they have small dicks,' but decided raunchy dialogue was off the menu with this lady. She definitely had class. My God, she was such a catch! Very rich, extremely beautiful, quite young and absolutely sweet and ador-able, with no side to her – how different was Carlotta from Lara and the coterie of rich bitches she surrounded herself with in New York?

'I think the super-rich need to set themselves totally apart from the rest of the human race,' said Fabrizio, remembering what Lara had told him about Jonathan. 'They live on planet "opulence". It's all they really care about. They only need to impress the tiny group of people that inhabit the same planet as them by achieving even more enormous wealth and making it grow each year. They only compare themselves to other mega-rich; no one else exists on that world.'

'What about their families – their wives and children?' asked Carlotta, who thought she knew the answer to that. Wives and children were definitely secondary in the lives of wealthy men.

'They must be of the best quality, just like their yachts or mansions or artwork. Why do you think they trade in their wives every ten years or so?'

Carlotta shuddered, remembering the times that Nicanor had screamed at her, *'You're old and ugly – I'm sick to death of you – get out of my sight!'* Well, death had claimed him just in time. She wondered how many more years he would have stayed with her. If it wasn't for their beautiful daughter Flora, she was sure he would have ended their marriage years before and seen to it that she had no money either.

While Fabrizio waxed lyrical, she observed him from behind her shades. He certainly was magnetically good-looking, tanned and toned – she could see that now he had taken off his shirt. He had a well-defined six-pack . . . it was almost an eight-pack, in fact. How many hours did it take at the gym to get abs like that? Maybe she had misjudged him by thinking he was just a cheap parvenu.

'Look at that.' Fabrizio was pointing at a humongous ocean liner a few hundred feet away. 'That's the sort of thing these guys like.'

'What is it?' asked Carlotta. 'I've never seen such a huge boat!'

'He'll tell you,' Fabrizio gestured towards Roberto, who was extolling the virtues of the monster ship.

'Ladies and gentlemen, behold the eighth wonder of the world. That, my friends, is a floating country, for those of you who don't want to live the great life I'm about to show you in Saint-Sébastien. It's called *The Planet*, and it's not only the biggest cruise liner in the world, it's also apartment living at its most glamorous and secluded.'

'Jesus,' gasped Monty, 'people *live* on that thing?'

'They do indeed – very *few* people. The owners thought they would be fighting them off to buy apartments, but sadly,' he laughed, 'very few takers. Nobody wants to live on a floating mega-hotel that is as long as the Shard and broader than the wingspan of a 747. It cost £800,000,000 to build, and at 225,000 tons, is 40 per cent bigger than any other vessel that's ever docked in France. It holds 550,000 passengers and 2,400 in crew. Problem is, only about a hundred people took up this golden chance, so the old girl cruises around the Med and the Aegean like the "Ship of Fools" in *The Dead Zone!*' He chuckled at his wit and his competitors' misery.

'It looks like a floating shopping mall,' said Nate, examining it through binoculars.

'Yeah, but how much time can you spend shopping?' laughed Henry Phillips.

'Ask your wife,' quipped Khris Kane, getting an ice-cold stare from Blanche in return. 'Anyway, you couldn't get me on it, let alone buy an apartment there.'

'Me neither,' chimed Harry Silver.

'So they *do* have some taste,' Fabrizio whispered conspiratorially to Carlotta, who smiled back.

The supermodel Zarina and her pop-star girlfriend Sin were cuddled up together, eyeing up Fabrizio and giggling, making it difficult for him to keep his focus on Carlotta. Carlotta noticed

Sin's pink-lacquered toenails, encrusted with sparkling gemstones.

'They're Swarovski crystals,' Sin explained, noticing her gaze.

'They're amazing,' said Carlotta.

'Yeah, I get them done in this place in the port.'

'Give me the name of the salon – I may try it,' said Carlotta.

As they passed the seven-storeyed high-rise abomination of a ship, Zarina and Sin, bored of talking to Carlotta, let out appreciative 'oohs' and 'aahs'.

'I want to see it, Uncle Monty,' whined Zarina. 'Let's go visit!'

'No, kids, sorry – only a couple of minutes before we arrive at the most beautiful island in the world,' Roberto said proudly as they zoomed past the floating monstrosity. 'And there she is, boys and girls – Saint-Sébastien in all her glory!'

∽

Meanwhile, Maximus sat fuming at the elegant Tahiti Beach restaurant, talking on the phone to Fabrizio. He hadn't been invited on Roberto's trip to Saint-Sébastien and he was beside himself to discover that Fabrizio was on the outing.

'*Bastardo*,' he hissed.

'Can't talk – I'm on a launch. Se ya later, Maxie – *Ciao!*' said Fabrizio breezily, then hung up.

'*Stronzo* – stupid asshole. He's made a major mistake leaving Lara at home,' he fumed to himself and took a gulp of his piña colada. Lying back on the comfy orange cushion of the beach lounger, he reviewed his strategy.

What to do about Fabrizio? He was becoming too big for his Gucci loafers. Didn't he realise how imperative it was for him to get Lara to commit? Maximus lifted his binoculars to study the horizon. The huge cruise ship *The Planet* was slowly chugging in towards Saint-Tropez, getting as close as it could.

'An abomination,' he muttered, and then commanded to a passing waiter, 'Another piña colada!'

The waiter acknowledged Max's demand with a smile, causing Max to take off his shades to examine the boy more closely. He looked familiar. In fact, he was familiar.

'Don't I know you?' he asked.

'Sure,' replied François amiably. 'I'm usually at the Sénéquier but one of the boys is sick so Madame Felix asked me to help out.' He grinned, showing a fine set of what were obviously his own teeth, and Max inspected him with an expert eye.

'You get around, then?' Max asked him.

'You bet,' he smiled. 'Gotta make a buck while the season is jumping. It's a long cold winter, you know.'

As he took Max's empty glass, the older man scrutinised the slim, lithe body beneath the uniform white shorts and T-shirt. The waiter had a profusion of tight black curls and a crooked nose that looked like it had been broken a few times. A fighter, Max mused. He was wearing dark mirrored aviators, but Max seemed to remember that he had black eyes, which were curiously flat and showed no emotion – disturbing.

Nevertheless Max thought he could be a potential candidate to add to his stud stable, which was getting smaller by the day. He handed François Lardon his card, along with a twenty-euro note as a tip.

'Call me,' he added, 'I might be able to offer you something that could be of interest to you.'

∞

LoBianco's speedboat docked expertly at the jetty of the island of Saint-Sébastien. They had passed several small islands – the Iles D'Hyères – but Saint-Sébastien was the furthest away from the main coast and very secluded.

'Ooh, fabulous! Look at the white sand!' giggled Zarina, as she and Sin started jumping about and throwing it at each other.

'C'mon girls, cool it – let's see the island!' yelled Monty.

'Oh, Uncle Monty, you're *such* a downer,' pouted Zarina. 'All I wanna do is have some fun!'

'And all I want to do is show you this amazing place,' said Roberto LoBianco, irritated by the two teenagers. However famous they were in their respective professions as a supermodel and a pop princess, they had no idea how to behave properly in public. They were rolling in the white sand – sand which had been specially imported from the Bahamas and which had cost him a fortune.

'Stop it, kids,' Monty ordered, sensing Roberto's irritation.

'Yeah, if you didn't want to see the island then why did you come?' asked Roberto.

'Well, you did ask us,' Sin shot back, smirking. 'Guess all you wanted was to show the folks what pretty young pussy looks like here on your magical island.'

'Girls like having fun,' giggled Zarina. 'And I don't wanna see your stupid island, I just wanna play in the sand with Sin.' She stuck out her tongue at Roberto in full Miley Cyrus mode. And then, giggling hysterically, leaned across to rub sand all over her girlfriend's now naked breasts.

'C'mon guys, let's go,' Roberto urged, conscious that the sandy floor show could potentially be more interesting than his island tour, and pissed off at the girls' shenanigans. 'Leave 'em, Nate – let them get on with their little lesbian cabaret.'

'Cool it, kids,' snapped Monty, aware that their behaviour could potentially reflect damagingly on him and his retail business. 'This isn't the Crazy Horse.'

'Oh, Uncle Monty, you're such a drag!' yelled Zarina petulantly as the group wended their way across the beach.

As she passed the girls, who had now dropped on to the sand and lit a joint, getting ready to feel each other up and make out, Blanche threw her beach towel over them.

'Disgusting,' she sniffed, hobbling across the sand in unsuitably high-heeled boots. 'Young people today – *really*. They have no idea how to behave.' This declaration was met with chortling and guffaws from the two prone bodies in the sand.

∞

The island tour was a great success, and Roberto LoBianco was absolutely delighted. Three of the 'titans of the universe' had asked for the investment papers and had called their lawyers in front of him, and Carlotta had expressed interest in purchasing a property, as had Harry and Blanche and Khris Kane. Everyone agreed it was going to be an elegant and fantastic resort.

CHAPTER TWENTY

Fabrizio was delighted to receive an invitation from Sophie Silvestri for yet another event honouring Marvin Rheingold. The legendary Hollywood producer was remaking *Suddenly, Last Summer* and Sophie really wanted to nail the Katharine Hepburn role. Fabrizio too had thoughts of Hollywood stardom with Mr Rheingold. He was still waiting for the perpetually elusive call from *The X Factor* in Kazakhstan, an offer Lara felt was beneath him.

'Y'know, I think I should try the big screen,' he said as they drove up a steep and winding hill to Sophie's remote villa. 'I'd be wonderful in the Montgomery Clift role.'

'Keep dreaming, honey,' said Lara. 'That ain't gonna happen.'

'You never know,' he said sulkily. 'They're talking Ryan Reynolds but he's far too old.'

'Oh, sure – about two years older than you, I bet!' she crowed.

It was a clear moonlit night at the villa, but the wind was starting up. Sophie was taking morbid pleasure in Lara's injury and acting up a storm by being exceptionally solicitous to her. That fateful night twenty-five years ago when Lara tricked her to go to the wrong venue at the opening of her new fashion line was branded indelibly in her memory. Sophie had been forced into hiding and, afterwards, she had become a joke. Lara had shown no scruples when it came to wrenching the society spotlight from Sophie and Sophie had sworn revenge ever since. She grabbed every opportunity to bad-mouth the Russian woman.

Frick and Adolpho stood like sentries beside Sophie, as she held court, greeting guests. 'It must be terrible to have a painful pussy,' she purred to Lara, stroking one of her newest Persian cats. 'What a hideous thing to happen, *cara*. Who could hate you that much?'

Lara smiled through gritted teeth. 'It was an accident, honey, everyone knows that.'

The old star gave a disbelieving smile, 'Well, all I can say is you show amazing recuperative powers down there . . . or perhaps the nerve endings have all been destroyed? Must be *terrible* not to have any feeling there any more,' she cooed sympathetically. Then spotting the guest of honour, producer Marvin Rheingold, she hastened to him.

'Bitch!' snarled Lara. 'It wouldn't surprise me if she did it.'

'Don't be silly, *cara*,' Fabrizio attempted to soothe her. 'She's much too famous in Saint-Tropez. Someone would have seen her go into the salon, you know that.' Fabrizio's role in placating and tending to Lara was becoming more and more difficult, and he was finding it hard to keep up the pretence of enjoying having sex with her. Luckily with her wounded vagina it was 'games off' in that department now and he was mightily relieved.

They walked to the edge of the terrace, surveying the illuminated pool and the dazzling view. Palm trees and parasol vines grew wild down the side of the steep rocky hill where a funicular was nestled into the rocks. A three-quarter moon lit the Mediterranean with a shimmering glow, but the mistral was starting to whip up the waves.

Several guests milled about, complaining about the wind. Charlie Chalk, in mourning for his lost lover, was trying to put on his happy face but he was only able to muster a weak smile. 'Spencer was the love of my life,' he wailed to those who offered sympathy. 'My wife, my partner, my best friend.'

Many of the guests sympathised, although aware that Spencer had been less than a faithful lover to Charlie. But this, after all, was Saint-Tropez, where hedonism reigned supreme and infidelity was a way of life. If bad things happened it's up, up and away on to the next fabulous fiesta, and put on a happy face. Robin Thicke's hit song 'Blurred Lines' was playing, and a few guests were clapping their hands and bouncing around to the catchy tune. Some of the Sénéquier waiters were there helping with the service, amongst them François, whom Lara vaguely recognised. Sophie breezed over to Marvin, who was singing along with a lissom blonde on his arm. Smiling archly at the producer, Sophie dismissed the blonde and cornered him, displaying her most feminine charms.

'Do you recall when we went to Las Vegas together?' she cooed, playfully toying with his greying chest hair with one hand while the other held one of her newest kittens. 'Remember we went to see Sinatra at the Sands and do some gambling, but we spent most of the time in my bedroom?' She looked up at him through a forest of false eyelashes.

Marvin, looking uncomfortable, gently untangled her talons from his hirsute chest. 'Of course I remember,' he said gallantly. 'No man could ever forget you, Sophie, my dear. I'll never forget your appearance on *The Tonight Show* when you came out with your cat.'

'Ah, yes, I remember,' she smiled. 'I asked Johnny Carson if he'd like to pet my pussy.'

'And he said yes, as soon as you get rid of the damn cat!' Marvin laughed loudly, and Sophie joined him with a tinkly girlish giggle. Lara, resting on the chaise longue with her leg up, glowered at Sophie. Fabrizio stood by solicitously.

'Stupid old bitch. She's too long in the tooth for that sort of come-on.' Her voice was thick with scorn.

But Fabrizio wasn't listening. Across the terrace he saw Carlotta enter, arm in arm with Nick Stevens. They appeared to be glowing with happiness.

As he casually took a step towards her, he overheard the Hollywood producer whisper to Sophie, 'You always had a trick pussy, honey, and now I see you're collecting them.'

Fabrizio grinned to himself. Good line. The old guy certainly knew his business. Lara, suddenly aware of Fabrizio's gaze towards Carlotta, grabbed his arm possessively.

After three 'vodka on the rocks with a slice of orange', Lara was feeling no pain when Sophie wafted over to suggest that Fabrizio take Lara down to the beach. It was Sophie's party, and after seeing the way Lara scowled at her, she wanted to avoid a confrontation while appearing to be solicitous.

'It's beautiful tonight with the moonlight,' she said.

Lara struggled to her feet, snuggling up to Fabrizio as he helped her, as did Frick and Adolpho. But as they all prepared to board the funicular, Lara groaned, 'Oh, my God, I'm in too much pain to go on that rickety thing.' She sank back into a chair again and signalled to Fabrizio for a drink.

The warm winds of the mistral were making Frick and Adolpho feel amorous. Seizing an opportunity to be alone on a moonlit beach, they boarded the funicular as Sophie waved them goodbye with a throaty, 'Now, boys, you'd better behave yourselves – there's a full moon.'

Fabrizio stared at Lara, who was splayed out drunkenly, lying on a chaise.

'For God's sake, you're embarrassing me! Lara, you've got to stop drinking.'

'Why should I? I like the taste of it. Don't tell me what to do, asshole!'

Suddenly they heard the sound of desperate screams and cries for help as the funicular plunged down 150 feet in a ball of fire.

'What's happened?' cried Sophie as she ran to the edge of the hill. 'Oh, my God – Frick – Adolpho, where are you? Are you all right?'

In six-inch heels, the distraught actress attempted to clamber down the ravine, but Marvin grabbed her arm.

'You don't want to go down there, honey,' he said quietly, holding on to her.

The guests clustered in helpless horror as they watched the carnage and the huge fire below. They stood in mute shock as they heard terrified screams from the burning wreckage. As sparks flew into the wind and began to ignite the brush, Fabrizio, François and some of the waiters tried to clamber down the steep cliff, but there was nothing they could do to help. They managed to pull a charred and blackened body out of the funicular as it writhed in death throes.

'I think he's still alive,' yelled Fabrizio. 'For God's sake, get a doctor down here to help him!'

Sophie's screams echoed across the hills and, as if on cue, the mistral wind blew even stronger. The fire department arrived and several gendarmes, led by Captain Poulpe and Gabrielle, clambered down to the scene, once again to investigate foul play.

∞

'This is a disaster!' Roberto LoBianco, the property developer, puffed on his Havana, trying to look concerned and watching as the firemen attempted to douse the flames. 'This kind of publicity is gonna kill Saint-Tropez.'

'You sound almost pleased about it,' said Captain Poulpe.

'Don't be ridiculous, of course I'm not,' blustered Roberto. 'But my God, there have been so many disasters before the proper season has even started. Are people ever gonna want to come to Saint-Tropez any more?'

'There will always be people who come to Saint-Tropez. It is a magical place,' retorted Captain Poulpe quietly. He didn't like this arrogant man but he would never let his true feelings show.

'Yeah, sure – sure was magical for him.' Roberto gestured towards two gendarmes labouring up the hill carrying a body on a stretcher.

The crowd moved closer to the edge of the cliff – even Lara managed to sit up and rouse herself.

'Oh, my God, it's Adolpho! He's alive!' screamed Sophie.

'He was in the bushes,' said one of the gendarmes. 'I think he must have managed to throw himself off the machine before it hit the ground. He's a lucky man.'

'But Frick, where is Frick?' asked Sophie fearfully.

The fireman shook his head. Sophie started screaming uncontrollably as Marvin held her.

'There, there, honey – I'm sorry, so sorry.' He felt her warm body shudder with grief. Her make-up had worn off and suddenly she looked vulnerable and softer. Maybe she should get the Hepburn part, he thought, but decided it would be inappropriate to talk about that right now.

'Let's all have a drink, for God's sake,' announced Lara, who seemed considerably cheerier than before, as she held up her glass for a refill from François. 'I think we all need one.'

∞

After Frick's body had been brought up, Captain Poulpe gravely addressed the group. 'The cables on the funicular have been tampered with. I'm afraid I have keep you all here for questioning once more. This is now definitely a murder inquiry.'

'Fuck this!' said Sergei Litvak quietly to Lilly, his trophy wife.

'We're getting on the yacht first thing tomorrow, honey, and out of this hell hole.'

'Can we come too – please?' Zarina, Chloe and Sin whimpered, huddled together, their bony knees knocking and their tiny mini-dresses blowing above their panties from the mistral, which was becoming stronger by the minute.

'You know what they say about the mistral?' grinned Fabrizio to Lara. 'If a man murders his lover, the judge will not condemn him during a mistral.'

'Bullshit!' snapped Lara. 'Don't even think about it. Let's get the hell out of this place.'

'No one can leave.' Captain Poulpe had found a megaphone to counter the whistling noise of the mistral. 'You are all suspects here. No one can leave here – in fact, none of you must leave Saint-Tropez at all.'

Chapter Twenty-One

'It's impossible,' said Jonathan Meyer to his wife Vanessa some days later, 'They can't just hold us here – it's illegal.'

They sat on the front deck of his mega-yacht *Yankee One* gloomily watching the scruffily dressed tourists wandering around the port.

'Look at them,' scoffed Jonathan. 'More than sixty thousand of them visit Saint-Tropez each year and none of them buys more than a bottle of water or a cup of coffee.'

'That's because a cup of coffee costs nine euros, darling; they can't afford it.'

'Then they shouldn't fucking come here. The tourists are ruining the place – Brigitte Bardot was right.'

Vanessa nodded as she always did. The couple had had the rare honour of dining with the other queen of Saint-Tropez the previous week. In her house on a promontory, hidden by pine trees and well away from the madding crowd, Sophie Silvestri held a meeting with various locals, members of the council of Saint-Tropez, and the Mayor. Their aim was to return Saint-Tropez to the halcyon days of the 1950s and sixties, when it was just a simple fishing village. Although Sophie was still in mourning and had barely set foot outside her house during daytime, she considered this long-planned meeting important enough to show her face.

191

She sat silently in a tall bergère in her dark sitting room, watching the big businessmen decide the fate of her village. She stroked one of her cats and several dogs clustered at her feet.

Roberto LoBianco had also been at that meeting and had agreed with Madame Silvestri that Saint-Tropez should return to its grass roots and former unpretentious simple glory. The Mayor had started to implement plans the previous year when he had closed down the popular beach restaurant, La Voile Rouge. The building had been bulldozed to the ground, in spite of entreaties from those who lived there and many of the regular visitors who loved the louche atmosphere.

'Voile Rouge was one of the reasons people kept coming to Saint-Tropez,' Charlie Chalk had insisted. 'Fifty people lost their jobs when it closed.'

'I agree,' said Sophie Silvestri. 'And now I hear they're closing Bora Bora Beach as well.'

'These beaches attract thousands of people who spend a ton of money every year,' chimed in Nate Kowalski.

'Well, you spent a ton at La Voile buying champagne by the crate and spraying it over all your mates and annoying the tables around you,' laughed Monty Goldman.

'You don't do too badly yourself in that department!' scoffed Nate. 'How much did you spend on "shampoo" last year – two hundred and fifty grand, wasn't it?'

'About that,' grinned Monty, 'maybe closer to three. Gotta give the plebs what they want – action, babes, plenty of theatre.'

'Whatever,' chimed in Charlie. 'The bloody Mayor of Pampelonne finally succeeded in getting La Voile Rouge closed, and it's a great pity because it was unique and people loved it.'

'Yeah, well, there's a lot of unique places in Ibiza and Sardinia,' said Monty. 'And if they start closing any more fun and crazy beaches, I just might piss off somewhere else for the summer.'

'Come to Saint-Sébastien,' said Roberto smoothly. 'You saw what a paradise it is.'

Charlie was enraged. 'How can you *do* that, Monty? We need people like you; people who spend money to keep this place going. You know the locals need you guys with your big boats and your big hookers to get them through the eight months when no one comes to Saint-Tropez at all.'

'Who cares?' said Nate. 'Never miss anything that doesn't miss you, matey. I'll find another trendy beach where I can chuck champers over people. Eden Beach is getting pretty hot now, so is Bagatelle, but they'd better not start closing them down otherwise I will be outta here . . . maybe I will try Saint-Sébastien. I'm beginning to think that in any case it might be an excellent investment.'

After the meeting had been adjourned, Roberto LoBianco and the Mayor of Pampelonne had been asked by Sophie to remain and join her for dinner. It had been one of the highlights of Roberto's life.

⁂

'You know that this mayor doesn't have the best interests of Saint-Tropez at heart,' mused Jonathan, gazing through binoculars at the crowded port. He was still fuming about Poulpe's directive to remain in Saint-Tropez, which seemed to have the backing of the Mayor. Idly he waved at Sophie Silvestri, who was sitting at a round table at the back of Café Sénéquier, surrounded by her coterie of hangers-on, minus poor Frick, of course.

'What do you mean, darling?' Vanessa was idly flicking through the *Daily Mail* on her iPad. 'How could he not?'

'I think he's jealous because so many people go to the beaches, which are all on Pampelonne, as you know, but with the exception of a few big earners like Club 55 and Bagatelle, everyone then goes into Saint-Tropez at night to spend most of their money there.'

'Makes sense,' said Vanessa, now flicking through *Paris Match*. 'Oh, look, there's a picture of Mina's coffin being taken off a plane at JFK. That took long enough.'

'Poor kid,' said Jonathan. 'I still believe someone had it in for her. Does it say anything in the *Mail* about us being kept prisoners in this goddamn place?'

'Nooo,' said Vanessa scrolling down. 'Nothing. I guess we're stuck here for a while – well, there could be worst places,' she smiled, secretly thinking about the handsome young man she had been flirting with at the beach and at last week's dinner party. Was she wrong to have given him her number?

∞

Khris Kane had insisted that Mina Corbain's body be flown to the US for autopsy. And even though the jurisdiction of Saint-Tropez wanted the body to stay, enough money had passed hands to ensure that Mina went home to New York. There the verdict was announced. Mina had not been poisoned as Captain Poulpe suspected. She had died from anaphylactic shock brought on by a tainted oyster. She hadn't received treatment in time because no one knew, not even Mina herself, that she had recently developed a serious allergy to seafood.

'You see it wasn't murder,' the Mayor of Saint-Tropez glowed as he announced the news to a table of friends at Sénéquier.

'What about my Spencer?' asked Charlie Chalk mournfully.

'You know our teams are still working on that,' hesitated the Mayor. 'You know the autopsy found that he suffocated because of the wasp sting to his throat. We just can't figure out yet how the wasp got in there, but we will, Charlie. I promise we will.'

'I really believe he was murdered,' insisted Charlie. 'I mean, who can swallow a wasp?'

'A can of soda was found nearby. Maybe the wasp was in there and he swallowed it without realising it?' the Mayor surmised, shrugging Gallic shoulders. 'Anyway, we won't rest until we get to the bottom of it.'

'Thank you, Monsieur Le Mayor.' Charlie's big blue eyes filled with tears. He gulped down his Guinness as Sophie put a comforting arm on his shoulder.

'And Frick? What about my Frick?' she asked.

'That was definitely an accident, my dear Sophie.' The Mayor, who had always had a tiny crush on the grand diva, hastened to assure her. 'You had been doing repairs on your funicular, had you not?'

She nodded sadly. 'Yes, and my workmen were itinerant Poles and Romanians who worked cheaply.' She gasped at the realisation, 'It was *my* fault!' A mascaraed tear ran down her cheek and the Mayor gallantly offered her his handkerchief.

'Nonsense, my darling, it's nobody's fault. Accidents happen. I mean, look over there.'

They glanced over to a corner table where Lara and Fabrizio were staring gloomily into their drinks.

'That helicopter crash could have been a lot more serious,' he continued.

The group were interrupted by a happy-looking Carlotta coming into the café and sitting at the table next to them.

After greetings and hugs, Carlotta turned to Charlie and whispered, 'You'll never guess . . . I'm not supposed to say anything, but guess who's coming to Saint-Tropez the day after tomorrow?'

'President Putin?' sneered Lara, leaning over.

'Don't be silly.' Carlotta did not rise to the bait. 'Much better!' She waited until she had all their attention, then announced in a hushed whisper, 'Prince Harry – ta-dah!'

'*The* Prince Harry?' asked Charlie excitedly, being a keen royal follower.

'Is there any other one?' said Lara sarcastically.

'Ah, the Prince! Yes, yes, I heard he might be coming here,' said Sophie, knowingly.

'Prince Harry! What? No, I don't believe it,' gasped Maximus, aghast that the movements of someone famous had eluded his finely honed radar.

'Well, it's true,' said Carlotta. 'And guess who's invited him to stay?'

'Do tell!' Lara tried to keep venom out of her voice. As soon as Carlotta had announced the news about the Prince, Fabrizio had hastily moved them to a table next to where Carlotta was now holding court.

'Henry and Blanche – he's staying at their villa!' Carlotta announced triumphantly.

'But why would a young guy like Harry want to bunk up with those old farts?' Maximus was contemptuous. 'My God, Henry's older than God, and Blanche and that horrendous new dog of hers . . . he'll be bored to tears.'

'Yes, what's the attraction?' asked Sophie, thinking that she might give Blanche a ring later on, invite her to dinner at l'Opéra, and make sure she got an invitation to whatever soirée Blanche would be throwing in honour of the young prince. There was no question that the old hag would pull out all the stops to make a social impact with the fifth in line to the British throne staying in her house.

Zarina and Sin, who until a few minutes ago had been sitting at a back table engrossed in each other, rushed over when they overheard the conversation.

'I *lurve* Prince Harry,' gushed Zarina. 'He's hot!'

'Yeah, he's soooo cool. Can we come please, pretty please?'

Without asking, the two girls, neither of whom weighed more than one hundred pounds, planted themselves on Charlie's capacious lap, covering his blushing cheeks in lipstick kisses.

'Darlings, I have nothing to do with the party,' he groaned as he tried to turf them off his lap, but they had wrapped their long tanned limbs around his body and he felt as if he was in the clutches of an octopus.

'We'll be your dates!' they cooed. 'A Charlie Chalkwich!'

'Oh, for God's sake, grow up!' snapped Sophie.

The girls made sulky faces and wrapped themselves more tightly to Charlie who, despite the asphyxia, was rather enjoying the attention.

'How do you know all this?' Charlie asked Carlotta.

'Oh, I have my sources,' she gave a secret smile. 'Can't reveal them though.'

'I must invite him to my masked ball. Shall I call Buckingham Palace to invite him?' said Maximus.

'No, no, you can't!' said Carlotta hastily. 'It's a private visit – a secret. We can't let anyone know, otherwise the press will find out and we will be inundated with them. There's enough of them here already as it is.'

Sophie piped up. 'It's strange that since that unfortunate event on the boat when her dog was squashed . . . by you, Blanche hasn't been seen around Saint-Tropez much.'

Maximus had the grace to blush. 'Well, she has a new puppy now,' he said, sounding defensive. 'And I sent her a massive orchid plant. She must have forgiven me by now, I hope.'

'Not good enough, Maxie – you should have sent her a new dog!' joked Fabrizio. Max threw him a withering look.

'I want to know why Prince Harry is going to stay with *them*?' demanded Charlie. 'I know Prince Harry, of course. I've attended many events in the UK where he was a guest. I think he likes me,' he finished plaintively. The initial novelty of having Zarina and Sin on his lap had passed, so he was now unsuccessfully trying to dislodge the two teenagers, who stuck to him like twin Band-Aids.

'You're so cuddly,' cooed Zarina.

'It's all because of Henry Phillips,' explained Carlotta. 'Harry is very involved in motor racing for one of his charities, and Henry has promised to attend the next one and drive one of his classic cars.'

Everyone nodded sagely as she continued, 'But no one must know he's coming and we absolutely must not mention we know about it to Blanche or Henry, otherwise they'll panic that everyone knows and who knows what could happen? They might blab it to Harry and then he won't come.'

'I should think they'd love to brag about it,' said Charlie.

'They can do that *after* the event. The Prince wants absolutely no publicity at all, and if word gets out, the world's press will descend upon us. If that happens, Prince Harry will cancel.'

'I see,' said Maximus. 'Who told you all this, *cara?*'

'A woman I met last week – her name's Serena Forsyth. She's a great friend of the Prince, and of Henry and Blanche too. So please, if you want him to come, do not tell anyone.'

'How can you trust this woman?' asked Sophie. 'Really you should vet people thoroughly before you agree to get involved with them.'

'I trust her. She's well-known,' said Carlotta.

'How will we know if we are invited? Are we? Are we invited?' Zarina and Sin jumped over to Carlotta to try to cuddle her now.

'When the Prince arrives, Blanche has an email ready to send to all of you. But you needn't RSVP – I don't think she needs to worry anyone will turn it down!' said Carlotta sweetly to the two young women, trying to extract herself from them.

'Wouldn't miss it for the world,' smiled Fabrizio. 'I really like the Prince. We're the same age – like the same things.'

'Yeah, girls,' quipped Maximus, as Lara shot Fabrizio an angry look. She hated to be reminded of the twenty-four-year age difference.

'Yes, well, that's about all I can tell you for now,' said Carlotta.

'How is he going to get here?' asked Maximus.

'Serena told me he's coming on some bigwig's yacht the day after tomorrow.'

'If we're all stranded here and not allowed to leave, how come he can get here?' asked Fabrizio.

'If anyone can get in, it's Prince Harry. He knows how to get into all kinds of things!' joked Charlie.

'Who's the bigwig?' Lara didn't want Fabrizio talking to Carlotta. 'I know most of the high rollers who have boats.'

'Serena didn't tell me. All I know is that the party for the Prince is at Henry and Blanche's villa next Thursday and you're all invited.'

Maximus looked at Carlotta approvingly. In the few weeks she had been in Saint-Tropez, she had certainly learned the ropes.

'Well done, *cara*,' he patted her on the back. 'You're becoming one of us now.'

Chapter Twenty-Two

There had been such an outcry from everyone who hadn't been allowed to leave Saint-Tropez that reluctantly the Mayor was forced to drop the ban. 'It's unconstitutional,' Jonathan Meyer had declared. 'Against human rights.'

Even Captain Poulpe, who would have loved to interview everyone over and over again, realised the ban was unrealistic. However, he felt he had enough information and was making headway on the murder case. Now, with the news of Prince Harry's imminent arrival, everyone decided to stay anyway, making his job much easier.

Carlotta was becoming so much a part of the Saint-Tropez social scene that Sophie had issued an invitation to her to come for an intimate tea one afternoon.

'It was not so much an invitation, more like a royal command,' Carlotta told Max nervously.

'But you have to go, *cara*,' he insisted. 'Just to see how she lives is an experience. My God, the dogs and the cats . . . *oh!* And the smell!' He did a pretend sniff holding his nose and Carlotta giggled.

'But she terrifies me!'

'Nonsense – she's just an old lady wearing a lot of make-up and too many jewels. Underneath all that she's really quite sweet!'

'You're joking!'

'No – you'll see, the diva act is just an act, and besides, she misses Frick, she's lonely. Maybe she sees in you the daughter she never had.'

'Oh, dear! That's rather hard to live up to,' Carlotta said. She paused for a second then added, almost to herself. 'On the other hand, that would be quite nice – I wasn't very close to my mother.'

Max expressed a touch of fake sympathy as he thought about how he could turn this unexpected social event to his advantage. 'Maybe I should come for tea?' he asked.

'Sorry, she told me I could bring a friend as long as it wasn't you!' Carlotta giggled.

Max made a disappointed *moue* then smiled excitedly, 'Fabrizio! Why don't you take him?'

'Oh, God, no – perish the thought! I've asked Nick, if he's back from the Middle East, and I'll ask Sophie if that's okay.'

'He's press,' said Max gloomily, 'she won't like that.'

'He's promised not to write about her – and besides, he's been commissioned by the *Mail* to do an interview with Henry Phillips, which he'll be working on when he's finished the stint he's doing now. Oh dear, do you think maybe the *Daily Mail* has heard about Prince Harry coming?'

'I doubt it,' said Max, sounding disappointed and sad, realising the opportunities that were being denied him. Had he known about an offer for a *Mail* interview with the racing legend Henry Phillips, he could have negotiated it himself and made himself a little bit of money. God knows he needed it. Everyone seemed to be getting a piece except him.

∞

When Carlotta and Nick entered the dimly lit entrance hall of Sophie Silvestri's secluded villa, Carlotta wrinkled her nose. 'It reeks of animals,' she whispered.

'Man's best friend,' Nick smiled, 'and obviously Madame Silvestri's best friend as well.'

A sombre figure sheathed in black with his arm in a sling appeared at the end of the corridor.

'Madame will see you now,' Adolpho, still mourning his lover Frick, announced gloomily.

The salon was dark, even though it was the middle of the afternoon. Sophie was ensconced in an enormous eighteenth-century gilt and red velvet bergère armchair. It had definitely seen better days, as had all the furnishings in the room. She was clad in a voluminous silk caftan in purple to pink ombré. It bore the signs of wear and tear from the menagerie of animals that drifted in and out of the salon and crowded around her chair looking curiously at the newcomers. There was a strong smell of cat's pee and Carlotta noticed several litter trays stashed around the room. Sophie held out her hand, smiling warmly at the young lovers.

'Sit, sit,' she commanded. 'Adolpho, bring tea. You like English tea?'

Carlotta nodded.

'I always have it every afternoon, most refreshing in this hot climate,' smiled Sophie.

'Out, out!' she barked at two enormous poodles that had taken over the cosy armchairs opposite her.

Incense burned on a rickety table beside Sophie, and the enormous grand piano was covered in a Spanish shawl, on which were stacked about thirty silver photo frames. Nick, with his reporter's eye, quickly spotted the famous star smiling with Reagan, Sinatra, Streisand and Nelson Mandela amongst many others. 'Shades of Gloria Swanson,' he mouthed to Carlotta as Sophie turned to throw off her lap the giant cat she had been caressing. Adolpho had brought in an old-fashioned tea trolley gleaming with exquisite china, and plates piled high with sandwiches and a selection of patisserie. Sophie poured the tea elegantly, in a passable imitation of how the Queen might do it and, without asking, sloshed a generous amount of milk into their delicate cups.

After a limited amount of small talk she said, 'Now maybe you are wondering why I asked you here?'

'Yes . . . I actually . . . I mean, I'm extremely flattered to be invited, Madame Silvestri.'

Sophie held up her hand and said, 'Sophie, please.'

'Yes, well . . . Sophie. I've seen so many of your movies and my mother really admired you.'

A slightly irritated frown crossed the actress's heavily cosmeticised face and Carlotta swiftly realised she'd crossed an invisible no-no line.

'But I loved you in *The Barefoot Bride*. It was on TV a couple of months ago,' she added hastily, trying to repair the damage. Nick shot her an affectionately warning glance and Carlotta decided to shut up.

'Ah yes, *The Barefoot Bride*, one of my favourites. Jack Lemmon . . . ah, he was such a sweetie, we had so much fun.' She sipped her tea and, taking a bite out of a chocolate éclair, fed the rest to a massive basset hound who had been lurking under her chair. She stared off into the distance for a few minutes, apparently lost in thoughts of high jinks with Jack Lemmon.

It was quite gloomy in the salon, the windows shielded from the afternoon sun by thick parasol pines. Another fierce mistral had been brewing since lunchtime and it started its familiar high-pitched whistle as the branches knocked against the windows.

'Ah, you know what they say about mistrals, don't you?' said Sophie with a thin smile.

'Yeah, they keep telling us!' smiled Nick. 'A murderer is forgiven if he kills during a mistral, right?'

'Exactly – except not any murderer: a man who kills his wife.'

'Archaic,' breathed Carlotta. 'Does that rule still exist?'

'In this part of the world, my dear, yes, it does. Although I must admit it hasn't happened recently. You see, what everyone perceives about Saint-Tropez is just the tip of the iceberg, the cherry on top of the cake. There are ancient mystical customs here that have been practised for hundreds of years since the village had to protect itself. We were invaded by Turkish pirates, Spaniards – even the Japanese, you know.'

'Is that when they built the citadel?' asked Nick.

'Yes, by order of the King in the seventeenth century, but the people of Saint-Tropez are still very superstitious, and they don't like strangers. Nor do I,' she said firmly. 'That is why I rarely go out in the daytime. I can't bear to mix with the hideous mobs that come here in their tour buses, and go camping next to our beautiful beaches, leaving all their filth and detritus everywhere. Sacrilegious!' she spat, almost choking on a pastry, and looked furiously out of the window. 'They come here on their boats and try to get a glimpse of me. I'm old now. I don't want them to see me like this.'

Nick glanced at Carlotta, who was completely fascinated by Sophie's recollections. The star seemed to shrink and lose her glamour as her anger started to engulf her.

'I have tried . . . Mon Dieu, how I have tried for thirty years to stop all of this trash coming here. It upsets me so much, but what do they care? All that interests the Mayor and all the councils of the whole of this part of the Côte d'Azur is money, money, money!' She banged her hand so hard on the tea trolley that the plate of pastries fell to the floor and several cats leapt to devour them.

Suddenly there was another huge gust of wind and somewhere in the back of the villa a door banged so loudly that several of the dogs started howling. Sophie grinned devilishly at Carlotta's nervousness.

'Don't worry, my dear, it's not a big mistral and you're not married! Now let's get started. There were two reasons why I asked you here today. The first one was because I believe it's more than a coincidence that both Mina's murder and Spencer's death occurred during the time of a mistral – *n'est-ce pas?*' She stared at them both as the cat jumped on her lap again and she fed it a piece of smoked salmon from her sandwich.

'Well . . .' Nick was hesitant. 'I'm not much of a one for superstitions, but it does seem like quite a coincidence.'

'And my party for Marvin Rheingold, when my dear darling Frick was killed on the funicular . . .' Sophie's eyes filled with tears and she dabbed at her cheeks with the cat's fluffy tail. 'There was a mistral then, do you remember?'

Nick and Carlotta nodded. It had turned much darker in the salon, and the wind blew stronger now.

'I wanted to see if you young people had any ideas about who would want to murder those innocent people? Because Poulpe and that daughter of his don't seem to have a clue.'

'I'm a journalist, ma'am, and believe me, if I had any suspicions, I would let Captain Poulpe or the Mayor know. But I'm sorry to say, ma'am, they all look like accidents to me. Gruesome, yes, and freakishly coincidental, but accidents nevertheless,' said Nick.

'The Mayor? Bah! He's useless, and he loves the fact that Saint-Tropez is full of trash!' Sophie leaned forward ominously. 'And I don't mean those shabby-looking people wandering around in their ugly clothes. No, the real trash here are the oligarchs – those billionaires with their obscene yachts, and their jeroboams of champagne that they spray all over their whores at the beaches and restaurants.'

'Well, yes, there are quite a few of those guys around, I admit,' Carlotta conceded.

'But the town needs those people for the season,' Nick pointed out. 'Otherwise the locals, the shopkeepers, restaurateurs, the owners of the bars and beaches – they would go broke.'

'So what?' snarled Sophie, suddenly back to behaving like a virago. 'Saint-Tropez should be the sleepy fishing village it was before that *puta* Coco Chanel started coming here with her fancy friends in the thirties. Then that Brigitte Bardot ruined it even more in the fifties, running around half-naked.' She took a sip of her tea and stared at them both, becoming even more wild-eyed. 'Perhaps you don't agree with me. Many people don't. In fact . . .' she stroked the cat and her eyes gleamed as she leaned forward, 'many people think I am a witch!'

There was a huge crash from upstairs and Adolpho's voice came down the stairs faintly. 'Sorry, sorry, *cherie*, I just dropped a vase.'

Carlotta shuddered. She was beginning to feel quite queasy, and the pastries Sophie had insisted she eat were weighing heavily on her. She wanted to leave but as she started to rise, Sophie grabbed her arm.

'You don't think I'm a witch, do you, my dear?'

'No, no, of course not,' Carlotta could plainly hear a tone of menace in the old woman's voice.

'Good, that's good, because I'm not – although I do foresee things.'

'What sort of things?'

'Ah, that would be telling.'

'I hope you don't foresee any more accidents,' Nick said jokingly.

'Actually I don't . . .'

'That's a relief,' he laughed.

'. . . but I foresee a few more *murders*,' she hissed.

'Oh God, no . . . seriously? When? What do you see?'

'I just think everyone should be careful because I sense something evil is happening in Saint-Tropez. But I think we can prevent it by the power of prayer.'

Nick rolled his eyes at this but Carlotta, whose arm was in the grip of Sophie's strong fingers, flinched.

'Yes, with prayer, and staying close to good people and thinking good thoughts, we can prevent any more deaths. So, Carlotta, of all the people staying in Saint-Tropez now, I believe it is you, *cherie*, who is truly good. That is why I want to be much closer to you. I want us to bond, like mother and daughter. I never had a child, you know – but then again I didn't want one. I was a selfish and spoilt bitch, I admit.' Sophie laughed and suddenly her face seemed relaxed, and warm. She released Carlotta's arm and started stroking the cat again.

'It's my birthday soon. It's a big one, and every five years I ask someone who is pure, uncomplicated and simply a good person to throw a small party for me. Ten years ago it was Charlie Chalk. Last time it was my poor Frick. This year I am asking you, Carlotta, with your youth, beauty and kindness to give me a party. Will you, my dear?'

'Of course. I'm honoured,' smiled Carlotta.

'Thank you, my dear. I always try to celebrate it, even if I find each half of the decade more and more depressing. I mean, cheese ripens with age, as does wine, so why can't people get better with age?'

It was a rhetorical question that no one was able to answer, but Nick chimed in gallantly, 'Just because a woman has a few lines on her face doesn't make her less beautiful – and you, Sophie, are still beautiful.'

Sophie smiled and preened. 'Silly boy! It's not true, but thank you anyway.'

'Are you looking forward to Prince Harry's visit?' asked Carlotta after a minute of embarrassed silence.

'Ha!' said Sophie. 'The soirée for Prince Harry that we're not supposed to discuss. Ha! How everyone is going to keep their mouths shut is beyond me.' She rang a bell and an elderly, stooped maid entered to clear the tea things.

The two stood up. 'Teresa, see our guests out,' said Sophie. 'Thank you, sweet things, you have been most amusing.' She sank back into her chair as the big cat jumped off her lap and three white kittens jumped eagerly on to it.

'*Jesus H. Christ!* Was that a trip?' Nick hugged Carlotta tightly against the wild winds outside the villa. 'I can understand why some people would think she was a witch – she's a touch scary.'

'No, she's not,' said Carlotta, pondering the visit. 'I think she's rather sweet and rather sad too. I will enjoy giving her a birthday party.'

CHAPTER TWENTY-THREE

Word got out, word always gets out, and by the time the massive yacht belonging to some global nomad that no one had ever heard of came into port, excitement was palpable.

Prince Harry was supposed to be on it, and that was the cue for the movers and shakers of Saint-Tropez to be casually sitting around at various cafés in front of the port on the day it was expected. It was a humongous vessel by anyone's standards. Five storeys high, it was equipped with all the latest toys.

The usual suspects were clustered together on a large round table smack in the middle of Sénéquier, and even they were impressed.

'It's a five thousand tonner!' It took a lot to excite Sergei Litvak, whose boat was one of the twenty biggest vessels in the world, but he had whipped out his iPhone 6 like a child and started snapping away furiously.

'Jeez, they've got two helicopters, at least two pools and four speedboats!' chimed Nate.

'And those are the latest speedboats.' Monty Goldman was looking through binoculars and read out the name *Dar El Salaam*. 'I've never heard of it.' He quickly scrolled through his phone. 'I've just googled it. It doesn't show up; it's obviously from the Middle East – some sheik or sultan from Syria or somewhere. Strange there's no record of it.' He scrolled down his phone again.

The men gazed with thinly disguised envy at the massive boat as it slipped effortlessly into its berth. Sailors in pale blue uniforms ran hither and yon like ants, and one of the staff raised a green and black flag, which no one recognised.

'Blue uniforms,' sniffed Lara, who considered herself something of an expert in *la vie maritime*. 'Tacky.'

The gangplank was lowered. 'Teak and chrome, the latest from Blohm + Voss,' said Monty admiringly.

After a few minutes, a jaunty figure ran down the gangplank, wearing khaki cargo shorts, a light green polo shirt and a NY Yankees baseball cap pulled low over his flaming red hair.

'It's him!' Carlotta was thrilled. She had met a few European princes when she was married to Nicanor, but to meet English royalty was much more prestigious and exciting.

As soon as his feet touched the quay, two nubile teenagers in the shortest of shorts, wearing matching red bikini tops and high-heeled hooker shoes, ran up to him. The man put his arms around them, said 'Hi, girls', and they started to walk towards Sénéquier. The group gasped.

They were followed by a petite dark-haired woman dressed all in black and wearing two cameras slung around her neck and a large necklace made out of diamond skulls. She was busy photographing Harry as he and the young girls walked briskly over to the group at the round table at Sénéquier.

'I'd love to see the Queen's face when she sees those pics!' said Charlie.

The dark-haired woman came over to Carlotta, who chirped, 'Hi Serena.'

'Hi, Carlotta,' said the woman. 'Your Royal Highness, I'd like to introduce you to some of my friends.'

'Pity we can't see his eyes,' whispered Carlotta to Nick. 'Those mirrored Ray-Bans hide so much.'

Prince Harry stuck out one hand with his famous cheeky smile as Sophie, Lara, Carlotta, Vanessa, Lilly Litvak and all the men rose to shake his hand, mightily impressed by the presence of royalty. Zarina and Sin threw themselves on him, elbowing the other teenagers out of the way.

Lara practically genuflected when she met the Prince, and Fabrizio had to hold her up to prevent her falling over. The teenagers, having managed to push Zarina and Sin aside, clung to him like limpets, posing and laughing and tossing their long blonde hair. Serena asked them to pose this way and that, and when Charlie Chalk went to meet the Prince she called out, 'Kiss him on the cheek, Charlie!'

'Oh, I couldn't dear, it's not respectful,' he said, but one of the girls, grinning, pushed him so far forward that he lost his balance and planted a smacker on the young prince's nose.

'Oh! So sorry, Your Highness,' said Charlie, turning puce with embarrassment.

'It's okay, don't worry,' said Harry. 'I'm a big fan.'

'Really?' Charlie puffed up with pride. 'Well, so am I, sir!'

The whole quay was now throbbing with people, cameras were out, cell phones held up, as were babies, and there was an atmosphere of bonhomie and jollity.

'Fifth in line to the throne – what an honour.' Lilly Litvak curtsied so low that her Roberto Cavalli mini-skirt rose up, thigh-high.

Then the group turned as one, as a very tall, elegant girl in jeans and a striped Breton top stepped daintily down the gangplank of the boat. Her long chestnut hair swung in the breeze as she walked swiftly towards Harry with open arms and a big smile, calling out, 'Hi, babes!'

213

'My God, it's Kate Middleton!' screamed one of the crowd.

'Kate, Kate, look here, look over here!' screamed another.

'Oh, my God, is that the Duchess?' They started to push towards her, but several policemen who had arrived at the scene held the crowd back. Cameras and cell phones went crazy as two of Britain's favourite royals hugged each other.

Serena seemed unfazed by being in the proximity of the popular young Duchess of Cambridge. 'Kiss Harry, Kate darling,' she commanded, and with a big grin the Duchess and Prince Harry embraced, then locked lips in a passionate kiss.

The crowd gasped.

'I don't believe it.' Charlie was aghast. 'It's not them. It can't be!'

'They're lookalikes!' screamed one of the crowd angrily. 'Shame on you!'

'You're right, there's no way it's them!' yelled another.

The crowd started booing.

Quickly 'Harry' and 'Kate', still entwined, turned and ran swiftly back on to the boat, followed by Serena, who was still snapping hastily.

'What the hell was all that about?' Sophie turned furiously to an almost tearful Carlotta. 'They were fakes!'

'I . . . I don't know. Serena's a friend – well, an acquaintance really. She called and told me the Prince was coming and he wanted a party and that no one should know. I don't know why she would play this trick on me.'

Nick put his arms comfortingly around her and she started to sob.

'How good a friend?' demanded Sophie.

'Well, actually I only met her once in Monaco – but she's been calling me a lot.' Carlotta was horribly embarrassed and crying copiously. The others rolled their eyes.

'You've been done, darling.' Lara was quite delighted to see the younger girl in hot water. She was becoming sick of everyone saying how wonderful, sweet and beautiful Carlotta was. 'Serves her right,' she whispered to Fabrizio, who looked determinedly neutral.

'It's a bit unfair, I admit,' said Charlie, 'but a jolly bit of fun. My, but those lookalikes were really good – we were all taken in by them!' He started to laugh uproariously and the others, getting the joke, started laughing with him.

'Look, the boat's leaving!' Monty was astonished at how quickly Serena, the two lookalikes and the girls had hopped onto the boat, which was already on its way out of the port.

'I notice Blanche and Henry aren't here. Were they in on it too?' asked Sophie sternly.

'No,' Carlotta was crying softly. 'Serena told me not to call them; that it had to be such a secret. I was supposed to tell them today and help organise the party. She felt that Blanche would maybe let the cat out of the bag,' she sobbed and Nick held her tightly.

'You're right about that, dear.' Charlie patted Carlotta's arm comfortingly. 'That woman has a bigger mouth than I have.' Everyone laughed.

'Carlotta, don't take it too seriously darling,' said Nick. 'I know that woman. She's a professional photographer who specialises in taking photos of celebrity lookalikes in compromising positions – just like that famous photographer Alison Jackson.'

After they had sat down and ordered a large bottle of rosé, Charlie said, 'I've seen her work, it's very original.'

'Well, she's going to have to get permission from all of us if she wants to use those photos,' said Jonathan Meyer, who was the only one of the group who didn't get the joke. 'It's not funny, for Christ's sake! In fact, it's a goddamn liberty.'

'Calm down, dear.' Charlie patted him on the shoulder. 'I think the pics will only be of him and "Kate" kissing in front of the mob.' He gestured to the people who were still gathered around them curiously. 'And of course Prince Harry with the hookers! My dears, that will go viral!'

And it did. Within hours it was all over the internet and the next day the picture of 'Harry' kissing 'Kate' hit the front pages of every tabloid in the Western world. So much shock and outrage followed that Buckingham Palace was forced to issue a statement that they were lookalikes and Serena Forsyth had to release a profuse apology.

∞

'Well, so much for asking our permission!' Charlie Chalk threw copies of the *Daily Mail* and the *Daily Mirror* on to the table and issued a loud, 'Harrumph! Shall I sue?'

Carlotta, Nick, Fabrizio and Vanessa were taking their morning coffee and croissants in a little café on the corner of the Place des Lices. It was market day, and the leafy square was jammed with tables and stalls full of goods ranging from cheese to socks, from pizza to art-deco tea sets. The place buzzed with hundreds of tourists. Language-wise it was like a league of nations, with German, Dutch, and Italians vying with the English and the French as to who could shout the loudest or be the pushiest. Dogs on leads and babies in strollers entangled themselves in the shoppers' legs as a strong mistral whipped through the stalls, sending sarongs and scarves fluttering like flags outside the UN. The stallholders were looking glum as the holidaymakers, carrying enormous rucksacks on their backs or pushing prams containing fretful babies, fingered their goods but then moved on.

'*Merde!*' said the woman who sold vintage Victorian pieces from the stall opposite the café. 'It gets worse and worse each year, no one is buying.'

Charlie leaned over sympathetically and patted her on the shoulder. 'It's the recession, darling. Never mind, I'll buy a set of twenty napkins from you. They'll be useful for my party.'

'I thought you were having a hundred guests,' laughed Fabrizio. 'Twenty napkins won't go far.'

Charlie rolled his eyes. 'Spread the wealth, darling, help the poor, then you'll go to heaven, although I don't know about you, dear.' He winked blithely at Fabrizio, who was making unsuccessful attempts to engage Carlotta with a few card tricks. Seemingly unimpressed but always polite, she smiled up at him and moved closer to Nick.

The Mayor came to their table to say hello. Nick stood up and asked him if he would like to join them. He sat down and ordered a café crème.

'What's happening with the ban?' asked Charlie. 'Why did they decide to lift it?'

'At a meeting with the city council and the gendarmerie, we realised it's impossible to implement. God knows what they were thinking in the first place. We don't know if these incidents were accidents or murders, but in any event we could not hold the whole of Saint-Tropez responsible. To keep everyone here who could possibly be involved was impossible.'

'Any more news? Do they have any suspects?' asked Charlie. A tear dropped on to his chocolate croissant as he sighed heavily. 'My poor darling Spencer, what a dreadful thing to happen.'

'I sympathise deeply,' said the Mayor. 'The gendarmerie are continuing their investigations. We'll give you any news as soon as we have it.'

Nick, who had just returned from a short business trip to Baghdad and had been filing articles with several US publications on the recent strange events in Saint-Tropez, added, 'What about this Prince Harry hoax – could there be a connection?'

Carlotta looked guilty, but Nick squeezed her hand and smiled comfortingly. 'It wasn't your fault, darling. It was a "sting" that this Serena woman perpetrated on you. Hey, you know, you need me to be with you more,' he grinned, and she smiled up at him. Fabrizio winced.

'Well, you should stop dashing to the Middle East all the time – I do need you with me.' It was true – Nick was a pillar of strength, always there for her; reliable, trustworthy and intelligent. He had not been pressuring her to go to bed with him; she knew how much he wanted her, but she felt that when she committed to the act of love again, it had to be for ever.

Charlie was still studying the front page of the *Daily Mail*. 'Look at this picture. "Harry" is kissing me! My God, I'll become the laughing stock of London.'

'Not at all,' said the Mayor. 'At the meeting today, all of the councillors applauded you, Charlie. And yes, it was a mean thing to do, but this Serena person is known for that sort of thing.'

'Did you read the caption? Listen . . .' Charlie grabbed the paper and read, 'Photographer Serena Forsyth scored another coup when she snapped a lookalike of Prince Harry kissing a lookalike of the popular comedian Charlie Chalk in Saint-Tropez last week. *They didn't even think it was me!*' he squawked resentfully.

'The woman's brilliant. I would tell her off but she won't return my calls,' said Carlotta.

'It could have misfired really badly,' said Charlie.

'Nonsense,' said the Mayor. 'Where's your sense of humour? No one was hurt, and in fact that picture will encourage more people to come to Saint-Tropez, I hope.'

'I guess it was quite funny.' Fabrizio, who had been frustrated in his attempts to interest Carlotta, had decided to turn his charm on to a smiling Vanessa Meyer.

'It's so great that the ban is over. Jonathan will be delighted.

We can finally take the boat to Capri, whenever he can tear himself away from the golf course.' Vanessa sounded delighted and exchanged a meaningful look with Fabrizio.

'Oh, that's too bad,' said Carlotta to Vanessa. 'I know that Sophie will miss you at the birthday party she's asked me to give for her. I'm a bit overwhelmed actually – there's so much planning. Thank goodness Maximus is helping me.'

'Ah – talk of the devil,' grinned Fabrizio. 'Here comes Dumbo now.'

'Now, now,' admonished Charlie. 'How many times must I tell you, we do not mock the fat! We can't help it, you know.' He patted his corpulent belly, sheathed in a wildly printed Dolce silk shirt, and moved his seat so Maximus could sit.

'I need a word with Fabrizio.' Max sounded out of breath and serious. He didn't take up Charlie's offer. 'Come.' He beckoned Fabrizio over to a quiet corner of the café, and he obediently followed.

'I had a call from CRAP today. Carina actually phoned me.' Fabrizio sat down, paling beneath his caramel tan. 'She says your brats Alberto and Pietro are starving, and so is she and your other whore, Raimunda.'

'What the hell am I supposed to do?' Fabrizio said despairingly. 'I sent them as much as I could last month.'

'She said the kids need clothes for school and lots of other things that kids need – I can't remember. Thank God I never had any of the little monsters!'

'School doesn't start until September,' snapped Fabrizio.

'Hey, don't shoot the messenger! They're making threats, Fabrizio – bad threats.'

'What threats? What can they do? They already threatened to stop me seeing the brats – like I care,' he laughed hollowly. 'I mean, Carina and Raimunda get a thousand euros a month each from me. It's all I can afford. Isn't that enough?'

Maximus shrugged. 'Lucky me, I never sired bastards – or screwed teenagers. You were stupid, Fabrizio.'

'Don't you think I know it – I was only nineteen, for Christ's sake, I didn't even know about birth control then, or the facts of life . . . I didn't even watch porn,' he laughed hollowly.

'But you were led by your dick as usual. Tut-tut!'

Fabrizio stared sullenly into the square.

Maximus continued, 'Anyway, their latest threat is that they will turn up here – the four of them – and present themselves to Lara. Now you know how she *loves* publicity,' he said sarcastically. 'And of course she is very famous in America. So your "exes" will relish telling the press about Lara's *fidanzato*'s two little bastards who are barefoot and starving, and that he doesn't support them.'

'But I do support them, as much as I can.' Fabrizio put his head in his hands and groaned.

'Lara will be put in the embarrassing position of being described as the thoughtless bitch who won't help her fiancé – it won't look good for you, my friend; not good at all,' continued Max.

'What the fuck – what can I do?'

'You will just have to face the music and tell Lara the truth at last. Get her in a good mood first, however you manage it.' Maximus winked lasciviously.

'And then?'

'And then you confess – put on your "poor little lost boy" look, you know she's a sucker for that; ask her for more money for your starving kids.'

'What if she refuses to give me any more money for them?'

'Play hardball – break up with her,' said Max firmly. 'Even I can see she's becoming more and more of a pain in the ass. Threaten to leave, and if she doesn't stop you, then go.'

'But what will I do, where will I go?' Fabrizio's voice was a plaintive wail.

'Oh, for God's sake, stop the Scarlett O'Hara act! You can stay with me for a few days. Then I suggest maybe you get to work on *her*.' He gestured to where tawny-haired Vanessa Meyer was looking over her designer sunglasses with barely disguised interest at Fabrizio's well-toned chest in a white designer shirt open to the waist.

'That would be the perfect irony, *n'est-ce pas?*' grinned Max. 'You dump Jonathan's ex-wife and hit on the newest one!'

A faint smile played around Fabrizio's lips. He was way ahead of the game. He and Jonathan's gorgeous English wife had already been exchanging long looks and phone numbers for the past week. Maybe soon it would be time to move in for the kill. It was obvious that Vanessa was bored stiff with Jonathan.

Max gave Fabrizio a little nudge. 'Go on, work your magic on her, big boy. You know you can.'

Chapter Twenty-Four

Carlotta, Nick, Sophie and Maximus sat on Sophie's terrace, over-looking the sparkling Mediterranean, preparing the guest list for the actress's seventy-fifth birthday party. Sophie fingered a battered Filofax into which she peered shortsightedly as she read out famous names.

'Deneuve . . . we must ask Catherine. I haven't seen her since Cannes but we've been friends for years.'

Max raised his eyebrows. Sophie's female friends, especially if they were famous actresses, were few and far between.

'Okay,' said Carlotta. 'She's in Paris, right?'

Sophie nodded, 'Always in Paris, always *working*,' she hissed then said, 'Brigitte – I'm sure she'll come.'

'Bardot never goes out socially to parties at night,' said Max, 'even though she's known as the Queen of Saint-Tropez.'

'*One* of the queens,' said Sophie swiftly. 'You know I am also known by that title.'

'Okay, well, I'll put her on the list anyway,' Carlotta touched the keys on her iPad, 'and send an invite.'

'Ah! Depardieu – my dear Gérard, such a darling. We made *Appointment in Baghdad* together; he must be invited.'

'Now we must invite Helmut Berger, and Jean-Paul Le Blanc,' said Sophie firmly, ignoring Max's sly dig. 'Ah, we had such fun together making *The Spy I Loved* in sixty-eight.'

'Have you seen him since?' asked Max.

'Well, no, but he was a good friend.' Sophie closed her eyes and let her mind take her back to a long-ago time in Paris, when for a brief moment in time she and Jean-Paul Le Blanc had conducted a wonderfully clandestine affair.

'Ah, he was so young, so famous and so good-looking – in a tough, masculine way, of course.' Sophie sighed wistfully, remembering how they had spent their afternoons entwined in silken sheets in her hotel on the Avenue Foch. 'Ah, those afternoons were the stuff that dreams were made of, until his wife found out. She came banging on the door one afternoon screaming, "I know you're in there with that slut, Jean-Paul. Come out of that *puta*'s clutches, you bastard!"' Sophie laughed, then whispered dreamily, 'He wouldn't go to her. He wouldn't leave my bed. He loved me so much. Oh, how we loved each other!'

'So what happened? Where is Jean-Paul now?' asked Carlotta.

'Well, like all affairs on movie sets, it ended when the director called "Cut". You know, it doesn't count on location.' Sophie came out of her reverie, 'I don't know where he went. Maybe Paris? I heard he made some films in Italy for a time. His wife left him eventually,' she grinned.

'Oh, but I think I saw him,' Adolpho excitedly blurted. 'Last week I was in Gassin, dining at Bello Visto, and I swear I saw him at the next table.' He frowned. 'I think he was with a couple of people – maybe with some kids? Yes, I'm sure it was him – great hair,' he finished, 'considering he's over seventy.'

Sophie's eyes lit up. 'Gassin, of course – he loved that village. It was where he was born.'

'Well, he shouldn't be too difficult to track down, then,' said Max. 'Gassin is only a tiny village.'

'I'll go tomorrow,' said Adolpho enthusiastically. Thoughts of a romance between his employer and an ex-lover excited him.

'What about Maximilian Schell?' Sophie was still flipping through her book. 'My God, what a stud! He could go for hours!'

'Too much information,' Max mouthed to Carlotta, who grinned then said: 'I'm sorry, darling, but he died last year.'

'Oh, too bad . . . I don't suppose De Niro and Pacino are still around?'

'Well, yes, they are, but I don't think they ever leave the States. I'll try anyway.'

Just then the doorbell rang and Adolpho jumped up to answer it.

'Don't bother,' said Sophie, 'Teresa will get it.'

The old maid was so crippled with arthritis she could barely walk towards the door. 'Ah, *madame*. It was a messenger with a big box of your favourite chocolates – Charbonnel et Walker,' she called as she tottered into the salon.

'I wonder who sent them?' said Sophie. 'Not many people know I love them.'

'Here's the note,' said Teresa, passing a tiny envelope to her mistress.

'I'm busy, Teresa, I can't open chocolates now – take them to the kitchen and put them on a silver platter to pass to my friends.'

The old woman waddled off, muttering to herself, as Sophie opened the card. 'To my idol, from your devoted pursuer.'

'Hmm, who could that be? I think I have quite a few devoted . . .' Just then they heard an almighty explosion from the kitchen, and a strangled scream from the maid. One of the windows blew out from the blast and Adolpho and Carlotta, who were the closest to the kitchen, were tossed to the floor.

'Oh, my God! It's a bomb!' yelled Maximus.

They burst into the kitchen to find it totally destroyed, and the poor old maid Teresa lying dead on the floor with a massive, bloody hole in her chest. The chocolate box was open beside her, smoke billowing out of it.

'Call the police,' Nick ordered Adolpho, and immediately wrapped his arms around a sobbing Carlotta, placing her face against his chest. 'Don't look, darling.'

Sophie was shaking with fear and horror. Adolpho helped her on to a lounge chair on the terrace and gave her a glass of brandy, which she sipped gratefully.

'That was meant for me,' she said. 'Someone wanted to kill me.'

'But why?' asked Carlotta, putting her arms around the shaken actress. 'Who would have wanted to kill you?'

Nick shook his head. 'I don't think it was meant for you, Sophie. I think for some reason someone is trying to frighten the fuck out of all of us.'

∞

After Captain Poulpe and Gabrielle had thoroughly questioned everyone in the house and allowed them to leave, Carlotta and Nick went outside again. She was still shaking from the shock of the explosion and the tragic death of Teresa.

'Do you realise there are no mirrors inside the house?' Nick said.

'Why is that?' asked Carlotta.

'I don't think Sophie wants to see herself during the day until Adolpho has put her together as she wants to look. It's tragic really, she's like stuck together with facelifts, fillers and wigs.'

'But I do like her,' said Carlotta. 'It must be horrible to feel so lonely, the last one standing of a great generation of true stars.'

∞

As soon as Jonathan Meyer learned that the ban on suspects leaving Saint-Tropez was lifted, he called the captain of his Gulfstream II and told him to plot a course for Paris immediately. 'I've got to close that deal with the Von Schreiber brothers,' he informed his wife.

Vanessa, who was lolling in their beautifully appointed stateroom watching a DVD episode of *Orange Is the New Black*, didn't look up.

'Why aren't you getting ready?' he asked, already in city mode – lightweight grey slacks, white-on-white cotton shirt from Charvet and a light blue linen blazer. He clasped his Breguet watch on his wrist, adjusted his shiny toupee, which he had recently switched from jet black to dark brown streaked with grey, and glanced at Vanessa. She yawned, stretched and, putting the remote on live pause, purred, 'Oh, darling, I really don't feel up to it. It's that time of the month. I'd like to spend some time with Jonathan Junior.'

'But honey, you love Paris. I'll have to be there at least three days – think of the shopping.'

'Darling, Jon Junior really needs to spend more time with me. He's been with Nanny far too much recently. I want to take him water skiing, sailing on the boat, and do some mother/son activities . . .'

'Sure, okay.' He checked his cufflinks, making a mental note to ring the gorgeous blonde courtesan he had connected with last time he was in Paris. God, she was hot! If he didn't know he was paying three thousand euros a night, he would have actually thought she had enjoyed sex with him.

Vanessa was still droning on '. . . and the weather's been so bad, that mistral blowing all the time, poor Jonny hasn't been able to ski at all.'

'Sure, sure, okay, honey – we'll keep in touch.' He blew her a kiss, checked his pockets and picked up his alligator briefcase. Vanessa lay back, a big smile spreading over her perfect lips. When she was sure her husband had left the boat, she picked up her cell phone and dialled a number.

∞

Fabrizio had pulled. It wasn't the first time, nor would it be the last, but the former Honourable Vanessa Anstruther-Formby, now Mrs Jonathan Meyer, was a major coup. At twenty-nine, she was a seasoned beauty at the peak of perfection. Her abundant hair framed an exquisite kitten-like face, with high chiselled cheekbones, a pointed chin and clear eyes. But it was her body that was truly superb. She was tall and slender with perfect breasts and a tiny waist. Whether the breasts were real or not, Fabrizio was about to find out.

Vanessa had given the captain and crew the night off. She had sent nine-year-old Jonny and his nanny to the funfair at La Foux, to meet Vanessa's cousin Louisa and her twin sons. They were the same age as Jon; he would be spending the night with them in Saint-Maxime. She was excited. She had only had one other fling in her nine years of marriage to one of the most influential and important moguls in America – and, after all, didn't everyone cheat? Besides, this was different. She was genuinely attracted to and intrigued by Fabrizio; knowing that he was the kept man of Jonathan's ex-wife made the assignation even more exciting.

Jonathan's boat was now moored in the less inhabited part of the port, far away from the throngs who gawped at the major yachts in front of Sénéquier, L'Escale, and all the other shops and cafés, which suited Vanessa perfectly.

At eight thirty it was practically deserted, except for a few empty sailing boats and a couple of empty mega-yachts whose owners were also away. The rich liked to save money, so when they were not on board the captains were usually told to moor their boats in the less expensive port at Cogolin. Mooring charges in Saint-Tropez were astronomical in the season from May to September, but still competition was rife for the best berths.

Fabrizio, wearing his deepest darkest Ray-Bans, ran quickly up the gangplank and into the gorgeously over-decorated salon. There, Vanessa waited, a vision in Tom Ford's sexiest black lounging pyjamas, her breasts barely covered by a thin strap of shining black bugle beads, her long legs visible behind transparent chiffon trousers. She handed him a glass of chilled Cristal and smiled seductively. Fabrizio felt himself harden. No need for the blue pill tonight. He raised his glass, took off his shades and locked eyes with her.

'To us,' he whispered.

'Yes, to us,' she replied huskily, and slinked closer to him.

Vanessa pressed her body to Fabrizio as if she was offering him pastries from a platter – and he was very hungry. She was far more beautiful and sensual than any of the trophy wives or young hookers he'd been banging since he had been living with Lara. Vanessa was top-of-the-line, A1 pussy, and Fabrizio was in his element.

The sexual tricks Vanessa had learned from Roman Scavolini, her first lover, always fascinated and enchanted any new lover. She tried not to think of Roman and his total rejection of her, but the pain surfaced like maggots on ripe fruit whenever she had one of her rare assignations. Maybe it was the feeling of a new man's body close to hers but the only way she could assuage those hateful memories was by a toke of coke. As Fabrizio prepared to enter her after what he considered to be an adequate amount of foreplay, Vanessa raised herself on one delicate elbow to reach into a silver box and offered him a generous line of the white powder and a crisp new hundred-dollar bill. Fabrizio didn't hesitate. Although he was fired with lust for Vanessa, he knew the magic powder would make the sex even more exciting. He sniffed deeply – and the game was on.

∞

Vanessa Anstruther-Formby had been born to Lord Charles and Lady Elizabeth Anstruther-Formby in a gloomy castle in the wilds of Gloucestershire. Her parents were aristocrats. Their lineage went back to the fourteenth century, when the family owned half the county. But by the 1980s many fortunes had tumbled and they were finding it difficult to make ends meet. They had to sell off great tracts of land and, as their final ignominy, opened part of the castle to visiting tourists, who wandered around in bug-eyed awe at the gorgeous artifacts and paintings in the exquisitely appointed rooms. The third daughter was a surprise, as Lady Anstruther-Formby was well into her forties.

'Another daughter!' Charles fumed. 'Another bloody wedding we'll have to spend a fortune on! Damn it, Elizabeth, couldn't you have produced another boy? My God, we have four children to bring up now.'

'Darling, it's the will of God!' She lay back in a nest of white lace pillows, cradling her baby. 'Look at her, Charles, she's beautiful. I've never seen such a pretty newborn – I don't think we'll have too much of a problem marrying her off.'

Charles barely gave a glance to the baby as his two elder daughters, Jessica and Jane, came bounding into their mother's bedroom to inspect the latest arrival. Brother Jeremy had no interest in the infant, and spent most of his time in his room drawing and painting.

'Ooh, she's got red hair,' cried Jessica, 'that's awful!'

'And dark eyes,' said nine-year-old Jane. 'Gross!'

'Most babies have dark blue eyes,' said Elizabeth with a smile. 'Don't worry, they will get lighter like yours, darling.'

And they did. By the time she was three, Vanessa was a gorgeous, blue-eyed, auburn-haired pin-up baby who could have been plucked from the label of a Gerber's baby-food jar. People stopped her nanny in the street to coo and comment about how cute and gorgeous she was. However, her sisters felt differently. They loathed the little girl and made no bones about letting her know just how much. Older and taller than she, they played crafty and wicked tricks on her. Since she didn't take to riding horses and playing the blood sports her sisters loved to indulge in, she was left to her own devices much of the time. She played with her dolls' house until she was almost fifteen. School friends were few, since she attended the village school and most of the girls were too intimidated to visit the castle.

'It's spooky,' said Beryl, one of her few friends. 'I'm sure it's haunted, Vanessa. How do you sleep at night?'

Vanessa had more than her fair share of 'apple-pie' beds and ghost-like apparitions in the middle of the night, when the older girls would come into her room covered in black from head to toe, making scary noises and waking her up screaming. Luckily the pranks stopped when Jane and Jessica were both married off, before they were twenty and within a year of each other, leaving Vanessa to sleep alone in the top wing of the castle. Even though they had been unkind to her, she missed her sisters. Worse was to come when her father Charles died, exactly on the day when his first grandchild, a boy, was born. Lady Anstruther-Formby took to her bed for most of the next year and the teenaged Vanessa was pretty much left to fend for herself.

The castle really did have an empty and intimidating feeling to it. When the winds whistled through the bare branches of the oak trees and barged relentlessly against the mullioned windows of the castle, Vanessa was scared. She started to keep a diary; she felt abandoned and alone and had the spooky feeling that her father was watching her. The diary became a means of support; she could commit her inner thoughts to these pages.

The winds have become ridiculously strong. Woke up, yet again, in the middle of the night and had to take a pill. For somebody who is anti-drug and anti-pill, this is becoming ridiculous, but I do feel that sleep is necessary, she wrote.

One night her mother rushed into Vanessa's bedroom. Both of them had heard a horrible, terrifying creaking in the walls.

'I've never heard anything like it,' her mother told her. 'It's awful, how can you sleep?'

'I can't,' Vanessa said simply. 'It's a continuing nightmare.'

'I'll send you to stay with your aunt,' said her mother.

'No, *please*! You always said I could go to art school to study design, like Jeremy.'

Lady Anstruther-Formby wasn't averse to the idea. Motherhood had not been her forte, and with her youngest daughter gone she could dedicate her days to riding and taking care of the tourist trade at the castle's shop, selling hampers, gift sets featuring the family crest and concocting delicious organic preserves and biscuits made from the finest ingredients. Trade had increased significantly, and Lady Anstruther-Formby was now in her element.

∞

Vanessa thrived at the London School of Art and Design and she made many friends, mostly boys. The male population at university hit upon her relentlessly, but she simply wasn't interested in men until she met Roman Scavolini. A little-known Italian artist, he had been giving a lecture to the students on post-Impressionist paintings. Afterwards they asked him questions, and when the beauteous Honourable Vanessa Anstruther-Formby cast her guileless blue eyes upon him, he was more than intrigued.

Although it was totally against college rules, Signor Scavolini managed to wangle a date with Vanessa. She was thrilled. All the girls in her class fancied him, and now he had actually asked *her* out – it was exhilarating. It was also inevitable that Vanessa would sleep with him. He was not only the most alluring and seductive man she had ever met, but he was a brilliant and expert lover and, at eighteen, she was the only virgin in college – a fact she didn't like to advertise. He played Vanessa as he would a fine violin and brought her to peaks of joy she had never known existed.

And then he dumped her. It wasn't gradual, it wasn't expected and it wasn't kind. One day she just couldn't reach him. After she had sweated it out for three of the longest days of her life, she found out he had left the hotel where he had been staying with no forwarding address. His phone went straight to voicemail and her texts and emails went unanswered.

Broken-hearted, Vanessa had no one to comfort her. At home with her mother, she couldn't admit what had happened, but a phrase Lady Anstruther-Formby had used many years ago kept resonating in her head: 'Men only want one thing.'

The following year, Vanessa won a scholarship to the Parsons School of Design in New York, and was delighted that her mother had no qualms about letting her leave England. Lady Anstruther-Formby's line was turning over a tidy profit so she could afford to help Vanessa along in her dreams. She hit New York feeling just like the song: 'I want to wake up in a city that never sleeps'.

That fall, Vanessa met the mega-rich mogul Jonathan Meyer. Although still married to the volatile Russian ex-dancer Lara, but unable to keep his zipper zipped, he wooed gorgeous Vanessa with every trick in his book. She was so cool, so English, so refined – he wanted her as he had never wanted any woman before; and what Jonathan wanted, Jonathan always got.

She gave him her body and showed him all the sensual tricks that Roman had taught her, but there was a part of her he could never possess. He wanted her to love him, but she couldn't. Her wounds were still too open. The hurt had healed but a part of her heart had been injured for ever. But when Vanessa became pregnant and Jonathan begged her to marry him, she decided to take on the life of a Manhattan trophy wife of one of the richest men in the world. Why not? Even a damaged heart can be fixed. He adored her, he was handsome, albeit somewhat balding, and he let her do anything she wanted, within reason. And when their son was born, Vanessa felt almost complete for the first time in her life.

CHAPTER TWENTY-FIVE

No one had any idea who had sent the bomb to Sophie. But whoever it was would have been delighted with the completely shocking effect it had had on everyone connected to her.

Still grieving over the death of Frick in the funicular, and now with the loss of her faithful old maid Teresa, Sophie felt so frail, weak and old that she took to her bed. Nevertheless, Captain Poulpe had gently tried to coax any information from her – she still had to be interrogated.

'Do you know of anyone who would wish you ill, *madame?*'

'Plenty,' she snarled. Lying on her bed in her over-decorated purple bedroom, she was swathed in cashmere and fox-fur wraps against the cold, even though it was eighty degrees outside. For her it was perpetually chilly in the old stone villa – it never really became warm until the July sun had penetrated the ancient walls and flies started buzzing in the main salon and in Sophie's bedroom.

'I have a lot of enemies.' She handed him an envelope. 'Read it.'

Poulpe took rubber gloves from his pocket and gently removed the note.

'You won't escape next time,' was printed in block letters on the kind of cheap lined paper that was available from any supermarket.

'When did this come?'

'This morning. Adolpho found it under the front door – now I'm having to hire security guards.' She started to weep and Gabrielle Poulpe, who had been standing quietly in the door, handed her a tissue and plumped the cushions behind the old actress's bewigged head.

'Of course I have enemies. Many people are – or were – jealous of me. I was famous, I was beautiful, I had many lovers, some of whom I stole from their partners.' She blew her nose and looked contrite. 'This I regret, of course.'

'Is there anyone in Saint-Tropez now who you believe might bear you a grudge?' asked Poulpe.

'Well, Lara Meyer, of course. She hated me when I was successful and she tried to ruin me with that debacle of my boutique opening.'

Poulpe wrote rapidly in his old-fashioned notebook as Sophie expounded on the long-ago event, while Gabrielle took notes on her cell phone.

'Hmmm, now is there someone else who is *not* persistently drunk and half-comatose who you believe might bear you a grudge?' enquired Poulpe with an edge of irony.

'Maybe that stupid gigolo she lives with – Fabrizio. He hates me too, I think.'

'You mean Fabrizio Bricconni. Why is that?'

'I rejected him,' Sophie said. 'Last month he came to me and asked if I would sponsor him in some TV show – that *X Factor* thing in a country I'd never heard of. Of course I said no. I would have had to go there to sponsor him and be on TV; become a laughing stock for *him*,' she laughed bitterly. 'He was quite angry – told me it would be a great opportunity to . . . how did he put it? Ah, yes – *to regain my fanbase*. Ha! As if I'd ever lost it!'

'But you are in the same social circle, are you not?'

'We are, unfortunately. I am always civil to him because, as the saying goes, "Keep your friends close, but your enemies closer".'

'What about Mademoiselle Martez?' asked the Captain.

Madeleine Martez was a somewhat mythical figure in Saint-Tropez. A major star in the 1950s, she was now rarely seen either out or at any of the parties. Rumour had it that she and Sophie had been enemies for years although no one ever knew why.

'That cow! She's always hated me, from the very beginning when I moved here. I'm younger than her, and I was more popular in Hollywood. She never made it in Hollywood, you know.'

'I did not know that; I thought she was a big star there?'

'Star? Bah! She did one Hollywood film and that was the end. No one could understand her accent. I speak perfect English, you know.'

'Yes, I know that – most impressive. Well, I think I must interview Ms Martez as soon as possible.'

'Oh, good luck with *that!*' crowed Sophie. 'She's more of a recluse than I am. Too ashamed to be seen because she looks so hideous.'

'Really – I see her photos everywhere,' mused Poulpe.

'Yes, you do, parading around in tiny shorts and bikinis. Yes, you actually do, Captain. What you don't see is that those photographs were taken over fifty years ago . . . when I admit she was good-looking,' she added grudgingly.

'Ah yes, of course!' He scribbled some more then asked, 'Anyone else you can think of, *madame?*'

'Deneuve,' she hissed. 'Catherine has always detested me.'

'Ah, yes.' *This woman is completely deluded*, thought Poulpe.

At over seventy, Catherine Deneuve was still one of the most popular Gallic actresses. The chances that she resented Sophie

Silvestri, who had definitely seen better days, were slim to nil. Still, he'd have one of his colleagues in Paris check her out.

∞

François Lardon stood naked in front of the mirror, admiring himself.

'You are gorgeous,' he said, smiling at his stunning reflection. Deeply tanned, six foot three of rippling muscles, black curly hair and a movie-star face, he was well aware of his genetic luck, and he spent plenty of time taking care of his gift.

He hummed as he anointed himself with Tom Ford's latest men's scent, and admired the tattoo on his shoulder, which he always kept covered with a shirt or a white T-shirt. It was a fierce black and yellow snake that coiled down one arm, its viperish tongue reaching out to devour a tiger's head etched around his left nipple. Underneath was a motto in Latin: *Causa Mortis* – cause of death.

Tonight he was going out with the luscious Gabrielle Poulpe, and he couldn't wait. Although he pulled girls regularly, young tourists from Scandinavia and America, they were all too easy. They were all suckers for a handsome waiter in white and he never slept with them more than once. Gabrielle was different. Conquering her was like flying too close to the sun and the danger was exhilarating. And besides, if he wasn't mistaken, she hadn't had much experience with men. He wanted her, and he was going to get her.

She had insisted that he pick her up at Le Gorille, a restaurant in front of the port, but he was late. He liked to keep them waiting just a little bit – it kept them insecure. She looked beautiful in tight pale blue jeans, sandals and a flowered top. She wore no make-up as usual, but her red curls had been freshly washed and framed her face perfectly.

He took her to see an old Fellini movie at the cinema in the Place des Lices and then he bought her dinner at a charming little *boîte* in one of the back streets of Saint-Tropez. Gabrielle found him amusing and intelligent, full of gossip and anecdotes about the rich denizens of the Côte d'Azur, where he claimed to have been a waiter for three years now, with an ambition to become a master chef, he told her.

When he walked her back to her car in the underground parking lot, he kissed her gently. Gabrielle was leaning back against her car and she enjoyed the touch of the handsome waiter's lips on hers, the feel of his body against hers. But when his kiss began to be more insistent she pulled back.

'No, I'm sorry, I can't,' she said.

'Why? Don't you like me?'

'Yes, but please, I'm working on a case and I cannot get involved with anyone. Try and understand.' She wriggled free and jumped into her car. 'But I enjoyed the evening, François, and I promise we'll do it again when this is all over.'

'Okay.' He slumped against a concrete pillar, watching the car's rear lights disappear up the incline.

'Frigid bitch,' he muttered. 'I'll get you yet.'

∞

Carlotta and Sophie had become extremely close during Sophie's recuperation. Sophie loved Carlotta's freshness and innocence, often remarking, 'You remind me of myself when I was young.' Carlotta had recently confided to Sophie the horrors of her dreadful marriage to Nicanor and Sophie had been most understanding and sympathetic.

'But now, my dear, you must forget all that distress. You must move on.'

'I want to,' said Carlotta, 'I really want to put that nightmare life with Nicanor behind me, but when I try to ... to become closer to Nick, those awful memories come flooding back. Oh, God! Nick is being so patient with me. He loves me and I think I love him, but I've still not been able to ... to ...'

'To have sex with him,' Sophie said firmly but gently.

'Yes. He wants to come and live with me but I'm frightened.'

'Of what?'

'Of giving myself and then getting hurt again.'

'My dear, you simply cannot go on reliving the past. The past is history, tomorrow a mystery, and today is the present – which is a gift! You must live for now, Carlotta. You're too young and beautiful not to have a rich, fulfilling life with someone who loves you. You know I'm an astrology buff and you and Nick are so compatible. Your signs – Gemini woman and Libra man – denote you are meant for each other.'

'I hope so,' said Carlotta haltingly. 'He has asked me to marry him.'

'One step at a time, my dear. Let him move in with you and then ... well, just let Nature take its course.'

'You know so much about men, Sophie,' said Carlotta admiringly.

'My dear, not at all. What I know about men actually could be written on the head of a pin. They are not all so different. Remember that book – *Men Are from Mars, Women Are from Venus?*'

Carlotta nodded.

'That about sums it up. I never married, Carlotta, because I became bored of my lovers too soon. And there were many, many men.' Reminiscences flooded Sophie. 'I've had many lovers from all walks of life, all ages, all nationalities and religions – and yet I still don't know what makes men tick.' She laughed. 'But an expert blow job usually pleases them all!'

Carlotta joined in the girlish laughter then said, 'Do you think it's true that men think about sex five times a day, like the research says?'

'Oh no, my dear, it's much more than that. I doubt they ever stop thinking about it!'

'Have you ever watched porn movies?' Carlotta asked tentatively.

'Oh heavens! I did once or twice, long ago, when they had some sort of plot and the sex scenes were quite erotic.' She shook her head. 'Now what passes for adult entertainment is nothing but filth.'

'Oh, I agree,' said Carlotta. 'Nicanor used to watch the most revolting images.' She shuddered. 'I can't even begin to tell you.'

'Don't,' said Sophie. 'I can imagine. I don't know what has happened to romance, my dear. It has been totally demystified, because sex is served up on a plate twenty-four/seven and it's as easy to get as a hamburger at McDonald's.'

Sophie looked at Carlotta with motherly tenderness, 'Give Nick a chance, dear. I'm sure it will work out for you two.'

∞

By dint of persuasion and coercion, Carlotta, Nick and Adolpho managed to get Sophie to agree to attend her own birthday party at Carlotta's rented villa.

It was a balmy warm night, and for once there was no mistral wind to blow the ladies' hair into disarray. The house was pretty and elegantly furnished, without the vulgar ostentation of many of the newer homes in Saint-Tropez. Sophie, having spent three hours with her 'glam squad', arrived early, looking beautiful in a 'Valentino Red' gown that showed off her creamy cleavage to perfection, and a blonde bouffant wig upon which Adolpho had fixed a white gardenia. Although she lived close to the beach, Sophie never took the sun.

'I don't want to look like a wrinkled hag like some actresses who live here,' she sniffed.

Needless to say, none of her celebrity friends had shown up for the event, with the exception of Dirk Romano, still coasting on the mischievous charm that had made him famous back in the 1970s. His cheeky bedroom eyes hidden by trademark shades, he came to the party alone, looking for action and not doubting for one minute that he would get some. He had always been catnip for females of all ages. Dirk walked over to the coolly beautiful Vanessa Meyer and unsuccessfully tried to charm her. Her husband was nowhere to be seen, but Vanessa seemed unconcerned as she chatted animatedly with the gigolo Fabrizio Bricconni. *What was he doing here without Lara?* Dirk thought. *That bitch is not going to take too kindly to her boyfriend chatting up her ex-husband's present wife.*

Dirk's thespian instincts were finely tuned and he noticed the definite body language between them. The way Vanessa smiled at Fabrizio while playing with her long hair gave the game away, and his hands lightly resting on her elegant waist, sheathed in silver silk jersey, left no one in any doubt. Not that anyone really gave a damn in Saint-Tropez. Flirting and affairs were rife, but none of them were taken very seriously.

'If Lara sees that she'll shit a brick!' Dirk whispered to Monty.

'Yeah, and if Jonathan sees it, ditto!' he grinned.

Zarina and Sin arrived fresh from Ibiza, wearing matching silk togas that barely covered their panties. Although they had announced they were 'in love' with each other, nevertheless they made a beeline for Dirk. He made no protest at all when they bundled him down to the pool-house to smoke a joint.

Sophie was doing the room in a flurry of red chiffon and feathers. The years had fallen away from her face, thanks to Adolpho's brilliant ministrations. She looked vibrant and was charming the pants off everyone. Marvin Rheingold stood in the doorway observing her and wondering again if it was perhaps not such a bad idea to cast her in *Suddenly, Last Summer*. Tonight she looked as if she could show the vulnerability that Katharine Hepburn had evoked so brilliantly. He thought he almost had a lock on Angelina Jolie for the Elizabeth Taylor role. 'That is, if she doesn't adopt any more kids,' he told his partner Joe Schwartzman, and he was hoping for Ryan Reynolds for the Monty Clift role.

'If I get those two it could be the casting coup of the decade,' he told Roberto LoBianco, who was investing some money in the project, as they smoked cigars while observing the fray.

'Yeah, but if you don't get Reynolds and Angelina, what do you do then? Aren't you supposed to start shooting in two months?'

'Sure, sure, I know. And we do need the weather, but it's still good down here as late as October,' said Marvin.

'How long did you say you needed to shoot in Saint-Sébastien?' asked LoBianco.

'Four weeks maximum. Then we'll do the studio stuff in Nice for six or seven. We should wrap by November.'

'Well, Saint-Sébastien is all ready for you,' said Roberto. 'It's an Eden – gorgeous beaches, unpolluted water and no goddamn tourists gawking at your stars. A producer's heaven.'

Marvin smiled. 'Talking of heaven, I can't wait to see Angelina on the beach in that white bathing suit Liz wore.'

'Wow, was she hot!' said Roberto.

'Yeah, well, Angie will be hotter,' said Marvin.

But he was worried. Miss Jolie's agent had told him an hour ago that he hadn't a hope in hell of getting the delectable actress to appear in *Suddenly, Last Summer*.

'Even if it is artistic shit, she's booked up till 2020 – writing scripts, directing scripts. No way, man, sorry,' barked the workaholic CAA agent.

Marvin's backers were banking on him getting a major star for the female lead. He had many contacts, and tomorrow he planned on calling some of them. In a conference call the previous night, one of his backers had said, 'None of today's bankable actresses have the "in-yer-face" sexiness that Marilyn, Ava and Liz had. Where are the broads like that today?'

'Gwynnie could do it,' Marvin replied.

'Yeah, but she ain't got no sex appeal,' the backer retorted.

Marvin reluctantly agreed, his mind working overtime. He'd tried to interest Cara Delevingne, but then who wouldn't? He was considering Margot Robbie, who was so hot in *The Wolf of Wall Street*. If he couldn't get her, he might have to cast an unknown.

Yeah, that might be the cool thing to do, Marvin thought. *Great publicity – the search for Scarlett O'Hara in* Gone with the Wind *had become the stuff of legend. The search for a beautiful fiery actress to replace Elizabeth Taylor in* Suddenly, Last Summer *could be mega.*

He strolled over to Sophie, who was gracefully accepting congratulations, compliments and presents from the guests. A burly security guard took each gift from Sophie and handed it to an even burlier security guard, both pre-arranged by Captain Poulpe. The gifts would be thoroughly checked before Sophie was allowed to see them. Marvin offered his gift, a tiny blue box from Tiffany.

'Oh, darling, thank you,' trilled Sophie. 'I always say the tinier the box, the bigger the present, and you know how I love presents.'

Marvin grinned. Boy, did he know! When Sophie was at the

top of the tree in Hollywood, she'd had a clause in her contract that the producers had to give her a gift every day of shooting. It could cost anything from a hundred dollars to ten thousand dollars, but she had to have one. Due to her immense stardom at the time, her gifts kept on coming, and some of them were legendary. She preferred jewellery, and often got it, but she was always delighted to accept a stuffed animal or a fine-art book or even a scented candle. But the producers knew that to stay in her good graces, toys were not enough all the time, so every movie budget had a contingency for 'Sophie Silvestri's treats'. To Sophie, the more stuff people gave her, the more she believed she was loved, and tonight, judging by the amount of gifts she was receiving, she was very loved indeed.

'How'ya doing, honey?' Marvin gave her the Hollywood hug and she gave him a kiss that left a big red lipstick mark on his cheek.

'I'm wonderful, Marvin, so happy. This is such a lovely party that sweet girl Carlotta is giving me.'

'Yeah, sure.' Marvin looked around for some celebrities but he could only see the usual suspects. 'I thought Lauren Bacall was coming?'

'Oh, poor Betty! She died last year, didn't you hear?'

'Shit, I've been down here too long prepping the movie! Y'know, I've been thinking about you for Violet Venable. Are you interested?'

Was she interested? Of course she was! Mrs Venable was a plum role made iconic by Katharine Hepburn. But she knew never to show too much interest when a prime role was dangled before one like a carrot. Negotiations would be necessary – as Bette Davis once remarked, 'I'm not to be had for the price of a packet of peanuts.' Although Sophie hadn't worked in years, the name Sophie Silvestri was still very well known, and she was considered a star even though many people believed she was dead.

'I might be a little old for the part,' she said coyly. The words stuck in her throat, but subtle self-deprecation was always attractive when talking to producers.

'Nonsense! You can play sixty easy. No problem. Honey, the studio is thinkin' about you!' *Even though Hepburn was fifty-three when she played it*, he thought.

'So am I . . . on your wish list?' she smiled.

He gave her a swift peck in the cheek, careful not to smudge the immaculate *maquillage*, and said, 'Keep the faith, honey. Keep the faith.'

She'd be good as the wealthy harridan Violet trying to bribe a young doctor to lobotomise her beautiful niece, he thought. In the story, the character of Catherine, who hopefully would be played by Angelina Jolie, had gone on holiday with Violet's son Sebastian, who died in such terrible circumstances that it had sent the young girl insane. Roberto had told Marvin that the beaches of Saint-Sébastien could certainly pass for the Spanish resort on film, where the Tennessee Williams play had originally been set. It was a torrid, terrifying plot with many twists and turns, and Marvin was convinced he could make it into a big, money-making blockbuster.

'But the cast, the cast,' he muttered to himself, thinking back to the phone call with Angelina Jolie's agent. The decisive 'no way' brooked no argument. 'Who do I get to play Catherine?' he mused. Of course if he could get Meryl or Mirren to play Violet that would guarantee immediate interest with the studio, who had still not committed to the extra millions he needed. 'Then we say bye-bye to Ms Silvestri,' he reflected philosophically.

Everyone at the party was milling about drinking mojitos, which were Sophie's favourite cocktail. The DJ was playing mellow mood music for the cocktail hour, and there was much gossip about the bomb in the box of chocolates that had killed Sophie's maid. They were surmising who could hate Sophie that much. The answer was a lot of people. Several of the Saint-Tropez regulars were talking about jumping ship and leaving for Monaco or Ibiza.

'I've had enough, I can't sleep at night,' announced Blanche Phillips to Charlie Chalk. She was cuddling her new pooch, an even uglier mutt than the one Maximus had fallen on and killed. 'Aren't you scared, Charlie? I mean your boyfriend was *murdered* in your own garden. How can you live there any more?'

'He wasn't my boyfriend, *dear*, he was my husband,' said Charlie frostily. 'We don't know for sure if he was murdered and I love Saint-Tropez, so no one is going to scare me away.'

'Well, Henry and I have had enough.' Blanche started kissing her dog's brown wet lips. 'We've put the villa on the market,' she whispered, 'and so have several of our neighbours.'

'No great loss to society,' Charlie said sarcastically. 'We'll be glad to get rid of the geriatric set,' he added under his breath as he walked over to greet Maximus and Fabrizio. He noticed the latter seemed quite taken with the lovely Vanessa Meyer who was standing between them. He observed that the two of them seemed at ease with each other; the kind of cosy camaraderie that lovers have.

Carlotta stood at the bar with Nick, impressed by the eclectic group of guests who had turned out to honour Sophie.

'Oh, look. Isn't that Tony Blair?' she asked.

Nick glanced towards the suntanned, middle-aged man surrounded by a coterie of sexily dressed young women.

'My goodness, he looks like a used-car salesman,' said Carlotta.

'Well, it's not used cars he deals in, it's new diamonds,' Nick replied.

'What do you mean?'

'That, my sweet, is Bert Burrows, otherwise known as "the diamond geezer". He carries bags of the jewels around with him like some people carry bags of Maltesers. No wonder he's so popular with those gals.'

They watched as Bert removed a huge emerald-cut diamond ring from his pocket and waved it in front of the women with a satisfied leer. They all passed it around with 'oohs' and 'aahs'.

'Just a little bait,' laughed Nick. 'A bit of a carrot to get them either into the sack or persuade one of their boyfriends or husbands to buy the thing.'

'And do they?' asked Carlotta.

'Sometimes – he's not called the "diamond geezer" for nothing.'

Lara arrived, slightly unsteady on her feet and wearing a mauve Lurex dress so tight that her breasts squeezed out of the top like toothpaste. Maximus saw Lara first. She seemed out of sorts and lost, but that was not unusual for her recently.

'Head her off at the pass – I'll take care of Vanessa,' he hissed to Fabrizio. 'Get your ass over to her now – *andiamo!* – or I think the brown stuff may hit the air conditioning!' He laughed at his wit and gave Fabrizio a shove, who reluctantly slouched over to his sulky mistress.

∞

Gabrielle was outside in the garden of Carlotta's villa, double-checking Sophie's presents, when François came out of the house.

'I'm taking a break,' he smiled at her and she smiled back. Then he offered her a cigarette. She shook her head and he asked, 'Mind if I do?'

She had been dodging his calls, but he was nevertheless extremely friendly.

'I had a great time last week. Maybe one day I can cook for you in my apartment,' he said.

'Maybe,' she replied enigmatically.

They exchanged pleasantries and Gabrielle subtly steered the conversation towards the murders, deftly probing his recollections about the various episodes. François simply shrugged, lit a cigarette, and reiterated that he hadn't seen anything suspicious at any of the incidents.

The bomb-disposal expert, whom Captain Poulpe had summoned from Paris, was examining the presents with the help of a large Alsatian trained to detect any signs of explosives. He looked up at François as he lit his cigarette.

'Move away, man – move!' he barked. 'This is a no smoking zone.'

François bowed sarcastically, moved a couple of steps and continued smoking his cigarette. 'So when *are* you going to let me cook my or coq au vin for you?' he whispered to Gabrielle who wondered if she had imagined him emphasising the word *coq*. 'I miss you – you've been avoiding me.'

'I've been very busy.' Gabrielle was flustered. She was attracted to this man but at the same time she knew that starting an affair with him – for there was no doubt that that was what François was aiming for – was a bad idea. There were four deaths that were keeping both her father and her awake at night, and several unexplained and terrifying incidents that seemed to have no rhyme or reason to them.

'Hold on a moment.' She turned as Gerald the bomb-disposal specialist held up a black gift-wrapped box bound with black satin ribbon. 'I don't like the look of this one. I think I'm going to have to open it.' Putting on protective gloves and goggles, he moved to an empty part of the garden. The dog followed, sniffing eagerly, and Gerald started cutting open the black box.

François stamped out his cigarette, blew a cheeky kiss to Gabrielle and went back inside to the party.

∞

The next morning, Sophie sat in an elegant wicker armchair on her terrace, surrounded by all the gifts she had received from the previous night's party. Carlotta and Adolpho sat nearby, exclaiming in delight over the gifts and, in some cases, mock horror.

'Oh my, look at this from Blanche and Henry!' crowed Adolpho. 'It's a jewelled salad bowl with matching servers. How on earth could you eat out of this? The Swarovski crystals would fall into the lettuce!'

'Crunchy – like bacon bits,' laughed Carlotta.

'Oh, that's nice!' Sophie had opened Marvin's Tiffany box and held up a gold heart encrusted by diamonds on a chain.

'Very pretty. Do you want to wear it now?' asked Carlotta.

'Oh, I am bedecked!' laughed Sophie, who had already donned various bracelets, rings and scarves gifted to her.

'Enough already – I've been spoiled . . . but where's that black box I saw?' Adolpho and Carlotta exchanged glances.

'What black box?'

'You know perfectly well, I saw it in the pile last night. Now, now, what have you done with it?'

'I don't think you will like it,' said Carlotta gently.

'Don't tell me what I would or wouldn't like,' Sophie snapped. 'Show it to me!'

Reluctantly, Carlotta handed it over, and Sophie opened the box.

'Oh, my God!' she gasped, staring at a framed portrait of herself. 'I can't believe someone would do something so horrible.'

The picture was an old cover of *Paris Match*. It showed a young Sophie lying on her chaise longue surrounded by seven or eight cats. Each of the cat's faces had been carefully cut out, and pasted on each was a picture of a hideous grinning skull. Where Sophie's face would have been, another paper skull was pasted – this one screaming hideously like the figure in the Munch painting, *The Scream*. There was also a note, which Captain Poulpe had already dusted for fingerprints along with the frame and glass. 'You are never safe, bitch.'

'Oh, my God!' Sophie threw the picture and note to the ground. 'Who hates me enough to have created this horror? Who? *Who?*'

In a café in Port Grimaud, a man sat sipping a café crème and smoking a cigarette. He smiled to himself, that should scare the old bitch, he thought, but it's just the beginning of what I've got planned next. . .

CHAPTER TWENTY-SIX

'Are you fucking my wife?'

Coming out of the shower of the Byblos hotel gym after his afternoon workout, wet and naked except for the gold medallions swinging around his neck, Fabrizio felt at a definite disadvantage. He quickly removed the towel from his neck and attempted to tie it around his waist, but Jonathan was having none of it. He ripped the towel from Fabrizio's hands and went nose to nose with him.

'Are you? Are you, you little punk? Are you screwing Vanessa?'

His tone was so ominously calm that Fabrizio's knees started shaking. Whether this was a reaction from his soaking wet body or from fear, he didn't know. He'd heard the stories about the legendary Jonathan Meyer. He took no prisoners, either in the boardroom or the bedroom, and if he didn't get what he wanted by fair means, force was his next power play.

Fabrizio stammered, 'Of course not – what a ridiculous idea!' He cupped his genitals then changed his mind. He didn't have to hide what he called his 'noble tool'. Vanessa had whispered to him last week, 'You have the most beautiful cock I've ever seen,' and Fabrizio had to admit, having seen a few himself, she had exquisite taste.

Nevertheless, how the fuck had Jonathan found out? Vanessa would never have confessed to their affair – not in a million years.

There was no question of that. She had even admitted to Fabrizio that he was only the second man she had slept with since marrying Jonathan. Well, it was only a tiny fib . . . Who the other man had been, he didn't know: she would only tell him that he was an actor. Fabrizio, immediately assuming she had been attracted to this other guy for the same reason she'd been attracted to him, and with the innate curiosity of the well-endowed, was curious to know who might have a bigger one.

'I don't believe you, you little cocksucker,' Jonathan roared as he shook Fabrizio and banged his head against the glass shower door.

'I swear to you, I didn't,' he gasped, surprised at the older man's strength. Although in his fifties, Jonathan Meyer had the powerful musculature of a man much younger and he was furious. *Like a mad bull*, thought Fabrizio.

'If you did, if you fucked her, you scumbag, I'll find out and then I'll cut your balls off and stick them down your throat until you choke to death.'

Fabrizio started to panic. Jonathan's hands were around his neck, and he was attempting to squeeze the life out of him as he yelled, 'Did you? Did you screw my wife, you asshole? Come on, tell me!'

'For Christ's sake, Jonathan, stop it! I didn't fuck her, I swear on my . . . on my . . . mother's life,' he croaked.

Just then an attendant came running over and tried to pull Jonathan away, saying, 'I'm sorry, sir, but this is a quiet zone.'

Jonathan gave the man a terrifying glare and shouted, 'Get the fuck out of here!'

'Oh well, if you're going to strangle someone, at least please keep it down,' stammered the attendant, and scurried away.

Jonathan took his hands off Fabrizio's throat, throwing him down on the marble floor like a used towel. Bending over him, he whispered menacingly, 'If I find out you screwed my wife, your life won't be worth living, you bum! I'll fucking ruin you, you little shit!'

Jonathan straightened up, adjusted his toupee in the mirror and strode out of the shower room. Fabrizio dragged himself on to a bench shivering with fear. What a fool he'd been. Yes, Vanessa was gorgeous and sexy, but the fucking he got from her wasn't worth the fucking-over he would get from one of the most power-ful and influential men in America. He didn't need this. He didn't need Vanessa, but he had to find out how – and more importantly *if* – Jonathan Meyer really knew about their affair.

∞

The two children pranced down Tahiti Beach from the hotel above it. Their mother had told them not to go near the water as it was too early for the lifeguards to be on duty, and the beach boys hadn't yet started setting out the bright orange loungers and matching umbrellas.

Emily and Alexander were shrieking with childish enthusiasm as they played along the wide expanse of clean beach. The temper-ature was already in the high seventies and it was such fun being the only kids down there. Alex was bending down to pick up their ball, which had rolled near the water's edge, when he saw something floating in the shallow water. He picked it up and looked at it curiously.

'What is it?' yelled his sister.

'It's . . . it's . . .' Ten-year-old Alex blushed as he held up a ripped black Lycra bikini bottom covered in golden hearts.

'Oh, silly – it's just panties.' Emily, who was a year older, scoffed.

'What are they doing in the water?' Alex asked.

'Who cares? C'mon, let's play ball before the beach fills up,' and with that she threw the ball to him, but it bounced so far away that Alex had to run across half the beach to retrieve it. As he bent over again he saw something that almost made him sick.

The naked body of a girl was lying face up in the water. Her long blonde hair was entangled in seaweed and crabs were crawling over what was once a beautiful face. Alex shrieked with fear; running to Emily, he grabbed her hands and together they went racing up to the hotel's beach restaurant, yelling for help.

'There's a girl in the water,' Alex screamed. 'She's *dead!*'

'What? What has happened?' The waiter François – still filling in for his sick friend – rushed out from the kitchen to the bar, where the hysterical children had collapsed on to a banquette in floods of tears. Within minutes everyone at the hotel was awake and clustered around Emily and Alex, who could only point towards the beach in horror-stricken panic at what they had seen.

Captain Poulpe and Gabrielle were on the scene quickly.

'There is no question about it. This time it is definitely murder,' said Captain Poulpe.

'Oh, my God! Who would want to kill Zarina?' Gabrielle felt faint.

'A very sick person indeed,' replied her father.

Within minutes a small group of gendarmes arrived and quickly shielded the naked body of Zarina with a tarpaulin tent; but, as if alerted by jungle drums, 'lookey-loos' and gawpers descended on the beach in droves.

'What hotel were they staying at?' Captain Poulpe asked Gabrielle, who had been keeping close tabs on everyone.

'The Tropezien Sun,' she replied.

'Go check out her room,' he said. '*Now* Gabrielle.'

Gabrielle jumped on her motorbike and, arriving at the girl's suite, found it empty, but a complete mess. Clothes, make-up and jewellery were littered around the room, but there was no sign of

Sin. Strangely, both their cell phones were still plugged in. Gabrielle carefully photographed everything, along with the girls' diaries, iPads, and anything else that could give any clues as to Zarina's murder. She then got on her cell phone to the gendarmerie to round up the forensics team.

∞

Vanessa Meyer came back to her boat from a morning at the gym to find the singer Sin's body trussed up in her closet. When she opened the polished blond wooden doors of her built-in wardrobe, she discovered it. She had no idea who the girl was, but whoever put her there had a sense of humour, for they had taken the time to wrap the corpse in Vanessa's newest gold lace Oscar de la Renta gown and thrown a sable stole over the girl's battered face.

Vanessa's hysterical screams brought Jonathan and most of the boat's crew running into her stateroom. Sin's skinny tanned legs were sticking out at an awkward twisted angle and a little mermaid tattoo was visible on her left ankle. Her toenails were painted bright pick with tiny Swarovski diamonds stuck on them, and she had a silver bracelet on her other ankle.

Jonathan cradled the weeping Vanessa. A take-charge guy, always in control, he immediately instructed Nanny to take little Jonny to the beach, away from all the furore, 'But be available to talk to the cops when they arrive,' he added.

It wasn't long before they got there. Captain Poulpe and Gabrielle, followed by several deputies and a swarm of gendarmes, descended on Jonathan's boat, which was moored at the far end of Saint-Tropez harbour. Although there were only a few boats nearby, the word got out fast on the streets, so within the hour the entire village knew about another dead girl and soon the jetty was swarming with the curious. Everyone was stunned, none more than the adrenalin-filled Jonathan and Vanessa, who sat in their elegantly furnished salon being interviewed by Captain Poulpe. Poulpe had cordoned off the boat as a crime scene.

'Where were you last night?' Captain Poulpe directed himself to Jonathan first.

'I had returned from a business trip to Paris in the afternoon,' said Jonathan. 'I went to the Byblos gym then I had dinner at the Café de Paris with a business acquaintance.'

'Who would that be, *monsieur*?' asked Poulpe.

'One of my NY partners, Sam Barton – he can confirm that.'

'Please give his details to Lieutenant Gabrielle Poulpe, *s'il vous plaît*, so we can speak to him. And after dinner?'

'Then we played *chemin de fer* at the casino until about three a.m. After that my chauffer drove me back here.'

'When did you arrive on the boat?' asked Gabrielle.

'About four thirty or five a.m. – I went straight to my stateroom and went to sleep. I only woke up when I heard my wife screaming.'

'And you, *madame*?'

Vanessa froze. How could she possibly tell Captain Poulpe, let alone in front of Jonathan, that last night she had met Fabrizio for a few hours at the discreet little *pension* he kept in a back street? She had meant to meet just to tell him that, because of Jonathan's suspicions, she couldn't see him any more, but when she told him that Jonathan was in Paris, one thing led to another and before she knew it he had cajoled her into bed for 'one final fuck', as he'd whispered.

No, there was no way she could ever admit this. It would be the end of her marriage and the end of this glamorous life that she loved. Jonathan would probably even take Jonny away from her.

'*Madame?*' Captain Poulpe was staring at her impassively, his pen poised over his old-fashioned notebook.

She felt herself flush and started to weep even more, but the Captain waited patiently, as did Jonathan.

'Yes, where were you, Vanessa? I called you twice but there was no answer,' asked Jonathan. He was suspicious now, but not for the same reason as Poulpe.

Vanessa was panicked. *Think, think, think – she had to think!* In between sobs, she said, 'I . . . I did a little shopping in the afternoon. I was at Dior for a while . . .'

Gabrielle busily tapped the screen of her iPad.

'Yes, I bought a dress, actually . . .' said Vanessa.

'Yes, and after that?' asked Poulpe.

'Oh, then I went to Sénéquier for an aperitif, at about seven o'clock.'

'By yourself, *madame*? Did anyone see you?'

'Oh, yes, several friends – Blanche and Henry Phillips. I sat with them for a while.' At least that part was true. Then she had a brainwave.

'And after that, *madame*?'

'And then I drove to my brother Jeremy's apartment in Gassin and we dined together.'

She slumped on to Jonathan's shoulder in another paroxysm of tears while frantically thinking. Could she get to her phone in time to call her brother to supply an alibi for her? And would he do that? They had never been close, and although he lived nearby, he was pretty much a recluse, only socialising with a small group of artisans and painters.

When Gabrielle heard that name she froze. Could it be? Could Jeremy Anstruther-Formby actually be Vanessa Meyer's brother? She surreptitiously googled Vanessa on her iPad and saw the Wikipedia entry: 'Vanessa Rosemary Meyer is the third wife of tycoon Jonathan Meyer, formerly the Honourable Vanessa Anstruther-Formby. Born in Gloucestershire, England on 20

August 1983, Vanessa is the fourth child of Lord and . . .' Gabrielle didn't need to read any more. She quickly deleted the search but her heart started to pound. She hadn't had any contact with Jeremy since that horrible afternoon five years ago. He had tried to call her several times afterwards to beg her forgiveness, but that vile scene in the back of his antique shop was branded in her mind and she refused to talk to him, much less see him again.

'Please don't ever contact me again,' she had written in a note she had posted to his shop. 'It's over.'

She always went out of her way to avoid his little shop on the Rue du Clocher, and whenever thoughts of him crept into her mind, she banished them with an iron will.

She had actually caught sight of him in the Place des Lices a few months ago. He looked puffy and decadent, his blond hair lank and laced with traces of grey, and there were lines running from his nose to his mouth. Even his usually immaculate clothes looked untidy, his jacket rumpled and creased, his shirt none too clean.

For the rest of the interview, Vanessa could only think of call-ing her brother before the police contacted him. Asking to go to the bathroom, she thanked God she had left her mobile there. Her brother picked up after the second ring.

'Jeremy? Darling, it's Vanessa.'

'Sister dearest! Long time no speak. And to what do I owe this honour, my dear?'

'Jeremy please, I need a favour. It's major. Please, please listen to me, darling, very carefully . . .'

∞

When the news broke of the deaths of two of the most famous young celebrities in the world, Saint-Tropez was swamped once again with camera crews and media from all over the world. Gabrielle and Captain Poulpe were inundated with paparazzi and reporters screaming questions at them wherever they went. The press was wild for any quotes from the other celebrities. Dirk Romano, after a painful interview where he disclosed that he'd had a couple of sexual flings with the two girls earlier in the summer, summoned a private plane and flew out to Ibiza.

'Who could possibly have murdered these girls?' asked Charlie as he took his morning coffee at Sénéquier with Adolpho. 'Because this time there's no question – not like my poor Spencer. Those poor little girls were viciously bludgeoned to death. It's definitely murder,' he said sadly.

Marvin Rheingold had headed off to Saint-Sébastien to scout locations for *Suddenly, Last Summer*. He had decided to cast Sophie in the Katharine Hepburn role, but was still holding auditions in LA with the half-dozen other contenders for the Elizabeth Taylor role. Sophie stayed in her house with Adolpho and began a rigorous regime of diet and exercise in an effort to shave fifteen years off her seventy-five. She was excited about her first important role in years and determined to be an Oscar contender.

Because Jonathan's boat was now cordoned off, he and Vanessa were forced to move to the Château de la Messardière hotel, with strict instructions not to leave Saint-Tropez. They were prime suspects, along with the rest of the boat crew.

∞

Vanessa had managed to slip away to meet Jeremy in the back room of his tiny antique shop by telling her husband that she had a standing appointment to get her roots done. Captain Poulpe had called Jeremy earlier that morning to confirm her story, but Jeremy, having spoken to his hysterical sister the night before, had been cagey and revealed nothing.

'We will need to interview you at our headquarters tomorrow morning,' Poulpe ordered.

'Of course,' he said in his most charming voice. 'I shall be at your sevice.'

∞

'You're a slut, Vanessa. You've always been a slut and you always will be.' Jeremy spat it out, his voice laced with scorn.

'How can you say such a thing?' Vanessa moaned. Her face was tear-stained and she looked exhausted.

'I don't give a fuck who you fucked, darling. I know perfectly well you could never kill anyone – you couldn't even drown the kittens we found when we were kids – *sooo* soft-hearted.' He laughed in his supercilious way and drew on a long brown cigarillo.

'Well, will you lie for me, even though you think I'm a slut?' she pleaded. 'It will be the end of me, you know. Jonathan will take little Jonny away from me – I know he will. He'll cut me off – I'll be destitute!'

'Well, my darling, we wouldn't want that, would we? Lovely aristocratic Vanessa Meyer bonking a gigolo at a filthy *pension* while another little slut gets murdered on her husband's boat? Tut-tut-tut! What will the papers say?'

Vanessa was silent. Jeremy seemed to be enjoying her humiliation – he always had, ever since they were children. He was in the driver's seat and he knew it and he loved it.

'Were you alone last night?' Vanessa asked tentatively.

'As luck would have it, my pet, yes, I was. Giorgio was out of town on business, so it was just me and my DVDs,' he laughed. 'You're a lucky girl, Vanessa, but . . .' He leaned back and laced his fingers behind his head. 'What's in it for me, sister dearest?'

'Whatever you want,' Vanessa gulped. 'Money?'

'Of course money, you silly goose – it's what makes the world go round, and haven't you got a lot? Does the old man give you an allowance?'

'Of course,' she said quietly. 'Jeremy, I can give you . . . whatever you ask for.'

'A million,' he said simply. 'A million dollars, darling – that's less than it would be in euros, and only what I deserve for perjury, even if it is for my darling sis.'

'A million?' Vanessa asked haltingly. 'I don't . . . I don't exactly have that much, Jeremy. I could come up with one hundred thousand in cash. I can give you the rest in jewellery if that would suit you?'

'Diamond jewellery?' he asked. She nodded. 'That would suit me just fine, darling. Perfect. Portable wealth. I shall see you tomorrow then at the prefecture, or wherever they want us to have our little get-together.'

He stood up to usher her to the door. 'Go get your roots done, darling – they need it.'

'Thanks, Jeremy, I really appreciate it.'

'*De rien, cherie*. What are brothers for? Blood is thicker than water, sweetie.' He bent down to kiss her and whispered in her ear, 'And don't forget the diamonds, darling – they're thicker than anything. I'll see you *demain*.'

∞

Saint-Tropez was in uproar. The ghastly murders made everyone a potential suspect since Zarina and Sin had rubbed many people up the wrong way with their cute but crazy behaviour and their devil-may-care attitude, rudeness and blatant drug-taking.

Vanessa and her brother Jeremy had sat for four hours at the prefecture being grilled by the French police, Interpol and the FBI. Vanessa wept through most of the sessions, much to the annoyance of Captain Poulpe, and the contempt of her brother.

Poulpe himself questioned François Lardon, the waiter who

had been working at Tahiti Beach, where Zarina's body was found. Because he'd been at the scene close to the time that forensics had provided for the girl's death, he was a prime suspect. After Poulpe's grilling, he was remanded to police headquarters in Nice, where he was interrogated intensely in a process known as *garde à vue*. He was placed in a holding cell and subjected to several hours of fierce, videotaped interrogation. At the end he was released due to lack of evidence, but Gabrielle and her father still had their suspicions about the waiter. François was still pressuring Gabrielle to go on another date and offering to cook for her. In an effort to probe further, she had decided to accept one of his invitations to sample his cooking and they set a date.

'I will fix you the most superb beef bourguignon you have ever tasted,' he told her. 'Or would you prefer my coq . . .'

'I think you should go,' said Captain Poulpe. 'Check him out; see if you can find anything – anything that could incriminate him. We've had no luck so far with anyone – all their alibis check out.'

∞

Having accepted François's offer, a few days later Gabrielle drove up to his home, which was actually a guesthouse on the estate of Roberto LoBianco. François answered the door looking handsome and fresh in white shirt and trousers, wearing a striped cook's apron.

'I'm so happy to see you!' he smiled.

She returned the smile, surprised at the almost monk-like severity of the tiny sitting room. There was little furniture – nothing but a black leather sofa in front of a forty-two-inch TV and a state-of-the-art music system that was playing some kind of weird wailing oriental music. From the tiny kitchen, however, a delicious smell emanated.

'Please, sit down and try some of this excellent Pétale de Rose. I just have to do a few more things in the kitchen and then I'll join you.' He smiled again. He did have a lot of charm, she thought, and beautiful teeth.

A small table in the corner was set for two, with elegant silver cutlery and cream candles flickering softly. Gabrielle sat on the leather sofa and put her hands down the back of it – nothing there. She asked if she could use the rest room.

'There's only one, I'm afraid, and it's in my bedroom,' he said, popping his head out of the kitchen.

This was lucky, as it meant she would have a chance to check out most of his living quarters by the end of the evening. She quickly opened the doors to his medicine cabinet but found nothing remarkable there, just the usual shaving stuff and a lot of different toothpastes. She checked under a pile of black towels and then went back to the bedroom. The bed was covered in a black and white striped cotton duvet with matching sheets. There was nothing remotely suspicious anywhere in the bedroom or under the bed. In fact, there was precious little of anything.

When François served the food, Gabrielle ate ravenously. She usually cooked for her father and rarely had time herself to eat.

'This is delicious. Where did you learn to cook like this?'

'In Marseille at a little restaurant I worked in. I want to open my own restaurant one day and Mr LoBianco said he would help me.'

'Is that why he lets you stay at his guesthouse?' Gabrielle enquired.

'Yes,' he smiled. 'He loves my cooking, so whenever he has a small dinner party or he wants a meal, I'm on call to serve him in exchange for lodging.'

'Really? I guess you would have cooked for him the night of Zarina and Sin's murders?'

'Yes. For him and a couple of friends.'

265

'And then you were at the beach the next morning when Zarina's body was found?'

He frowned. 'Yes, I was subbing for a friend of mine who was ill. I already told the police all this. Are you interrogating me again?'

'No, no, of course not. I'm police too, you know. I can never switch off,' she laughed. 'So where and how did you meet Mr LoBianco, if that's not too intrusive a question?'

François started to look irritated. 'In Marseille, at the café where I worked. I told you already. Can we talk about something else?'

'Sure,' said Gabrielle lightly, and they started discussing movies they both loved, music and their childhoods. Gabrielle realised as he kept refilling her glass that dinner was not the only thing that François had on the menu that night. But she had prepared herself for this eventuality and the timing could not have been more perfect.

As François placed a glass plate of crème brûlée in front of her and casually brushed an auburn curl away from her cheek, her cell phone rang. She put the call on speaker and her father's voice rang out with great authority. They both heard him say:

'Gabrielle, there has been a break-in at a small villa – you must come and meet me there immediately.'

'Yes, Papa,' she said obediently. 'Of course, I'll be there as soon as possible.'

She took the address and disconnected the call, then turned apologetically to François. 'I'm so sorry, François – duty calls . . . literally. I really enjoyed your bourguignon. You are an excellent cook.'

He looked so crestfallen that she felt a slight twinge of pity for him. He was sweet and funny and he had made an effort with dinner, but she wasn't ready for an affair. In fact, she was not really interested in him at all, except as a possible suspect.

∞

Gabrielle knocked on Lara's door. 'Can I speak to Signor Bricconni?' she shouted through the door.

'What the hell do you want him for?' Lara grumbled, then opened her front door. She looked a total wreck. Her red hair, matted like a bird's nest, stuck out in spikes, her lipstick was smudged around cracked lips and her make-up streaked. She wore a terry-cloth robe that hadn't been washed in many moons.

'We need to know his whereabouts last night. May I come in?'

Reluctantly Lara moved to let her in and Gabrielle caught a strong whiff of stale vodka and some exotic perfume. The woman looked haggard, as if she'd been dieting too much, and her face was gaunt in spite of the Botox and fat injections. *She searched for the fountain of youth and got the fountain of fillers*, Gabrielle thought.

The living room was dark and dirty, and although the furniture and fittings looked expensive, they had a worn-out look. There were ashtrays full of butts and empty glasses everywhere.

Lara lit a cigarette and motioned for Gabrielle to sit.

'Last night my fiancé was here with me,' Lara said flatly.

'Would that be Mr Fabrizio Bricconni?' asked Gabrielle.

'That is correct,' said Lara firmly. 'We were here, we watched TV, I cooked – I can cook, you know – and we went to bed early.'

'I see. Mr Bricconni – where is he now?'

'Here,' said a sleepy voice in another room, from which Fabrizio appeared, bleary-eyed. 'I went for a run this morning but I've been here all night. *Ciao*, darling.'

'*Ciao*, sweetie.'

Was it Gabrielle's imagination, or did Lara shoot a mean and meaningful glance towards her lover? Nevertheless, after a few more questions, Gabrielle left. Their alibis checked out and there were many more people to interview.

'Thank you for your time. You've been most helpful,' Gabrielle said as Fabrizio gallantly escorted her to the door.

As soon as the door closed on Gabrielle, Lara threw the book at Fabrizio.

'*Stronzo, bastardo!* You little shit! Where were you last night, you faithless piece of scum?'

'Okay, okay, okay, I admit it. I was with a woman. For Christ's sake, Lara! I'm sorry, really I'm sorry, but you know I'm just a man – I have needs, Lara my darling, my love, and you have been . . .' He struggled for the words. 'Off games for a while,' he finished lamely.

'Oh, so you can't go three weeks without pussy?' she hissed. 'What's wrong with watching porn and fiddling with your perfectly healthy right hand, huh?'

'For Christ's sake, Lara, you know I hate doing that.'

'Did you fuck those two little sluts?'

'No, absolutely not.'

'So who were you with last night then?'

Fabrizio knew Lara would probably kill him if he told her that he had been with Vanessa.

'Err, well, you don't know her.'

'Try me, I know everyone.'

Fabrizio racked his brain. God, what could he tell her that wouldn't cause even more of a major eruption? He'd have to confess to some indiscretion to get Lara's cooperation. He had been on a long morning run around Saint-Tropez' coast road when he had seen the crowd of onlookers scurrying towards the port. He had stopped a girl to enquire what was going on, and when she told him there had been a murder on Jonathan Meyer's boat he had almost had a heart attack. He'd hotfooted it back home and begged Lara to say that she had been with him if the police came.

Eureka! He had it. 'She's nothing – not even that good-looking,' he confessed humbly.

'I though you were particular about who you fucked?' she sneered.

'It's Betty,' he said.

'Who's Betty?'

'She's the English girl who's been teaching me to sing and dance.'

'Little bitch! I'll give her a piece of my mind. Give me her number.'

'No, no, you can't. She . . . left on a cruise ship . . . to Norway . . . this morning . . . and, and,' he stumbled and fumbled for words, 'I just went to see her for a last lesson . . .'

'And a quick fuck?'

'Yes . . . I mean no – it wasn't meant to happen but it did. I'm so sorry – it was the first time,' he lied lamely.

'Oh, fuck you, Fabrizio, you testosterone-filled asshole!'

'Look, it was just a quickie. It was nothing special!'

'That's too much information,' snapped Lara. 'You know, Fabrizio, I believe this is the end of the line for us.'

Suddenly Lara took command of the situation. She seemed to grow in stature.

'What are you talking about?' Fabrizio said desperately. 'I love you, Lara. You know I do.'

'I don't think you do, sweetie,' she said sadly. 'I'm just a meal ticket for you. You're a pathological narcissist, not to mention a pathological liar. I think you only love yourself. It's sad but true.'

'Not true. Not true at all.' He grabbed her by the collar of the stained dressing gown and tried to kiss her, but she pushed him away with surprising strength.

'Go away, Fabrizio – I don't want to see you any more. Go to Paris – go live with that pimp Maximus. Go to one of your girls, your baby-mammas, and your bastard kids . . .'

Fabrizio looked stunned.

'Yes, I found out about them – all your dirty little secrets. I've had it. So take your silk shirts and your tight pants and get the fuck out of my life!'

With that Lara turned and wearily limped into the bedroom. 'I'm going to go to sleep and when I wake up I don't want to see you or any of your stuff ever again.'

'You're kidding, Lara – you don't mean it?'

'Don't I? We'll see. Right now I'm tired. Tired of life and tired of this pain and I'm really tired of Saint-Tropez. I just wanna go to sleep.'

'Well, you know that they say when a man is tired of Saint-Tropez he is tired of life . . .' Fabrizio tried a touch of humour but it failed.

'That's London, you stupid cunt! Just go, please.'

∞

Gabrielle spent two hours questioning Roberto LoBianco. She thought he was the typical mega-wealthy Eurotrash, but his alibi checked out with François Lardon's and also with one Guido Franciosa, Roberto's other dinner guest that night – the night of the murders.

Gabrielle was not convinced by Roberto's blustering innocence. He appeared to be far too cocky and self-assured, and she disliked his boastful talk of the wonders of Saint-Sébastien island. She was suspicious.

'Before I leave, may I use your rest room?' she enquired guilelessly.

'Of course. In fact you may use my bathroom.' He escorted her gallantly to an over-decorated suite, heavy with black velvet curtains and golden silk hangings around the enormous bed.

She locked the bedroom door, donned some latex gloves and

270

quickly checked out the bathroom cabinet and the chest of drawers. Nothing of interest there, other than the usual sex toys. She knelt on the black and white zebra rug next to the bed and, holding a small flashlight in her teeth, peered under the bed to discover a giant black dildo. She shuddered and then ran her fingers expertly over the fur carpet. She didn't know what she expected to find until her sensitive fingers felt a tiny metallic object stuck on the rug, half hidden under the silk valance. She gently prised it free. It was some sort of little glittering object, which she immediately put into a plastic evidence bag. She would look at it later with forensics and her father.

She then went to interview the other guest, Guido Franciosa, at the Château de la Messardière. A very large Italian man, he was completely bald, with muscles that bulged, just like his eyes. He came from Marseille, where he ran a successful import/export business.

François Lardon's alibi had fitted perfectly with Roberto LoBianco and Guido Franciosa's, as he had been the waiter at the intimate dinner and then claimed to have slept in the little maid's room off the kitchen with one of the local call girls. LoBianco vouched for it, as did the lanky Russian call girl who had stayed in Roberto's bed all night. The fourth guest was Monty Goldman, who had left his sexy wife to her own devices that night in order to help Roberto entertain the hookers.

'But the girls seemed so stoned and out of it that I don't know if I can believe them,' admitted Gabrielle Poulpe to her father, back at the Prefecture.

∞

And then, after the paparazzi and the press had their day, the Twitter and Facebook trolls came crawling out of the dark undergrowth of the internet to spew forth their filth online. The anonymous scum sat in their lairs and conjured up the most vile and frightening messages with which to skewer their victims.

Fabrizio was the first victim. 'You filthy wop, you raped those two girls and killed them. Die, monster, die!'

Fabrizio, who, after his fight with Lara, had holed himself up in his tiny *pension* room was freaked out. He rushed over to Maximus's hotel only to find him packing.

'What the hell! Where are you going?' he demanded breathlessly.

'Out of this place. The police are letting me go – I'm not a suspect.' Max was throwing shirts and pants indiscriminately into a duffel bag. 'I'm taking the train to Paris until this whole thing blows over. Look, look at this,' he threw his smartphone towards Fabrizio, who read the text message with horror.

'Get out of town, fatso, or I'll put a bomb in your house like I did with that old bitch actress.'

'Jesus!' Fabrizio groaned, 'who sent it?'

'No idea. Scroll up – there's more,' Max said breathlessly. Fabrizio, in his haste, hit a wrong button, and saw with dismay an email from the mothers of his children.

'Tell Fabrizio we've come to Saint-Tropez to find him. We are hungry – we need clothes for the children – we need help. Tell us where he is now because that Lara woman doesn't know, or won't tell us. Help us, Maximus, or we talk to the press, and the police.' Both Raimunda and Carina had signed it.

'Maximus, why didn't you tell me about this? Oh God, they must have gone to see Lara and that's why she kicked me out!'

'Fuck you! I have bigger problems than your CRAP.'

'Oh shit, oh Christ! What can I do? I'm broke, Max. I have nothing to give them.'

'I can't help you, *caro*, it's your problem now.' Max closed his suitcase and walked to the door. 'I'll be back when things have calmed down, although I don't expect it will calm down for you for quite some time. Face the music. It's time, my friend.'

The door slammed and Fabrizio stood in shock. He had lost everything. Lara had dumped him, Max had abandoned him and was getting out of what had now become a dangerous hell-hole. He was being threatened by an online monster and his two ex-baby-mammas had turned up in Saint-Tropez with his kids. What else could possibly go wrong? And to make matters worse, he could potentially end up as a suspect in a murder case if Lara squawked and told the truth about where he was that night.

'What to do, where to go?' he muttered to himself. Then, catching sight of himself in the mirror, he started to smile and flick his hair. He was still handsome, still young, and still a great lover. Maybe it was time to go full throttle for Carlotta.

∞

Charlie Chalk removed his old string bag from behind the kitchen door, patted the pockets of his orange safari shirt and baggy shorts to make sure he had euros and credit cards, and set off down the winding lanes behind the Place des Lices to go to the Saturday market.

The weekly jaunt to the market had been one of his and Spencer's favourite outings, browsing the bustling market with its stalls filled with everything from ceramic ashtrays to tacky 'I heart Saint-Tropez' T-shirts and all manner of dresses, blouses, sarongs and skirts, made in developing countries and sold for hugely inflated prices. The open-air market was unusually busy and bustling this Saturday. Although it was early, the hot summer sun already dappled the cobblestone streets and there was little wind to shift the plane trees that provided shade over the hundreds of stalls of the traders who plied their wares.

Charlie paused at one of the first stalls in the narrow street leading to the main square to peruse an abundance of cheap watches and pendants newly arrived from China or Korea. He tried on several while chatting to the stall owner and then handed over ten euros for his selection – a bright orange plastic watch that matched his shirt and which he immediately clasped on to his wrist.

Before he took off towards the bustling crowds, he checked his reflection in a small mirror that hung from a pole that in turn supported the stall's awning. Was it his imagination, or was someone in a black hoodie leaning against the bank's ATM machine staring at him? He turned to look but the person had disappeared into the crowds.

Shaking off a feeling of foreboding, Charlie strolled into the main square, stopping to admire a selection of vintage Louis Vuitton luggage for sale, only slightly less expensive than a new set. While he chatted to the stall owner, an old acquaintance, he was startled when someone roughly bumped into him and almost made him lose his balance. He glimpsed a hooded figure melting into the crowds around a stall selling straw baskets.

'Did you see who that was?' he asked the stall owner.

'*Non*. I saw no one,' he shrugged in that inimitable Gallic way. 'Just the crowds, Charlie – so many people today,' he sighed, as if to forgive all manner of transgressions. 'But no one's buying.'

Slowly Charlie strolled into the midst of the bustling throng. The air was filled with a delicious aroma and he realised he hadn't eaten breakfast. He and Spencer had always breakfasted together on the terrace of their little villa. Charlie reminisced about the croissants oozing butter, soft-boiled eggs and strong coffee they shared together, and it made him sad, and hungry at the same time. His stomach grumbled as he walked to the stall where the smell came from and ordered a slice of pepperoni pizza.

He took a bite, closing his eyes as he relished masticating the gooey cheese and meat with the delicate crust, and when he opened them again he saw the hooded, bearded figure, eyes covered by aviator shades, boldly staring at him from the opposite stall.

Maybe he's a fan, thought Charlie, conscious of his status as a popular British 'national treasure'. He smiled at the man and waved, but was stunned when the man in response raised his middle finger in the international sign for 'fuck you'. The hooded apparition then magically evaporated behind some passing tourists. Charlie began to feel decidedly uncomfortable. He didn't like the feeling that he was being stalked. He decided he needed a cup of coffee, maybe something stronger, and so, dodging the scooters and honking lorries, he crossed the street to the Café Clemenceau across the square, the popular market café on the corner of Rue Clemenceau.

The tiny café was cramped and bursting to the brim with tourists, but Charlie was offered an empty seat by a couple of middle-aged English tourists who were more than delighted to share a table with this British legend.

Charlie gratefully squeezed his vast bulk into the rickety aluminium chair, and to his dismay glimpsed the hooded figure outside the café performing a macabre dance. He had put on a skeleton mask over his face now, and started moving maniacally, giving everyone in the café the finger. Some children were laughing but the adults ignored him and admonished the youngsters for encouraging the bizarre street performance. Charlie and the couple next to him were appalled.

'Well, I never,' said the lady, whose name was Mags. 'That's a 'orrible sight, innit? Scares me to death, 'e does!'

As the hooded figure began to push his way into the café, a policeman suddenly appeared and dragged the dancing weirdo into the road. Charlie breathed a sigh of relief until he saw the figure apply a neat judo move on the policeman, leaving him stunned on the ground as he once again magically evaporated, drawing a gasp of wonder from the crowd, who thought it must be a magic act.

Charlie threw back his aperitif gratefully as soon as it was put down in front of him. He was surveying the room in case the horrible apparition decided to reappear, when he saw behind him, huddled in a corner at a small table, Roberto LoBianco, Nate Kowalski and . . . could the young man in the white shirt with his back to him be that cute young waiter, François from Sénéquier?

Whatever – he'd had enough today and he didn't care any more. He dropped money on the table, said goodbye to the tourists and wended his way home, looking over his shoulder nervously all the way.

'Oi, look Mags. 'E's got the Hattie Jacques,' said Mags's husband, Barry.

∽

When she read the tweet, 'Kill yourself, you ugly old bitch, before I do,' Sophie decided to hole herself up in her villa with Adolpho.

'Ridiculous! It's some deluded fan. Maybe the same one who sent the photo with the skeleton faces. Don't check my Twitter feed any more, Adolpho. I refuse to be intimidated.'

'Don't you think we should leave Saint-Tropez?' Adolpho asked nervously. 'All these deaths – the murders – it's not safe here any more, Sophie.'

'Nonsense! We have the dogs to protect us.' Adolpho cast a doubtful glance at a tiny Pomeranian, who yelped at him. 'We have plenty of food. We will just batten down the hatches as they say in the films and stay put. I'm sure Captain Poulpe will find whoever has committed these terrible crimes, and I hear Interpol and the FBI are here too because those two little sluts were Americans.'

'But everyone is leaving!' cried Adolpho. 'Blanche and Henry have sold their house and bought a place in Saint-Sébastien. Nate Kowalski was so upset by Zarina's death that he's put his house on the market – so has Monty Goldman and many others.'

'But Charlie is staying, is he not?' she enquired.

'Yes, he said he would never leave, even though he was followed by some crazy guy. He's received horrible threats too.'

'What threats?'

'Oh, emails about how he would be killed like Spencer – poisoned or horribly stung by wasps or something like that.'

'And Carlotta?'

'Yes, she is staying, and she and Nick see each other every day now. They are very much in love.'

'Hmm, good! It's time she had some happiness. Well, we are staying here too, Adolpho. I have my regime to follow every day. I must prepare for the movie.'

'Okay,' whispered Adolpho. There was no arguing with his mistress when she felt like this. Maybe he could make the best of it and have a fling with Charlie? He was always the life and soul of every gathering and Adolpho adored him.

∽

Fabrizio's exes had been given his cell-phone number by Maximus and he went cold when he heard their long-forgotten but familiar voices.

'*Caro mio*, it's us. The mothers of your babies,' cooed Carina.

'I'm here too!' crowed Raimunda.

'So are we, Papà!' two childish voices joined in, yelling, 'Papà, Papà, we want to see you. Come and see us. We're hungry, Papà – we need food. We want our papà!'

Fabrizio dropped his phone on to the bed as the yelling and entreaties continued. Finally he picked it up again and decided he had to say something.

'Where are you?' he croaked.

'We are in a caravan in the camping area next to Port Grimaud,' cried Carina. 'Please come to us, Fabrizio – we've come all the way from Rome. Please do come – we need you. Our life is in your hands.'

'Okay, okay, okay! I'll be there. Give me a bit of time. Look, I promise. I'll try and bring you some money.'

Fabrizio had remembered the joint bank account that Lara had opened several years ago when they had just started seeing each other. They had never used it as they paid for everything on her account, on Amex or other credit cards. Could there possibly be any money left in it?

He rummaged frantically in the Gucci holdall that he always travelled with and found the chequebook in a zippered side pocket. Then he jumped on his bike and zoomed to the Place des Lices. It was nearly four o'clock and the bank was crowded as it was about to close.

Fabrizio requested his balance from the teller and to his delight he saw he was in the black to the tune of twenty-seven thousand four hundred euros. He drew out the whole amount. Saved, he thought. Saved for a little while. Twenty-seven grand would not go far, given his lifestyle, and he knew he was obligated to give a substantial amount to his exes, but he calculated that, having pleaded poverty to them, giving them ten thousand euros should buy them off until he could get on his feet again.

Kazakhstan X *Factor* had finally called last night and told him to hang on for a few more days, as he was really close now to being one of the fourteen final contestants.

Fingers crossed, he thought. It's time my luck changed.

∞

Along with the FBI and Interpol, who were trying to solve the murders, a team of internet crimes specialists had been brought into the investigation in an effort to see if the Twitter and Facebook threats had any connection to the murders but, aside from a few known trolls of no relevance, some of the more menacing messages were so well hidden behind firewalls and proxy servers that the investigators threw their hands up in frustration. Two weeks had passed since the murders of Zarina and Sin and the teams were no closer to discovering the killer, or killers. Captain Poulpe believed there was a conspiracy, since forensics thought it likely that the girls had been killed around the same time, but in different places by a different person.

Meanwhile the hordes of holidaymakers that normally swamped the village in July and August had drained to a trickle. Not so the press and the paparazzi who, sensing one of the biggest stories of the decade, were making hay while the sun shone.

'Saint-Tropez: Murder Capital of the World,' screamed one tabloid, while other press outlets and media revelled in every juicy detail. They rehashed stories about Mina and Spencer's deaths and the tragedy on the funicular at Sophie's house, and generally made up articles arguing that every high-profile denizen of Saint-Tropez could be a suspect.

'Business is terrible,' confided Patrick, owner of the popular Tahiti Beach, to Charlie. 'They're cancelling reservations in droves – look at the beach, it's almost empty.'

Charlie surveyed the vast expanse of golden sand with only a few orange loungers and parasols on it.

'And the mistrals we've been having all year only make it worse,' he sighed. 'Well, things can only get better,' he added optimistically. But they didn't.

∞

Lara opened the door on her way to Sénéquier for her morning vodka cocktail and almost tripped over a package that had been left outside. Without thinking she opened it. Inside the box, which was strangely wrapped in Christmas wrapping papers, lay a dead rat oozing with maggots on top of black tissue paper, with a scrawled note that read, 'You're next, bitch'.

Chapter Twenty-Seven

Fabrizio found the shabby little caravan easily. It was parked in a scrubby piece of land next to several others on the camping site. Two women sat outside on broken beach chairs. The vestiges of prettiness still clung to their faces, but they looked tired and worn out. When they saw Fabrizio tanned, toned and handsome in white linen pants and black silk shirt, their faces lit up.

'Fabrizio, *caro, mio amore!*' they cried and ran towards him.

'*Guarda, guarda i tuoi bambini!* Look at your children!' said Raimunda, as two strapping young boys shyly approached. Fabrizio shook hands solemnly with his sons, whom he could see had inherited his dark good looks.

'*Piacere,*' he said as the boys studied him with interest.

'Sit, sit,' said Raimunda, eagerly brushing imaginary dust off the rickety chair. 'Sit down and talk to us, Fabrizio. We've missed you so much.'

'Yes, we still love you,' said Carina wistfully. 'We want to be with you again.'

Oh, God! Fabrizio felt totally out of his depth. That two girls he had slept with and impregnated by mistake when he was eighteen or nineteen and then never seen again had come back into his life was a major pain in the ass, to put it mildly. He had to get this farce over with as quickly as possible. He was raring to go to work on Carlotta. As for these women, my God, they didn't even shave their armpits, let alone their legs!

He tried to explain that anything to do with them in the future was out of the question.

'You see, I'm off to Kazakhstan tonight,' he said desperately, 'to be on *The X Factor*.'

'Oh! You gonna be a star, Papà?' asked one of the boys innocently.

Fabrizio winced. The word 'Papà' made him feel old.

'Yeah, well, I hope so.'

One of the women later brought out a huge steaming bowl of spaghetti and calamari. Fabrizio realised he hadn't eaten since the previous night.

'*Mangia, mangia,*' said Raimunda as Carina brought out a platter of delicious-smelling garlic bread. Second to sex, good food was one of Fabrizio's passions, and he dug in while the women watched him, cooing with delight.

∞

Fabrizio sped on his Harley through the darkened hilly streets of Saint-Tropez, towards Carlotta's villa, which was owned by a French banker who had never used it and only rented it out. A small modern mansion, it was next door to Roberto LoBianco's villa. It was nine o'clock but the nights were drawing shorter now that it was July. Fabrizio hadn't realised how fast the time had flown while he was with Carina and Raimunda and his sons. Following the excellent meal, he had presented the women with a big stack of euros and they were delirious with joy. After promising to come and visit them in Rome, he let each boy ride pillion with him on his motorcycle, which he really quite enjoyed. Lara called him on his cell twice but he didn't pick up. He was actually having fun.

Fabrizio parked on the street and then moved swiftly through a garden full of parasol pines, hibiscus, hydrangeas and rose bushes. There were so many bushes and plants that he got entangled and tripped over a couple of times, cursing under his breath. Finally he found the thick gravelled path that led to Carlotta's house. Lights were glowing from the ground floor and he could hear mood music emanating from there, something mellow by Diana Krall. She has good taste in music, he thought, but then – having observed her for the past few months – he realised Carlotta had good taste in just about everything.

He noticed a nondescript cheap rental car in the driveway. So, she had a visitor – who could it be? Maybe this wasn't a good idea after all. The adrenalin rush that had led him to race off to Carlotta's house was wearing off. He was tired and he was angry with himself for spreading himself so thin with so many women, and even angrier with the person who had killed Zarina and Sin causing him to have to confess his infidelity to Lara.

He peered through the window of the living room. Carlotta and Nick were entwined on the sofa listening to the music. There was a bottle of champagne on the table in front of them and they seemed totally engrossed in each other. Nick was wearing a white terry-cloth robe and she was in a silky clingy negligee.

So the rumours were true – he was definitely her boyfriend. The body language was intimate – obviously that of a couple who had just made love. Fabrizio stared for a few moments then shrugged to himself, thinking, *What the hell, she's taken. No use barking up that tree. Time to start a new life. Kazakhstan, here I come.* Then his cell vibrated and Lara's name came up on the screen with a plaintive message.

So she wanted him back, huh? Well, she can fucking think again, he thought. Let her stew. He had given CRAP ten thousand euros so he still had seventeen left. That should last until Kazakhstan *X Factor* started paying.

As Fabrizio clambered back down the hill, he noticed a motorbike zooming up the drive to Roberto LoBianco's house. Was he having a party? No one was giving parties in Saint-Tropez now, not with the threat of a savage murderer at large, but Fabrizio's curiosity was piqued. He quickly scurried across Carlotta's lawn and, crawling on his hands and knees, peered through the window into LoBianco's living room. What he saw took his breath away.

∞

Carlotta and Nick had been growing closer and closer. After her chat with Sophie, she had called Nick and asked him to dinner 'à deux' at her villa.

'It will be just you and me,' she said. 'I hope you won't be bored,' she added shyly.

'Never with you, my darling. You know I adore you.'

Nick had been incredibly understanding about Carlotta's reticence to consummate their relationship. They had spent many evenings together at quiet, out-of-the-way bistros, well away from the Saint-Tropez gossips, but this would be the first time they would be spending the whole evening alone at her house.

Nick had brought a bottle of vintage Cristal and an enormous tin of beluga caviar, which he knew Carlotta loved. She answered the door wearing a long, cream-coloured satin caftan embroidered with tiny seed pearls. Behind her ear she'd placed a gardenia and her dark hair fell in a profusion of tumbled curls. She smelled utterly delicious and looked even better.

As soon as she saw him she was on him. She threw herself into his arms, covering his face with kisses and breathed, 'I want to wake up next to you tomorrow morning and every morning, Nick, my darling.'

'Whoa, whoa! You won't get any arguments from me on that score,' he laughed, then embraced her in a long and passionate kiss, which they held until they almost ran out of breath. He pulled back for a second and looked quizzically into her eyes, 'Why this change of heart?'

'There's been no change, no change at all. My heart just got bigger and let you in. I've realised I've been a fool for not seeing that you're the most wonderful, terrific, greatest man I've ever met.'

'C'mon now, Carlotta,' he said with pretend modesty. 'How about handsome, witty and clever?'

'Oh, that too – that too!' She kissed him harder and more passionately, then whispered in his ear, 'Come with me; follow me.'

'I'm following you to the ends of the earth.'

Carlotta held Nick's hand and led him down the hallway into her bedroom. Golden candles flickered and gleamed on every surface, the air was thick with some exotic aromatic scent and pink rose petals had been scattered on the floor leading up to the bed, which was covered in pure white Porthault sheets.

'Oh, my God,' said Nick. 'I do believe you are seducing me, Contessa.'

'You bet I am.' Carlotta pulled him towards her by his shirt and started undoing it, button by button. Then she pulled it off gently and started kissing his tanned chest all over until he couldn't stand it any more. He took her face between his hands and gazed into her eyes.

'I want you, Carlotta. You're the woman of my dreams – my soul mate. Will you marry me?'

'Yes, yes, yes, oh yes!' she whispered as she moved them closer to the bed. 'But first . . .'

She took off her cream silk caftan and Nick drew in his breath as he saw her exquisite caramel-skinned body for the first time.

'First . . . this.'

∞

For Carlotta it was as if she had never made love before. Except for a few times at the beginning of their relationship, all she had known when married to Nicanor were sexual assaults with no foreplay or loving tenderness beforehand. Nick was a gentle and inspired lover and Carlotta's gorgeous body and sweet disposition made him extra considerate. He kissed her everywhere until she moaned with desire for him to enter her, but he made her wait. With his tongue he brought her to peaks of pleasure. She had forgotten such rapture existed. Twice, three times he made her come until she begged for him to be inside her. She was avid for him, longing to feel him, and when he finally sensed it was the right moment, she melted into his body as they joined each other in erotic, joyful gratification.

'I never . . . ever . . . I . . .' she gasped later when for a moment they were satiated.

'Shhh, my darling!' he put a finger over her moist lips. 'I know, my darling – oh, how I know! This is how it will always be for us from now on, my sweet.'

Carlotta closed her eyes in bliss. She had finally found it: true love at last. Better than anything she had ever heard about or ever believed existed.

'The only thing that matters – to love and be loved,' she whispered. 'I belong to you now, Nick. I've kept my heart to myself for so many years, but now I'm giving it to you and I'm never going to leave you.' They went downstairs together to celebrate with the Cristal.

∞

'*Madonna mia*, I don't believe it,' Fabrizio muttered.

Lying splayed out on the couch, swigging from a bottle of beer lay François Lardon, grinning widely at Roberto LoBianco, who was raising a glass of cognac in a toast. Although Fabrizio was no lip reader, he understood that Roberto was congratulating François. The men were smoking cigars and laughing and it was obvious they were in cahoots over something. Fabrizio stared at the heavy-set LoBianco. He was typical of some of the nomadic super-wealthy species who flooded the Riviera in the summer. With his private Gulfstream, gin palace boat, multiple mansions and high-flying party style, he loved entertaining packs of high-end hookers and wannabe starlets at his lavish parties, plying them with exotic drink and drugs and making them do what he wanted.

As Fabrizio started to crawl away, he felt a large meaty hand on his shoulder and a harsh voice said, 'What the fuck are you doing here? You don't belong here, asshole!' When the meaty hand connected with the back of his neck, Fabrizio passed out.

Chapter Twenty-Eight

Fabrizio came to groggily in what appeared to be a fully equipped wine cellar. He was trussed up in a chair, his feet and hands manacled together with plastic strips, and gaffer tape gagging his mouth. His head felt like cotton wool and there was an agonising pain at the back of his neck. The burly six foot five, three hundred and fifty-pound heavyweight who had punched him stood in front of him, arms crossed and a pleased gleam in his piggy eyes. Beside him stood Roberto LoBianco and the waiter François.

'What the fuck are you doing here, Bricconni?' spat LoBianco.

The bruiser Guido leaned over and tore the tape from Fabrizio's face, causing him to scream in pain. Guido then put his hand over his mouth and shouted, 'Shut the fuck up, motherfucker, and answer him!'

'Nothing, nothing, I wasn't doing anything.' Fabrizio wasn't ashamed to admit he was shit-scared.

'Whaddya mean nothing, asshole? You were spying on us, weren't you?'

'No, no, no – I was visiting the Contessa Di Ponti. I thought this was her house . . . I got lost when, when . . . I was looking for my bike!'

'Oh, that silly cunt,' sneered François. 'She's been banging that journalist guy – stupid bitch.'

'Who knows you're here?' snapped LoBianco.

Fabrizio was stumped. If he told the truth, that no one knew where he was, who knew what these three obvious villains would do to him? His mind was racing and then, as Guido grabbed his balls and squeezed, he screamed out, 'My girlfriend, Lara Meyer. She . . . she knows where I am. I told her I was seeing the Contessa.'

'Oh yeah, sure.' François tossed Fabrizio's cell phone up in the air and caught it. He pressed the play button on the voicemail screen. Lara's plaintive voice screamed, 'Fabrizio, my darling, where are you? I need you. I'm so frightened, Fabrizio. I didn't mean what I said. I want you – I miss you. Please, please, come home. I love you . . .'

LoBianco grabbed the phone and hit the delete button. 'I guess you fucked up, buddy.'

He pressed play again and they listened to the next message. Lara was even more hysterical now. 'Fabrizio, where are you? Please, please, come home. The most horrible thing has happened to me,' she started sobbing. 'A rat . . . a dead rat outside my door and a terrible note – Oh! Please, Fabrizio, sweetheart, come home. I need you – I really do, my darling.'

'Yeah, I sent that.' François looked pleased with himself. 'Took a bit of planning to catch the rat, but I learned all that in jail, 'cause sometimes we had to eat them.'

François – real name Alain Millet – had spent five years in one of the most notorious and squalid jails in France, Baumettes in Marseille, for aggravated assault and the attempted murder of his then-employer. François Lardon was a fictional being he had meticulously created with the help of a powerful patron – Roberto LoBianco – and it was how he had avoided detection during the investigations.

Fabrizio felt sick. 'Did . . . did you kill those girls?' he asked.

'Sure I did,' grinned François. 'When you spend five years in Baumettes Prison you learn how to do all sorts of things.' He started to laugh and Fabrizio stared at him in horror.

'Don't tell me anything more; I don't want to hear anything,' Fabrizio pleaded, his eyes full of tears.

'Why not? I'm proud of my work – all of it – and you aren't gonna be around to tell anyone, bitch.'

'All of them? You mean . . . Spencer . . . Mina too?' Fabrizio's voice was a dull whisper.

'Yeah, all of them! And don't forget the fucking faggot I burned to death on the funicular. "Crispy", I call him!'

All the men laughed. François seemed to grow in stature as he boasted of his achievements. 'I'm quite an expert in the art of orchestrating an amusing death. They taught me good in jail. Taught me a lot of things, like how to cook.' His face clouded. 'I know a lot of crazy, interesting things to fuck people up.' He grinned at LoBianco who gave him a thumbs-up.

'But tell me why,' whispered Fabrizio, 'why did you do all those terrible things to innocent people?'

'Yeah, sure, well, why not? You're never gonna be able to talk to anyone again. I don't wanna brag but I think we did a fabulous job and it's worked.' He smiled at LoBianco. 'You see, we had to scare the shit out of everyone in Saint-Tropez so that they would clear out. I mean, fucking Saint-Tropez, what a fucking cesspool . . . and the people in it! Scum – you included – Moby fucking Dickheads!' He laughed at his own humour. 'You tried to fuck everyone, didn't you? Even that ancient witch, Sophie Silvestri.'

'Never,' Fabrizio replied, offended. 'I'd never sleep with anyone *that* old!'

'Bullshit, you'd fuck a snake, you would!' François was on a roll now, bragging about his brilliance. 'But I gave you a bit of a break, didn't I? Pouring hot wax on Lara?' He laughed maniacally. 'She was always dissing me, so I zipped down the skylight and evened the score. You should be thanking me!'

'Nevertheless,' LoBianco bent low to whisper in Fabrizio's ear, 'whether you fucked the old hag or not, we don't give a shit, but you made a *big* mistake coming here, my friend. I'm afraid your days of rutting and strutting are over, pal. *Finito – basta* – end of story for our little gigolo, right, François?'

'Right, boss,' François grinned. He loved showing off his perfect teeth. 'End of the line for this old stud.'

'How long have you been planning this? And please don't call me old.' Fabrizio needed to stall for time as much as possible. He remembered his second cell phone secured to the small of his back. When you lived a double love life, you always needed two phones, and thank God they hadn't discovered it. His hands were still tied behind his back but, as François talked and grinned (and oh, how he liked to grin), Fabrizio kept straining his fingers to action a button, any button, on his cell.

'Yeah, how long ago was it when we met, boss?' François asked.

'Six or seven years,' said LoBianco. 'I met François in Baumettes Prison – the filthiest, most overcrowded shithole jail in France. You ever heard of it?'

Fabrizio shook his head, playing for time. 'No, was it horrible?'

'Well, not only was it so crammed with cons that we had to sleep five to a cell, but the fucking rats were everywhere.' LoBianco shuddered at the memory. 'They were in our beds, in the showers, in the kitchens. It was overcrowded, violent, and most of the inmates were murderers and rapists. All I did was a little bit of embezzlement,' he laughed bitterly. 'But they put me in a freezing cold cell, fucking exposed electric wires hanging over our bunks, with two wife killers, one child rapist and this young man here. You saved my life, buddy.'

'We saved each other's, Robbo.' François grinned at the older man, and for a moment they seemed to be lost in reminiscence of prison life.

'Yeah, the Gallic Alcatraz. Everyone said it was impossible to escape from the most notorious motherfucking jail in France.'

'Did you escape?' asked Fabrizio, still working on his bindings.

'Nah, too tough. We saw what happened to a lot of the cons who tried it. You know who they sent there?'

'Who?' Fabrizio asked. Having suddenly become the confidant of ex-felons, it suited him fine if it bought him enough time to call anyone who could help him. He had to get to the keypad of his phone.

During LoBianco's discourse on prison life, Fabrizio had managed to separate his silk Valentino shirt from his waistband and locate the phone. He felt around for the home button and clicked it once with his thumb, which should have brought the phone to life. Then he visualised the distance from the home button to the phone icon, always on the far right. *Tap it once and tap it again to get favourites and pray that it worked.* He reached as far as he could to where he thought the first number should be, and was about to tap it when he thought, God, no – what if it started playing 'Happy' at the top of his playlist? That would give it away. Wait a second, he thought . . . using his voice to instruct Siri, the phone system's virtual assistant, should work – all he had to do was hold the home button down. If he could only find the right moment to yell out an instruction . . . it had to be something that made sense. He had to keep them talking.

'The fucking Count of Monte Cristo, that's who!' laughed François, baring his teeth again.

'Wow, that's amazing!' Fabrizio applied his minimal acting skills to feign intense interest as his mind churned – *what would make sense, what could I say on the phone that won't give me away?*

And what if Siri replied? He could almost imagine her high-pitched female voice coming out of his butt, to the amazement of the felons surrounding him, declaring, 'Hmmmm, I didn't get that?'

I have to lower the volume, he thought, feeling around for the two buttons, pressing the lower one in relation to the home button and reaching up to make sure the mute button was engaged. It was simply caution because he kept it always on vibrate.

'So you met in the Count of Monte Cristo's jail – wow! Like . . . wow! That's fascinating! How long were you there?'

'I'll tell you.' François was enjoying this. He pulled up a stool beside Fabrizio. 'I was sent to fucking jail when I was just eighteen.'

'What for?'

'A lot of things,' he shrugged. 'You know, break-ins, aggravated assault, possession, attempted murder. Judge had it in for me, even though I was barely past a juvenile. You know what happens to a guy like me in that hell-hole?'

François's face clouded over. Fabrizio attempted a sympathetic look, which seemed to work, as he launched into a litany of the perverted degradation and constant rapes he had had to endure.

'Four years they did it to me – all of them, the scum of human-ity. Guards too. I was so pretty – too fucking pretty,' he said bitterly. 'I tried to kill myself – twice. That's when Robbo here came in. He was connected, so he managed to keep the pervs who were shoving their dicks and other stuff into my ass night and day away from me.'

'How so?' Fabrizio was thinking what he could yell at Siri . . . *Call Lara?* He didn't know if he had Lara on this phone. Maybe he did, but what could she do? She was probably sozzled on vodka by this time. Vanessa? She'd never take a call from him, and if Jonathan saw it he would probably happily come to help Roberto. Betty? She was on the high seas anyway. 'Call Police'. That's it.

I'll keep yelling 'Call Police' – perfectly normal when you're about to get killed, even if it was strangely phrased.

'Because I'm a *very* powerful man,' said LoBianco proudly, 'and I have *very* powerful friends, both on the outside and on the inside. A few threats, a few promises, and François's abuse stopped.'

'Yeah, we became bosom buddies,' laughed François. 'Then we plotted this scam. Roberto wanted to create a big resort on this Saint-Sébastien place that he had bought. He needed the high rollers and big spenders from Saint-Tropez to buy villas and apartments, but he couldn't figure out how to manage it, until he met me.'

'Yes, François came up with the idea of frightening everyone off. I had tried for years to figure out how to get people away from Saint-Tropez and over to my island, and François's simple cunning mind came up with the solution in seconds. So we started with a "dress rehearsal" – poisoned oysters. All we wanted was to create panic, but we exceeded our expectations when Mina dropped dead.'

'Yeah, and we had no idea the one who dropped would be one of the biggest singers in the world,' François shrugged. 'Who knew the combination of a tainted oyster, botulism and her own allergy would have such an instant result? Well, accidents happen, eh?' He snickered.

'The queer guy was easy,' laughed François, continuing. 'He fancied me so it was "Hey, you wanna hang out at my place and smell the roses?"' He mimicked a bizarre limp-wristed sashay. 'I was going to shiv him but when I got there and saw all those wasps I thought of a trick I learned at Baumettes when they want to end someone. They stick a razor in your food and you swallow it. There were plenty of wasps in that garden – and there was the can of soda he was gulping. It was no problem, trapping one of the critters that had perched on the can, then shoving it in while he wasn't looking. Wasps! They're so stupid they just sit inside the can swimming around, so when the faggot took a deep gulp . . . God, you should have seen his face. It was comical! I should have taken a picture.' He laughed hysterically.

'It was brilliant,' LoBianco snorted, laughing along with him. 'You're a genius, François.'

Fabrizio laughed hollowly along with them, but his thoughts were far away from the hilarity the three men shared. *When do I do it? When?* he thought frantically. He only had one chance and it had to be perfect. He hoped it would work, because shortly after he did it, he would either be dead or as close to death as he could ever be. He found himself laughing alone, the three men staring at him curiously.

He recovered quickly. 'And the funicular?' he asked. 'How'd you manage that?'

'You don't need to be a brain surgeon to figure out how to screw up a funicular,' said François.

'We hoped to kill the old actress – that would have had great press, but we had to settle on that pouf assistant of hers,' explained Roberto. 'We tried again with the chocolate-box bomb we sent her, but it killed her maid instead. That Silvestri bitch must have used up all her nine lives by now.'

'Yeah, we didn't get enough press coverage on that,' agreed François. 'The bomb on the boat was good, though. That made up for it. You couldn't move for the media.'

'That was great,' laughed LoBianco.

'But why kill the two girls?' asked Fabrizio, panicked that they were tiring of recounting their exploits.

'We needed a biggie. You know the press. They were getting bored – bigger things were happening in other places and we still weren't getting the right fear effect. People kept wondering if they were pranks and the deaths accidental. We needed to make a definite statement to finally scare the residents out of Saint-Tropez. It was collateral damage. They were all low-lifes and sluts anyway!

But boy, did I have fun with those two skanks before I throttled them,' he laughed. 'They were up for anything. The two of them gave me a really great sex show, then I brought Roberto in with me and a giant black dildo,' he giggled. 'It's called "Steely Dan".'

Fabrizio felt sick at the perversion of these men. He didn't want to hear any more but he had to buy time and François seemed happy to brag about every sordid detail.

'Yeah, I fucked them with Steely – they screamed like the little pigs they were. Then when they were all worn out and begging for mercy, I gave it to them.'

'What,' Fabrizio gulped, still working his fingers towards his phone, 'did you give to them?'

'Mercy, you schmuck! I put them out of their misery – we both did!' He laughed at the memory of the horror he had inflicted on the beautiful girls and all the men chortled.

'Okay, I guess it's about time to say *adieu*, Fabrizio.' François lifted his gun and pointed it towards their prisoner.

'CALL POLICE!' screamed Fabrizio as he held down the home button on his phone. 'CALL POLICE! CALL POLICE! CALL POLICE!'

'What the fuck are you screaming for? No one's going to hear you down here,' barked Guido, who spoke for the first time.

'Calling emergency services,' a disembodied electronic voice replied.

'You motherfucker!' François suddenly realised what Fabrizio was doing and dropped the gun to his side. 'Search him, Guido.'

They quickly untied Fabrizio's hands and found the phone strapped to his spine. François grabbed it and stamped on it until it smashed, then punched Fabrizio in the face.

'Now you've done it, asshole.'

∞

As soon as Captain Poulpe received the forensic results back from analysing the tiny glittering object Carlotta had discovered under LoBianco's bed, it was all systems go. The sequin had traces that matched the nail lacquer that Sin had worn. Not enough to go to court with, given how the sequin had been found, but at least enough to start building a case and make LoBianco the prime suspect. At least they didn't have to waste time on anyone else.

'Let's go pay him a visit,' said Poulpe. 'Looks like he's our man.'

He walked rapidly to the police car followed by Gabrielle and two other gendarmes. They sped up the dark hilly streets and, when they were three blocks away, they heard the police dispatcher announce, 'Reports of disturbance at Villa L'Orangerie, Cap Tahiti. All units respond.'

'That's Roberto LoBianco's villa,' cried Gabrielle.

∞

'What was that?' asked Carlotta.

Nick and she were now lovingly entwined on her terrace, admiring the almost full moon. She was still glowing in the aftermath of the most wonderful lovemaking she had ever experienced, feeling warm, safe and thoroughly amorous.

'Did you hear that? It sounded like someone screaming from next door.'

'Yes,' Nick replied, jumping up. 'I'd better find out. That pervert LoBianco could be hurting one of his hookers.'

Before Carlotta could object he was racing across the terrace, and just as he got to LoBianco's lawn he saw two men coming out of the house, carrying a body between them.

∞

François and Guido held the semi-conscious Fabrizio up between them, while dragging him outside towards LoBianco's car.

298

'Get him the fuck out of here, and kill him somewhere else!' LoBianco had hissed at them. 'I don't want any trace of Bricconni in my house. Get him out of here *now*! I'll clean up. Hurry the fuck up!'

Suddenly Guido and François saw a figure in a flowing white terry-cloth robe flying towards them.

'What the hell are you doing?' yelled Nick, recognising the unconscious Fabrizio. 'What's going on here, for Christ's sake? Put him down now – I mean *now*!'

'Get the fuck out of our way,' warned François. He pointed his Glock pistol at Nick. 'Fuck off, Nick, or you're gonna get hurt. Get out of here, asshole – I'm warning you.'

No way, buddy, Nick thought, then bending low, he ran towards them in zigzags as he had learned in Afghanistan, when reporting during battles. François fired several shots in his direction but Nick managed to take cover behind a stone pillar.

François and Guido continued dragging Fabrizio's body down the grassy slope that led to the pool area and the carport. Nick followed them, yelling to Carlotta, who had run after him.

'Go back and call the police right now, Carlotta, *call them*!'

Carlotta ran back into the house for her phone. As she called the police and tried her best to describe what was happening, she watched in terror as she saw Nick positioning himself to . . . *what on earth was he doing?*

Nick had skirted a low hedge around to the edge of the pool, on the blind side of Guido and François, who were busy trying to drag Fabrizio's limp body down the slope. He launched himself in a rugby tackle worthy of a professional, praying that gravity would do the rest. It did.

I've just agreed to marry a lunatic, Carlotta said to herself as she watched helplessly.

The four men tumbled down the grassy hill towards the pool,

which was glimmering in the moonlight, when suddenly LoBianco lumbered out of the house and ran to the middle of the slope.

'Stop it or I'll shoot, motherfuckers!' he yelled as the three men recovered and stood up groggily. François pointed his Glock at Nick, while Guido picked Fabrizio up. Then they heard the police sirens approaching.

LoBianco, sweating profusely, realised he was in deep shit. He quickly did calculations in his mind about how to minimise the damage. François had spilled the beans to Fabrizio, who knew everything now. But he was the only witness. He had to shut him up permanently, otherwise he was ruined. If he killed him, his lawyers could argue that Fabrizio was an intruder who had startled Roberto, who had shot him involuntarily. Guido and François would back him up. He had no choice.

He raised his gun and fired at Fabrizio twice. Guido, startled, jumped back. Fabrizio's body convulsed and he fell to his knees, then tumbled into the pool, his blood turning the water dark around him.

'Jesus Christ, Roberto's gone fucking insane!' yelled Guido, scrambling across the grass to get to his car. 'He's killed him in front of a fucking witness!'

'Oh, I don't think so . . .' said François, as he watched LoBianco take aim at Nick Stevens's heart. Carlotta screamed, making LoBianco and François turn. The realisation now that he had a third witness to deal with was written all over LoBianco's face.

'What's the stupid prick think he's going to do? Kill half of Saint-Tropez in one night?' muttered François.

Just then Gabrielle Poulpe's voice rang out.

'FREEZE, POLICE! PUT YOUR WEAPON DOWN OR I'LL SHOOT!'

EPILOGUE

Fabrizio spent a month in hospital recuperating. The two bullets had torn through his stomach and hip but fortunately damaged no vital organs. The enormous press attention he received made a successful singing career happen quickly after he left hospital. In September Fabrizio made a hit record that went to number five. Ghastly Derek Flukle came out of the woodwork to claim his 20 per cent, but Fabrizio could now afford a good lawyer to put him in his place.

Soon after he released a very entertaining video that went viral. The video was a cover of Barry Manilow's big hit 'Copacabana'. In a twist that made the video popular, Lara had been persuaded to be in it and was cast as the old Lola of the story, who was the showgirl past her prime who drinks herself half-blind thirty years after the disco closes. Ironically, Fabrizio re-enacted being shot by LoBianco.

Fabrizio soon gained hundreds of thousands of screaming female fans because of his good looks and charisma, and was booked solidly for European singing tours for the next three years. He also gave generous child support to his children and alimony to the baby-mammas.

Maximus decided to give up pimping and dedicated himself solely to being Fabrizio's manager. With his manipulative cleverness, along with his elephantine memory of indiscretions carried out by many of his show-business colleagues, he was able to make a great deal of money for both of them.

Lara, after unsuccessfully begging Fabrizio to marry her, sold her apartment in Saint-Tropez and decided that in future she would spend her summer in The Hamptons, 'Where they speak English,' she spat to Blanche and Henry, who became her new best friends and neighbours. There she met a handsome young actor who had a couple of bit parts in horror movies and she promptly decided to become his mentor as well as his lover. 'He's going to be the next Brad Pitt,' she boasted to everyone.

And when he did, he left her.

Jonathan and Vanessa Meyer hotfooted it (by yacht) back to Manhattan, where they continued as one of the most popular couples on the social and charity circuit. At one of Vanessa's charities in the fall, she entreated Jonathan to pay Fabrizio to sing.

'He will be a huge draw,' she insisted.

'No way, honey,' said the ever-pragmatic Mr Meyer. 'I don't trust that guy within an inch of you.'

Vanessa at least had the good grace to blush, but continued to follow Fabrizio's career in the gossip columns with great interest.

Charlie Chalk and Adolpho fell in love, discovering during their time together that they had a lot in common. However, Adolpho was so loyal to Sophie that he would never leave her, so Charlie sold his villa and moved in with them, replacing Frick as stylist, companion and confidant. He planted and tended a beautiful rose garden at the bottom of the funicular track, and he made sure that no wasp nests were allowed to take hold anywhere near it.

Sophie Silvestri got the role of Violet Venable in *Suddenly, Last Summer*. She gave such a true, gritty performance that there was major Oscar buzz about her portrayal. Marvin Rheingold didn't make the film in Saint-Sébastien, but instead shot it in the charming village and beaches of Le Lavandou, just a few kilometres away from Saint-Tropez. He didn't get Angelina Jolie in the end, but discovered a new young actress fresh out of RADA who, he announced, was going to become the 'new Elizabeth Taylor'. Thanks to the steamy sex scenes between her and a hot young actor, the movie was a smash hit.

The entire resort and complex of Saint-Sébastien was allowed to fall into ruins when Roberto LoBianco was sentenced to life imprisonment in the notorious Baumettes Prison in Marseille for the murders he had committed. François also received a long sentence, but the thought of returning to Baumettes horrified him so much that after the trial he hanged himself in his cell.

Gabrielle and her father decided to take a winter break from Saint-Tropez and went skiing in Courchevel. Gabrielle had never skied before, so took lessons from a handsome ski instructor. Free from the responsibilities of being a housewife to her father, she allowed herself to fall in love with the ski instructor, to the delight of her father. They had a quiet winter wedding in a little chalet in the middle of a snowstorm. Although she loved Saint-Tropez, Gabrielle adored the peace and tranquillity she had found in the Alps and she decided to live there with her new husband.

'I'll miss you, Papa,' she said after the wedding, 'but I will visit you often. You're not going to get rid of me so easily.'

'My darling,' Captain Poulpe said, 'you are a wonderful daughter and you've done enough for me. It's time you live your own life now, and look after your husband as you have looked after me.' *And I won't miss your bouillabaisse*, he thought to himself.

Carlotta and Nick were married at the ancient little church in Ramatuelle. All their friends from Saint-Tropez attended the beautiful traditional wedding and the celebration afterwards at a gorgeous villa nestled in a valley overlooking the bay of Saint-Tropez.

'I've never been happier,' murmured Carlotta to Nick as they stood gazing at the panoramic view and the sunset on the terrace of the villa.

'Oh, I think I can make you happier,' he said. 'We are going to be happier and happier with each passing year.'

Sophie, who had been Carlotta's matron of honour, sighed as she watched the happy couple's embrace.

'Ah yes, marriage,' she said, turning to Captain Poulpe. 'The deep, deep peace of the double bed after the hurly-burly of the chaise longue.'

'You can say that again,' replied Captain Poulpe, as they exchanged a meaningful glance.

Looking down on the village and the bay in all its glory was a breathtaking view. The shining, peach-coloured roofs of the village houses glistened in the late afternoon sun and the small yachts skipped along atop the glimmering deep blue Mediterranean, their sails flapping gently in the light breeze. With the dreadful murders solved, Saint-Tropez soon returned to the glamorous, idyllic paradise that everyone loved. The residents went back to their homes and, with its reputation restored, Saint-Tropez looked forward to the following summer and another sizzling season of sun, sex, and maybe just a little bit of scandal.